COLOR BLINDED

COLOR BLINDED

K S GRAY

CONTENTS

PREFACE

COLOR *BLINDED*

K S Gray

ABOUT ME AND WHO HAS HELPED

ABOUT THE AUTHOR:

Writing has always been my passion. K S Gray is a pen name which has been used for the author's privacy. If you want to talk about this book, you can contact K S Gray at graykasam@gmail.com or on Instagram @ksgrayauthor.

DISCLAIMER:

This is a work of fiction. While COVID-19 is very real, the names, characters, places and incidents are the product of the author's imagination or are used fictitiously. Any resemblance to actual events, locations or persons, living or dead, is coincidental.

ACKNOWLEDGMENTS:

The author wishes to thank his/her family for all of their love and support throughout the years. Much appreciation is given to my editor, who also prefers to remain anonymous. And thank you to my longtime friend Nancy, which may or may not be her real name.

PRINT ISBN: 978-0-578-94112-7

EBOOK ISBN: 978-0-578-94113-4

PREFACE

In the first two decades of the 21st century, the United States together with the rest of the world faced unprecedented and simultaneous challenges. Racism exploded. Exclusionist political populism reached the highest levels of elected office. As 2020 opened, rather than being a year for reflection and optimism, it became a time of widespread fear and lock downs. A unique deadly virus caused a global health pandemic, quickly killing hundreds of thousands of people and infecting millions more. Skilled researchers raced to find a vaccine, while social scientists struggled to stem the spread of hate-filled divisiveness. One exceptional immunologist developed a vaccine that could alleviate the destructiveness of Covid-19, but would simultaneously disable people's capacity to discern race. What this vaccine offered was shockingly simple: it could be delivered by raindrops. But it also forced the world to confront a profoundly complex question: is being color blinded the right solution to the devastation being caused by a rapidly spreading disease and racial hatred?

| 1 |

Chapter 1: August 2020: In the garden, at a crossroads

Ricky and Caihong sat on a bench within the White Dagoba, the highest point in Beihai Park, having taken a comfortable stroll from Ricky's parents' apartment in Beijing. Resting under the 14 bronze bells hanging around them, they soaked in the history of this shrine first built in 1651, on the site of a former palace where Kublai Khan received Marco Polo. They sat silently taking in the beautifully landscaped flowers and plants enveloping the vista before them. They had already walked through three of the five dragon pavilions, monuments to a centuries' earlier time. Both were aware of the history and the lore of this 175 acre tribute to three magic mountains, and the legend that deities in those mountains possessed an herbal medicine that would help humans gain immortality.

The walk had given them time to catch up, some, on the 20+ years since he had graduated from the academy early. Caihong knew a lot about Ricky's incredible work around the world from many stories published in China which lauded his work as a Chinese scientist. He helped stem multiple public health crises around the world, ending a lot of suffering, and saved many lives. Ricky had only had the past two hours to learn of Caihong's work as an environmentally focused urban planner, helping with much of the redevelopment of residential portions of Beijing and Shanghai. At 5 foot 6, several inches taller than most Chinese women, she stood a half inch taller than Ricky. Her mother for years insisted she learn how to walk and sit such that her head did not top her male companion; a silly Chinese tradition she often thought, the woman should look up into the eyes of the man. But she respected her mother's wishes. She always thought Ricky cute when they were teenagers. She found him physically suitable now, but intellectually a strong force drawing her to him, even after all the time that had passed.

Caihong asked, "so, Ricky, would you like to explain your dilemma to me? I have read many of the news reports of your work around the world. But this most recent project, it is very... well, just incredible, really." Ricky leaned back against the wrought iron, looked up and exhaled.

"Of course. I know that this project has been very controversial, what we have discovered. Many have told me we should not pursue this, that it is not right, not ethical. Others have said this vaccine is a miracle, we should be proud and excited that it will save many, many lives and end so much suffering." Caihong nodded, placing her left hand on his right. Ricky looked down and smiled.

He continued. "And, maybe, maybe it will make people less hateful, more tolerant. I have heard all sides of this. My work with infectious diseases has often involved ethical issues. We are always examining how we will treat a disease if there is an outbreak; should we quarantine people, restrict their movement; how do we test potential treatments? Who do we help first, who will have to wait?"

"That has always been your way, Ricky. You search, you test, you explore, and you find answers. Many amazing answers." Ricky blushed.

"You are very kind, Caihong. Thank you. But, I have never faced an ethical dilemma like this before."

"Well, then tell me what you think are the choices we face and why. You know, Ricky, there are often many answers, but not one right answer. Come, our parents will be telling stories for hours. Let's stroll some more in this beautiful park and talk. As much as you would like. There is so much more to catch up on." With that, they rose up, and headed towards the two dragon pavilions they had not yet visited.

Ricky resumed explaining how he came to this crossroad and where he now stood, even if most of the world had pushed on. Caihong placed her left hand in his right hand, which he accepted, a bit awkwardly at first.

Chapter 2 : March 2014: Ebola fears

On March 17, 2014, President John Lewis "Kareem" Bursan stood at the lectern at the center of the entrance to the White House's East Room. He had prepared for a prime time address on Ebola, a disease most Americans knew little about. He knew he would be competing with March Madness, the annual NCAA basketball championship. People would be annoyed. They would be tuning in to watch hoops, but instead would be staring at a reed thin black man in a dark blue suit and sober blue tie. By agreement with the NCAA and the tournament broadcasters, the speech would delay that night's "Sweet Sixteen" tipoffs by seven minutes.

"Good evening my fellow Americans. I am speaking to you tonight about a deadly disease that has been spreading in other parts of the world, and to assure you of our plan to keep it from coming here to America. Earlier this month, the World Health Organization reported an outbreak of the Ebola virus in the West African country of Guinea. Additional cases have since been reported in the countries of Liberia, Sierra Leone, Nigeria and Senegal. Even though we have had no reported cases of Ebola in the United States, the CDC has declared this disease a public health hazard. This virus is deadly, and it spreads easily."

President Bursan kept his eyes laser focused on the camera. With his peripheral vision he found the aide on the left side wall who was to hold up a large cue card with "1 Minute" in large black letters.

"In working with our partners around the world, we have implemented a multi-government, public-private plan to address this disease, to contain it at its source, treat it there as best we can, and protect our American citizens from it coming here. Specifically, we are working on a multi-pronged approach to prevent or at worst limit Ebola exposure in the US by taking the following steps: first, to control the epidemic at its source in West Africa; second, to minimize the secondary impacts of the epidemic that aren't directly caused by the disease, such as access to food and clean water in the affected areas; and third, taking the lead in building a robust global health security infrastructure focused on avoiding spread and rapid treatment. I know this is not the type of news you wanted to hear tonight as many of you are tuning in to watch your favorite teams vying to win the NCAA championship. I get it, I do. But we cannot afford to turn a blind eye to a public health crisis of this magnitude." The aide held up the one minute warning sign, so Bursan decided not to talk about which team he was rooting for. He had released his tournament bracket weeks ago, a tradition of his since being sworn in as President. He didn't think levity would work well for this occasion. "We pray for the citizens of West Africa, and assure you, my fellow Americans, that we are doing everything possible working with the best minds in the world to defeat and contain this terrible disease. May God bless you, and may God bless America."

It was concrete and sincere. President Bursan meant every word of it. His staff would tell him that the speech was outstanding, a three-point buzzer-beater to win the championship. People are predictable, even the men and women who surrounded him, almost all of whom he hired because they were willing to speak their minds, not just kiss up with "yes sir, you did great sir." Thankfully, he had cleared his schedule to watch the games tonight, along with millions of other Americans.

| 3 |

Chapter 3: Racism on the rise

In July 2014, fascists, neo-fascists, Ultra-Populists and plain old fashioned racists from America, Europe, Asia and Africa gathered in central Europe. This three day confab was a rare secret, shielded from the prying eyes of the press and omnipresent social media. Quietly, cautiously, 37 of the world's most racist leaders gathered with no outside attention. They shared certain prejudices, but could not agree on a catchy name for their movement or loose affiliation. So sparing originality, they called themselves The Leaders. While they agreed to operate with something of a charter, the testosterone and conceit ran so high among them that the group could have no single president or chair. Instead, they acquiesced to three vice-chairs. For good measure, they began drafting by-laws. One easily agreed upon motion was that Latin America would be excluded from representation.

The first day's agenda revolved around electing the three vice chairs. John Barron "JB" Clark, the long time, powerful American political advisor and right wing cable news force, established himself as a first ballot choice. The Leaders understood that without a forceful American presence, their mission would fail.

Clark had developed a large following at home and abroad with his racist dog whistles. Most in attendance accepted his need to maintain plausible deniability when confronted on television about his views; they knew his true feelings.

The second vice-chair was Ulf Knutsson, a Central European. He had strong-armed his way to a position of authority at home. There, he ruled with force. His detractors sat forgotten in jail.

Knutsson had boasted on many occasions that he descended directly from King Cnut, the fierce Danish warrior king who conquered vast portions of northern Europe and ruled over England in the 11th century. Rumors had circulated that Knutsson's birth mother was once a prostitute. Those who heard him speak of his lineage knew it was best to suppress their smirks or ask about his mother; it was okay to talk about his father, who had served 20 years for brutally beating a black man to death, allegedly for standing too close to him at a soccer match.

"One day, we will again rule as Vikings did long ago. It is our heritage, and our right." Among these haters on steroids, he had to use his harshest and angriest tones to scale the ranks of leadership. And he possessed no remorse. He believed every word that passed his lips.

The third vice chair, chosen on the third ballot, was the systematically brutal Deng Xu-Pei, a prime minister in name but dictator in reality from Asia. Deng made sure that even a whiff of dissent resulted in immediate punishment, often a disappearance. While Clark and Knutsson loved the idea of putting all non-whites under their boot, they understood the need to make concessions for Deng, a man who ruled 80 million Asians. Clark told Knutsson on several occasions to think of yellow as another shade of white. "Remember," Clark had said, "even Hitler learned to get along with Hirohito."

The second day's agenda was straightforward. Each vice-chair had been allowed to choose one topic to lecture on. Deng chose how to complete the subversion of Western style democracy, so that autocratic rule could continue its spread. Knutsson's topic of choice was halting the march of human rights so those who opposed The Leaders could be crushed. And then there was Clark, always the crowd-pleaser. He ended with the need to suppress the inferior races. Like mutts in a pound hoping to be adopted, they had to understand who the masters were, who they must obey.

Following the speeches, the vice-chairs agreed to present The Leaders with a color chart as the central plank in their self-described philosophy of race purity. Clark thought of it like a paint store color wheel, like deciding on a new color for a den, but with real life consequences. They called it The Palette: people whose skin tone was one of the six agreed colors could live and move about freely. The rest would be dominated and disenfranchised. Women, of course, were inferior to this gathering of all men, so there was never any dispute about gender oppression. But their central passion, their basest and basic rule, centered on ending and reversing the fiction of equality under law.

When the Palette came up for a vote, everyone was given a paper with each color displayed: porcelain white; ivory; warm ivory; sand; beige; and warm beige. After many hours of debate spilling into the third day, they agreed on the Palette and two additional precepts for their by-laws. First, "Divide et impera" – follow Julius Cesar's theory of divide your enemies and conquer them all, an ancient axiom of politics and war. Second, make the division by race as attractive as possible to those who would be naturally inclined to follow, even if they did not realize where they were being guided.

At the closing session, Clark quoted Niccolo Machiavelli: "One who deceives will always find those who allow themselves to be deceived." They would never recognize the philosophy of Abraham Lincoln, "You can fool all the people some of the time and some of the people all the time, but you cannot fool all the people all the time." Lincoln freed American slaves. By definition, he was a traitor.

The final hours were spent on strategies to install leaders in so-called democracies who would spirit and channel divisiveness, race warfare, hatred of others. While individual members had made great progress in various parts the world, America, they said, was making things hard for them, especially with a black president. Clark described that as an opportunity, not an obstacle. "Bursan is not setting us back. Rather, he will launch us forward faster than any of you have done in any of your countries. You think our way is dead in the United States? You are very, very wrong my friends. Having this black man in the White House is like getting a flu shot; you have symptoms for a few days, but you emerge all the stronger, all the more resolute to defeat this enemy. America is boiling with enthusiasm for our way, and the next election can cause an explosion of new followers. We will culti-vate the right man to follow our way, to build our strength, to get us ever closer to the path to domination." Cheers erupted; applause went on for minutes. Clark sat down and pulled his crumpled sheet of yellow paper from his pocket, staring at the three names he had penciled in on his flight over. One of these three, he kept thinking, one of these three.

| 4 |

Chapter 4: The six foot sky hook

John Lewis "Kareem" Bursan had been elected President in 2008, a fresh, young face in a world of old politics. His father, Jean, served as a police officer in Niger, and had volunteered to help provide protection for international youth who came to various parts of Africa as members of the Peace Corps. His mother, Eunis, was an American of French descent who grew up outside Atlanta. Eunis met Jean while she was working in West Africa for the Peace Corps. They married in 1963 in Maradi, Niger, Jean's ancestral home, and immediately settled in Atlanta. While most states had repealed their laws criminalizing interracial marriages, and the Supreme Court would soon make those laws illegal, Georgia in 1963 was still very much the Old South. Eunis had grown up a devout Christian, but when the flock at her childhood church consistently gave her and Jean disapproving looks, they found a home at Ebenezer Baptist Church.

Their son was born in Atlanta in August 1964. His name was a combined tribute for his father, for the recently assassinated President John F. Kennedy, and for an up-and-coming civil rights leader named John Lewis. Eunis had read of Mr. Lewis' fight against discrimination, his rise to become president of the Student Nonviolent Coordinating

Committee, and his relocation to Atlanta in 1964 to head the SNCC office there.

Five months pregnant, Eunis was walking to an Atlanta department store shopping for baby clothes when she noticed a commotion. She stopped as police cars arrived to break up a sit-in at the lunch counter inside. She witnessed several young black men dragged out by the police, including, she was pretty sure, a young John Lewis. Before she went into labor, she thought about that scene at the department store, as she clutched the picture she kept in her purse of Mr. Lewis standing alongside President Kennedy and Dr. Martin Luther King, Jr. in the White House in 1963. One day, she prayed, her son would stand in the Oval Office alongside the President.

The Bursans lived and raised young John on what many called the wrong side of Atlanta. Jean found work as a security guard, after his application to serve as an Atlanta police officer had been rejected. Eunis took a job as a social worker. John picked up the nickname "Kareem" during college at Yale, which he attended on a full scholarship. He loved playing basketball, and tried to mirror Kareem Abdul Jabbar's sky hook, a much less effective shot at 6 foot tall than it was for the 7 foot 2 inch future NBA Hall of Famer. Still, his persistence at is made it an effective weapon for him, thus landing the nickname, which he embraced.

John wanted to return to Atlanta after college. Jean was sick on and off during John's junior year at Yale, with the illness that would later take his life. John turned down several scholarship offers at the most prestigious law schools to attend Emory University law school on a full ride. John also wanted to intern for Congressman Lewis. One day in his first semester at Emory he took the bus to the Congressman's office, and sat patiently until they could speak. Within a few weeks of interning, he had so impressed the Congressman that he told his namesake, still just 21 years old, that he would love to see him in the US Congress one day -- just not his seat. They enjoyed a hearty laugh. Young John, who was always looking ahead, rented an apartment within the portion of the 4th Congressional District which bordered and overlapped Atlanta. This location strategically placed him close to bus routes to the

Emory campus, his parents' home, and Congressman Lewis's office. He rode buses and walked everywhere, until his second year of law school, when he saved up enough money from his job at the law school library to buy a rickety car.

With inspiration and encouragement from his parents and the Congressman, John successfully ran for Atlanta city council at the age of 24. His JD became a credential, not a lifestyle.

That victory marked a string of successes. Atlanta elected John mayor at 33, and to the US Congress in 2002 at the age of 38. The honor of his lifetime, he would later say, was taking the Congressional oath of office standing next to John Lewis.

In November 2006, he won a third term with a stunning 73% of the vote. Days later, on a plane ride from Hartsfield-Jackson Atlanta International airport to Ronald Reagan Washington National airport in DC, Congressman Lewis leaned to his protege and half whispered, "John, you running in 08?"

"Congressman" which he always called him, whether in the halls of Rayburn House Office Building or at a birthday party in Georgetown, "I will run and serve as long as the fine people of Georgia's 4th will have me." Congressman Lewis laughed.

"Aim higher, much higher; think bigger, much bigger." With that, the Congressman opened his briefcase to read through several draft committee reports that would need to be finished up before the holiday recess. Young John's mind wandered about a higher run for a few minutes, maybe the Senate? From red Georgia? Then he took out his work.

A few weeks later, the Congressman told John his vision was for him to announce a run for President in 2007. A young black man from Atlanta, running with no incumbent President. The field would be wide open in both parties. Congressman Lewis assured John that his meteoric rise, intelligence, mild manners, and unbridled youthful optimism made him just what the country needed and would embrace. "The time is right, but I am too old," Congressman Lewis softly stated. It took young John a few weeks to embrace the confidence the Congressman showed in him, and to begin his exhaustive due diligence.

The rest became history as John quickly rose from Atlanta city council to the White House, becoming the first black man to take the Presidential oath of office on January 20, 2009.

In his first inaugural address, he credited so many who had paved the path for him. He included Congressman Lewis in that great litany. President Bursan expressed great hope for a post-racial America, for better days and years ahead, and for a healing of a nation once so divided that it went to war with itself. "We have walked from the Edmund Pettis bridge to 1600 Pennsylvania Avenue, all in the lifetime of so many who stand with us here today. Not as white Americans or as African Americans, but as proud Americans." Everyone present cheered; thousands and thousands cried. Many who were not there steamed and cursed, and plotted how to ruin this man's presidency.

| 5 |

Chapter 5: August 2014: Build a movement, pick the mover

On a humid August 1, 2014, Clark waited in the private lobby on the 52nd floor of NewsFirst Tower in midtown Manhattan. The crimson red couch was as soft as any he'd sat in, even with the buttons of the pattern striking his bloated frame in several undesirable places. He had to assume this couch and the rest of the plush décor was meant to look rich and inviting yet feel uncomfortable after a couple of minutes. The white carpet was thick and plush yet made his feet feel hot and sweaty. The Victorian era coffee table was too far to reach without lurching forward, with the most recent daily and weekly NewsFirst publications sitting teasingly just over the beveled gold filled edge. If you reach for either, you have to be balanced enough to not run your wrist across the dull protrusions. He had declined the offers for water or coffee, knowing he wasn't planning to stay long enough to drink either. He checked his American made watch for the third time. "I'm very sorry Mr. Clark, he is just finishing up." Glenda or Brenda or whatever her name was - she'd said it, he just wasn't that interested – emphasized the "is" again, third time. Clark just leaned back, the buttons digging into his shoulder blades. While she was strikingly attractive, he was on a schedule.

Two minutes later, the red mahogany door opened, and another gorgeous Glenda or Brenda welcomed him in, simply waiving her left arm for him to pass, like a restaurant host motioning him towards his usual table at his favorite restaurant. "Right this way." More plush carpet, similar furnishings, another waiting area, but she led him to the final entrance door, which was open. Clark walked in, and she closed the heavy door behind him.

Fritzy didn't bother to get up. His long arms stretched out onto his bawdy desk, the white pin stripes of his tailor-made navy blue suit popping in an almost blinding manner. Clark eyed the gleaming gold cufflinks adorning a dark blue dress shirt, closing the French sleeves just below the FSS monogram. His neatly cropped, slicked-back hair was as silver as his tie, and at 6 foot 4 he was an imposing figure, even sitting down and even at 76 years old. "JB, please sit down. Coffee? Tea? Juice? Did the girls offer you something?"

"I'm fine Fritzy. Really, thanks. I'm just ..."

"I know, meetings backed up all day, running late already and it's only 8:30am. So let's get right to it. What can NewsFirst do for you?"

Clark shoved his 285 pounds into the George Washington chair on the left side of the desk, the one strategically placed further away but better angled to look at his host. "Fritzy, you know the primaries are just months away."

"I do. And of course I know we cannot coordinate a media campaign for or against any candidate you love or hate without the FEC and FCC rummaging around where my gastro guy usually is." Both smirked.

"Wouldn't dream of it."

"So who's your guy? We hear Danzinger." Clark was savvy enough to know that meant Fritzy preferred Otto Danzinger, the son of a World War II hero, himself a two star general in the Army who commanded in theater during Desert Storm. Fritzy's intel was good, as always. Otto was on Clark's list of three.

"Almost. We looked long and hard at Danzinger. Incredible record, impeccable credentials, and shares our philosophy – he just obviously couldn't be public about it. You know the military has been half battle preparation and half PR the last 15, 20 years. We have a lot of guys who would love a Danzinger type but we can't find one acceptable to The Leaders." Fritzy was disappointed, but was more concerned about increasing NewsFirst's power and influence over the election than who the candidate is. He kept his facial expression the same.

"So who?" Clark cleared his throat.

"Drake Richards." Clark let the name settle in the thick air of Fritzy's office. Fritzy leaned forward, started to open his mouth, then reclined back in his red plush, button patterned, roller desk chair. He swiveled a bit atop the plastic carpet protector, pursed his lips, clasped his hands and brought his well-worn, wrinkled pointer fingers together to his lower lip. He more slightly exhaled "Richards" than repeated it audibly. Clark could see the decision trees running through Fritzy's sharp and savvy brain.

"Polling?"

"Nothing meaningful yet. I mean, we have seven years of Nielsen ratings and popularity polls to work from."

"Yeah, but that's TV stuff. You can't translate game show viewers to how he'd do as a politician." Clark nodded his head, and then Fritzy did. "Which is precisely why you're here. You think you can."

"You've evening TV guys have had him on several times."

"Oh, I know, I know. He and O'Day really hit it off. Richards is a buffoon, but man, what an electric personality. He had the number one game show for three years running, pulled 14, 15 million viewers in..." "He calls it a reality show."

"They're all reality shows. He can call it the state fair for all I care. His numbers were off the charts -- in spite of being a complete asshole in his personal life. I care about viewers not labels. And you're right, his cross-over ratings are strong. O'Day pulled huge shares the nights he was on." Fritzy pursed his lips again. "Age? He'd be 70, 71 by the election, right?"

"Yup. But The Leaders are mostly guys in their 60s, 70s and 80's, so his age doesn't scare us. I know it doesn't bother you. And I think the country is ok with going older, especially the demographic he plays to and coming off a younger guy."

"You've talked to him?"

"We've talked, my top team, vaguely. He had no idea why – he thought we were lining up an endorsement, which is what we wanted him to think. But his ego is so huge that he said he'd only endorse himself, how he knew more than any politician on what America needs right now, blah blah. We let him bloviate – couldn't really stop him. Most important, we share the same values. We believe the same core. He's had all types on his show, network makes him and pays him tons of money, but if it was up to him, it'd be all white all the time. I'll talk to him myself but wanted your non-coordinated, totally legal just TV type thoughts if we run him." Again, they both smirked.

"I'll rewatch some of him on O'Day. We'll run some analytics through our Austrian affiliate – more freedom there to do the research and not run afoul of US election law. What's your timing, JB?" Clark smiled, pushed his large frame out of the chair and stretched out his chubby arm to shake hands.

"Same as yours, Fritzy. When you're all in, we are ready to rock and roll. I'll show myself out."

"Call me in 3 days."

"No calls. I'll be here Friday at 7:30am. Work for you?" Fritzy nodded, and Clark left. Both were glad that the subject of Fritzy's idiot son as the third candidate on the list did not come up.

| 6 |

Chapter 6: Toothy shiny grinning

That Friday, Clark went straight from seeing Fritzy to Drake Richards' palatial offices in midtown Manhattan, which had been described by the New York Times Sunday Magazine in 2012 as "what gawdy and ostentatious look down on." The aura Richards had been going for was uncompromising affluence. When he gave his now former third wife an unlimited budget, he was aiming for a "big splash." Instead, she made his private office look like what the New York Times called "the set of a movie about a Russian oligarch who installed a very high end brothel in the Kremlin."

New York's upper crest and intelligencia would never accept this ham-handed buffoon, in spite, or perhaps because of, his "champagne wishes and caviar dreams" display of wealth. No matter how successful he became, he would always be a Coney Island huckster, an outer-borough vulgarian. He could wave his barely earned MBA and propped-up financial statements at dinner parties as much as he wanted. Richards could never sandpaper down the rough edges of his roots or persona.

Regardless, Richards gloated that he had been featured in the Times. While the story did not question his publicly stated wealth – a subject on which Richards had brought several lawsuits and threatened many more – the pictures shouted mission accomplished to him. He projected wealth and success. That was all Richards cared about. The hell with the inside crowd.

From 2011 to 2014, Richards had hosted the most popular prime time game show in television history, in terms of consistent Nielsen ratings. The concept behind "Pitch Me" was simple. Wealth wannabes would bring a new product or business idea to Richards, the self-declared king of the sales pitch. The sell could be for anything. Vitamin supplements, a real estate project, balloons that played music. The network would stake the winner to $10,000 in seed capital. Richards' company would nab a one year consulting agreement and an extra fee for helping bring the concept to market. Even better, any deals that became successful were highly touted, and the rest buried under non-disclosure agreements until forgotten.

As often occurred with TV programming, the show's popularity began to slip after four years as the highest rated game show. "Pitch Me" did not have the sustaining power of Law & Order, Jeopardy or even General Hospital. That measurable fact did not stop Richards from continuing to claim the "#1 show in all of television," a boast that was never true.

In 2013, a former show winner sued Richards for allegedly stealing his concept, a mixed use, gated development in Arizona. There, cars would be forbidden and instead residents had to walk, ride bicycles or drive golf carts everywhere. The development would be outfitted with grocery stores, pharmacies and its own post office. In other words, no one would need to exit the gates and enter the outer world for anything they wanted. The absence of cars would make the project the most environmentally friendly development of its size, bar none.

Richards couldn't care less about the environmental impact, but it made for a great sales angle to those uppity yuppies who had more cash than brains, in his opinion. Plus Richards thought he could somehow restrict the development to white residents only, without expressly advertising that of course.

He loved the idea of profiting from everything in the development, including home, golf cart and bicycle sales almost as much as he loved racial purity. He even had his in-house lawyer research how to charge the US government rent for running a post office. But since Richards knew he couldn't raise the funds to undertake such a huge project, he purposefully sabotaged the winner's efforts until after the year-long consulting agreement ran out.

Three weeks later, Richards clandestinely signed a licensing deal with a Russian investor who had acquired 1,200 acres near Scottsdale, Arizona. Richards slipped under the radar through various single pur-pose entities formed in Arizona to do exactly what the contestant had spent over a year planning out. He knew it would take a few years to pull the permits and approvals together before the first house went up. The project that would be called Richardson, Arizona. As expected, the groundbreaking featured an ostentatious ceremony, with a walk-through of the model home hosted by a runway model, a former Miss USA, and Richards declaring himself the genius behind the whole pro-ject.

When news of the lawsuit broke, Richards went on his favorite night time talk show, the "News of the O'Day Hour" on NewsFirst, to proclaim that his licensing deal was "totally and 200% different from what that loser had brought me. His idea was so bad, so terrible, I spent a year trying to get him to fix it, He couldn't. Loser. Cry baby. Plus he wanted to do Yuma – Yuma – who the hell would want to live in Yuma? I got this deal done in Scottsdale, which is totally, totally beau-tiful. It's like Manhattan, just in the desert."

The geographic reality that the project was closer to Yuma than Scottsdale was not a distraction to Richards. Facts usually weren't. Of course, since O'Day was not a journalist, he never asked about the Russ-ian money behind the project. He did focus on the resident profile Richardson would attract. They said everything about the homeowner Richards wanted to come live there, stopping just short of putting up a highway billboard that would say "Blacks Need Not Apply." Richards was actually okay with Jews living there. He thought of them as marks, terrible golfers whom he could fleece in tournaments. Plus, he wanted to open a bank there to finance the home purchases and thought they would be perfect to run Richards National Bank.

To Clark, the history of the guy he was about to offer to make the most powerful man in the world was exactly what The Leaders wanted. He looked around at the many pictures of Richards outfitted in frames of varying style, size, darkness, and material. The only consistency of anything hanging on these walls was each one had Richards flashing a gleaming, somewhat childish, full toothed smile. Clark almost laughed out loud when he looked at the redwood framed magazine cover that proclaimed Richards "Man of the Year". In it, Richards was wearing a golfing outfit, standing on the set of "Pitch Me," and leaning on a driver. The detail work was shoddy, and, of course, Richards never won such an award. But this reflected the man Clark knew well – the consummate media hound, obsessed with his own popularity.

No one knew his actual net worth - it was a huge mystery - but Richards always went out of his way to proclaim himself a billionaire. He actually sued Forbes for not listing him among the 100 most wealthy people on the planet in 2014. Clark also knew Richards had pursued many failed business enterprises, had been sued dozens of times, bankrupted several companies, and had a reputation of stiffing contractors and employees.

Those were big negatives for any serious businessman, which Richards most definitely was not. But he didn't drink and had no public sex scandals - thanks in large part to Fritzy's tabloid division. For a politician those were huge plusses, despite the fact that he was on his 4th marriage. He and his company also donated to Democrats and Republicans alike. Where those dollars went was usually based on the location of a pending deal when connections counted.

Richards' frumpy looking personal assistant came out to bring him in. This was a big change from the last time Clark was here, which was before wife #4, when Richards surrounded himself with leggy, ex-models. Clark assumed that since Richards' current wife was a former cover girl, she had dictated the personnel change.

Inside Richard's executive office, the king of his domain sat perched on his yellow gold leaf encrusted chair. . Richards didn't bother to stand or shake hands. Wearing an expensive suit and tie, the jacket extra-long to hide the girth he usually lied about when asked – "totally fit, 8% body fat" - Richards simply pointed to the chairs on the visitor side of the desk, flashed his pearly whites, and barked "sit sit." Clark settled himself into a chair that must have cost $10,000, and assumed there was still a balance due. "So, JB, what are we talking about? How big a donation, and what does it get me?"

"Take a deep breath, Drake. It's much bigger than that."

"Miserable damn day. Good thing for you the rain made me cancel my golf game."

"Yes, pity," answered Clark. Richards was known for his impatience, so the extra five seconds Clark took to answer the why they were meeting question left Richards squirming in his noisy leather chair. "Drake, how would you like to be President of the United States?" A question as momentous as that, requiring quiet and sober study, reflection and introspection, evoked none of that in Richards.

"What's the angle?" In Richards mind, being asked to be the most powerful person running the most powerful country in the world was not a matter of doubt. Asking "am I qualified" was a loser's question. Instead, Richards' thoughts were laden with "what's in it for me".

"No angle. We've done a lot of work on this, focus groups, private polling, talked to the right people, and we think we can you can run credibly. Better yet, we think you can win."

"Of course I can win. Tell me why I should do this? 'Pitch Me' is still super-hot" (it was not; the ratings had been waning for three years, but it was still a top 30 game show) "and my town in Arizona is taking a lot of my face time. The luxury condos in Turkey, the hotel in Peru, the spa in Chacararcas, all take a lot of my time." He never learned how to say Caracas, Venezuela. "I've got my hands full, flying all over the world. Plus I'm making a shit load of money." Debatable, thought Clark, but no one really knew. "Why would I want this job? What's it pay? Two hundred grand?"

"First, it pays $400,000 per year. More important, you can keep your business deals, and when you go to visit them you'd fly on Air Force One." Richards looked up. He loved the image, flying on Air Force One, jet-setting around the world. And for free. He started to think - press following him everywhere, glued to his every word. The geeks with their fancy college degrees having to analyze what he said to see how it might affect the stock market or the world economy, like they do for this awful, miserable SOB black so-called president we have now.

"Tell me how this works; and keep it quick. I've got a massage in 10 minutes." Ten minutes, thought Clark; 10 minutes to explain the details of federal election law and process, building a staff, grueling primaries, campaigning, and debates, the states he would have to carry to get 270 in the electoral college. With a mind like Richards, a waste of eight minutes, and nine minutes longer than his attention span. Clark has already boiled it down to three nouns; power, money, fame. All he needed do was put the adjective awesome in front of each. Richards was in.

With too much now to do to walk back the four city blocks to NewsFirst's offices, Clark texted Fritzy "he's in. talk tomorrow. Call me 7am." He checked his calendar; August 2, 2014; the first primaries would be in February 2016, so he had 18 months to build an organization and a movement. If anyone could do it, Clark told himself, it's you.

| 7 |

Chapter 7: August 2014: Ebola and the development of a quiet leader

On the morning of August 8, 2014, the WHO issued a health advisory. The agency announced a total of 68 new Ebola virus cases as well as a total of 29 deaths in Guinea, Liberia, Nigeria, and Sierra Leone, Africa. This advisory followed an Emergency Committee teleconference to determine whether the current outbreak constitutes a "Public Health Emergency of International Concern." After discussion and deliberation, the Emergency Committee advised of possible serious consequences of further international spread. The virulence of the virus, the ease of transmission, and the weak health systems in the most at-risk countries complicated the task of tackling the disease. Tsang Yi DeeLu, "Ricky" to his western friends, fully agreed with issuing this advisory. He was already months into studying the outbreak and well understood its lethal potential.

Ricky was one of a kind, even among the highest levels of advanced medical experts. Born Tsang Yi in 1984 to affluent parents in Shekou Residential District on the banks of the Sheshui River in Hubei province, China, he had the heart of a public health scientist despite being the only child of a communist capitalist. His father, Tsang Wai, was a pioneer of the Chinese business practice of guanxi, a method of building personal trust and a strong relationship with someone, with the added advantage of being able to convince them they had a moral obligation to extend you a favor.

When China began opening its markets to outside investment in 1978, Tsang Wai saw a tremendous opportunity to leverage traditional guanxi with Western capitalism, and entered into consulting contracts with several US companies that were eyeing entry into this enormous Asian market.

By the time Ricky was ready to leave the academy years early for college, at the age of 14, his parents had enough money to send him to any university he wanted to attend.

His father also agreed to Ricky incorporating his mother, Mae's, maiden name, DeeLu, as part of his legal name. While Tsang Yi was primarily a traditionalist, he understood how the future may be unfolding economically and socially, and valued domestic tranquility. By 1998, some affluent couples began using a mother's surname for a second child. At the time, Chinese law specified that a child could have either their father's or mother's surname, with the vast majority taking the father's name. Tsang Wai was able to use his influence to obtain an exception for their only child, having to agree in writing to having no more children, which he and Mae had already agreed upon. As a result, Ricky's legal name was changed before he was issued his first passport.

Ricky earned a scholarship to Kings College in London, where he met Professor Edmund James Dorchester, an impeccably dressed, oddly mannered, obscenely brilliant bioethicist and virologist. Professor Dorchester had won a British Wolf Prize for his novel work in gene editing. The bronze medallion hung on a shelf below his several medals for competitive ballroom dancing earned in his 40's and 50's. "Anyone can win a Wolf," he often joked, "but not everyone can master the Argentine Tango." After just a few days together, he told Ricky that he had a once-in-a-generation mind – almost, not quite, but almost the equal of his – but he should be more flexible and at least learn to waltz.

Another of the Professor's bad jokes: "you have to waltz before you can run."

Ricky stayed and studied under Professor Dorchester. He was on track to earn his PhD at the age of 22 when, in 2005, he read of a strange outbreak of infections in certain birds that was also attacking farm animals in China and other Asian countries. Knowing the long tradition of Asian countries underreporting bad news that might reflect poorly on their culture or scientists, Ricky asked to pause his PhD studies and turn his full time attention to working on what later became known as the H5N1 avian flu. With his father's political connections, and after signing lengthy nondisclosure agreements, he was able to secure temporary work permits for himself and Professor Dorchester to study with Chinese scientists at the Health Ministry Lab. This was a rare break in China's medical and scientific secrecy, but with China having long been a WHO reporting country, the political leaders allowed for this collaboration as long as it was conducted through the WHO China Representative Office. Ricky was pleased to do so, as this would be his first collaboration with the WHO.

While in Shenzen on a field inspection, Ricky met his parents for dinner at their roomy new home. By then, Wai was working with Ten-Cent, an internet company that was trying to apply the personal dynamics of guanxi to the less personal connections made via computer through an application called the Xiaonei Network. Wai asked his son if he would consider moving back home to China and help TenCent develop its algorithms for human interconnectivity. Wai saw algorithms that could predict social interactions and the ability of guanxi to modify relationships through emerging social media platforms as the future – as opposed to discovering what was killing birds and farm animals..

"Dearest father", Ricky began. He remained a humble and most respectful son. Continuing in his infrequently practiced but perfect Southwestern Mandarin dialect, "I cannot speak much of my work here, as you must know and can understand. But what kills birds today could kill us all tomorrow. What good is making personal connections on the computer when the friend on the other end may become ill and die?" His father simply nodded, as did Ricky. His mother, Mae, smiled, beaming with pride. Wai retained his stoic exterior, bursting with confidence that if anyone could find the cure to this bird flu, it was his Tsang Yi.

Three weeks later, in May 2005, Ricky was with Professor Dorchester at the US National Institutes of Health (NIH) headquarters in Washington, DC, meeting with their chief immunologist, Dr. Seymour Cooper, "Dr. C" to his students, friends and colleagues. For years Dr. C had been the leading infectious disease doctor in the US. Ricky's departure from China was under very controlled, very methodological circumstances. Two Chinese Health Ministry scientists and three political attachés were part of the delegation. Their presence was mandatory at every meeting. While China shared a multi-national commitment to finding a safe cure for the avian flu, it did not want to be blamed for its outbreak or spread. Ricky felt pride and humility. He was only 21 and attending a meeting with some of the world's best known immunologists and virologists. Dr. C, having now spent 25 years as a career public health expert, saw potential parallels between himself and Ricky. After the first day's discussions, parts of which Ricky led without fear or boasting, Dr. C took him aside and, in his still strong Brooklyn accent, said "kid, you've got a great future in this incredibly important work." That night, Dr. C introduced Ricky and his "posse" to knishes and pastrami sandwiches at his favorite deli in Georgetown.

The next dozen or so years of Ricky's life felt like he was drinking water from an intermittent fire hose. For months at a stretch, he would study and develop immunological theories, finish and defend his PhD, read and write distinguished papers on virology and bioethics, and attend conferences. Then he would pivot to months of emergency calls, meetings, long flights, tests and studies for another crisis, another outbreak, a new strain.

By the time the August 2014 WHO Ebola advisory was being reported on NewsFirst and other 24 hour cable news networks, Ricky was landing in Sierra Leone. He had been dispatched to help lead an international team of virologists and epidemiologists to continue working towards finding a safe and effective treatment. Ricky's team was joined on the ground by public health mitigation experts who worked toward containment strategies. They knew that the WHO would shortly convene a panel of medical ethics experts to begin looking at the use of experimental treatments to offset the ongoing Ebola outbreak. Time was of the essence. There were no approved medicines or vaccines to fight this deadly virus.

That summer Ricky had been named as a senior member of the White House Ebola Response Task Force known by the acronym ERTF. Where would Washington be without its acronyms? As a Chinese national, Ricky needed a special O Visa issued by the State Department, as a person with extraordinary ability or achievement in science, to allow him easier entry into the United States, and to associate with the ERTF. President Bursan personally intervened to make that happen. For months, the ERTF had been at the center of the president's four-prong, multi government, public private approach to this disease. Ricky provided much needed help in designing and overseeing implementation of this global strategy. The same vetting process that resulted in Ricky securing an O Visa allowed him to obtain select visitor status for meetings at the White House, the Eisenhower Executive Office Building (EEOB) , NIH and CDC.

Not much progress was being made on a cure or vaccine, and, after the agreed 60 days, Ricky and his team were back in Washington, briefing the Ebola response team at the White House, with the President in attendance and asking questions, clearly engaged. The numbers of cases were growing and public concern was on the rise. Certain news networks and social media sites run by rightwing agitators were spreading fear and heightening paranoia about a yet unseen massive Ebola outbreak in the US. They raised the specter of infected water supplies and the potential for tens of thousands of deaths. Darker corners of the internet chattered about the coming "black plague." President Bursan knew that many Americans were gripped with fear about an Ebola pandemic, so he decided it was time to speak to the country.

| 8 |

Chapter 8: October 2014: Control Ebola at its source

On October 26, 2014, President Bursan held a press conference in the White House briefing room, surrounded by Dr. C, the head of the CDC, Ricky and several other members of the White House Ebola task force. Ricky and Professor Dorchester stood off the raised briefing area to the right, but still visible in the wide angle shot. Bursan began: "In March 2014, the World Health Organization reported an outbreak of the Ebola virus disease in the West African country of Guinea. Immediately at that time, we implemented a four-pronged approach as part of our task force game plan to limit Ebola exposure in the US."

The president explained: "First, controlling the epidemic at its source in West Africa. Second, minimizing the epidemic's secondary impacts that aren't directly caused by the disease. Third, leading a coordinated international response. Fourth, building a robust global health security infrastructure. To date, our response has been highly effective. While there have now been more than 22,500 reported Ebola cases in West Africa, with more than 8,900 deaths, here at home, US medical teams have treated a total of just 12 Ebola patients, and all but two recovered." He went on to assure the American public that while many were suffering in West Africa and a few other less fortunate countries, and that such suffering anywhere was tragic everywhere, Americans were safe. He then took questions. He called on CNN's Dr. Taupee, their chief medical correspondent, but a newcomer to the press briefing room. "Mr. President, what have we done to treat patients in West Africa and help contain the disease there?"

"Thank you Dr. Taupee. We are focused on science, not fear. The United States has sent more than 3,000 U.S. health officials to Liberia, Sierra Leone, and Guinea to assist with response efforts, as part of a 10,000-person U.S.-backed civilian response. The best way to stop this disease, the best way to keep Americans safe, is to stay the course we have been following since March - to stop it at its source in West Africa."

A Wall Street Journal reporter was next. "Mr. President, we have reporting that World Health Organization officials are concerned that the global response is inadequate to keep the Ebola virus contained, and these officials think we should limit or suspend all travel from Africa until this deadly disease is fully contained. Do you plan to suspend travel from Africa to the United States?"

President Bursan responded. "Linda, we are controlling the epidemic at its source in West Africa. Our scientists - and we have the best minds in the world working on this - they do not believe that right now a travel ban is the right way to go. Plus that would potentially strand our doctors and other health workers who are there helping fight this disease." The reporter from NewsFirst, who only had received his credentials two weeks earlier, kept thrusting and jabbing his harm up in the air, but could not get the President to call on him. So he just jumped up and shouted out his question.

"Sir, Joe O'Day, NewsFirst. We have multiple reports that the number of Ebola cases here in American is already in the hundreds, maybe thousands, and that your administration has directed the health agencies to report those cases as unconfirmed. Do you care to comment?" President Bursan wheeled his head and eyes to glare at the reporter. While decorum required that you be called on before a question would be addressed, the reporter shouted loud enough and at the right time for the question, more of an accusation, to be clearly heard by the world-wide audience that was listening.

"In unsettling times like this, there is often fear and apprehension that can breed conspiracy theories and misinformation. Whatever sources you have, whatever reports you think you have, I can tell you categorically are false. Dr. Copper will now address the remainder of your questions. Thank you everybody." With that, the President bounded out of the room, questions still bouncing off of him as he left. Dr. C stepped on the podium and took over the lectern, Ricky and Dorchester now flanking him.

Fritzy called Clark. "You watching." Clark was in a black car on his way to Richards' offices.

"Oh yeah."

"Is this it? This the moment?"

"Oh. Hell. Yeah."

"Meet you there."

Clark could barely make himself wait until the driver had opened the door, then launched himself out of the car, and sprint-waddled to the entrance. Fritzy was in his private elevator heading down by the time Clark was in Richards' elevator bank going up. This would be the moment, the opening they had been building towards for the past two months of having their untraceable social media exploiters spreading fearful and mostly hateful propaganda about Ebola, this "black plague," coming to America and killing millions of innocent hard working, tax-paying, true Americans.

| 9 |

Chapter 9: Until we figure out what the hell is going on

Of course Richards had watched the press conference. He spent most of his day watching TV and all the major stations covered the event live. While waiting for Fritzy to arrive, Clark listened to more of Richards babbling about what a crappy job "he" had done, how much better Richards would have done as President, how the lighting was wrong, the staging amateurish. Clark looked up from his smart phone to catch some of the meaningless banter, realizing that Richards had yet to refer to the leader of the free world as the President. Clark liked that – a lot.

Once Fritzy arrived and the frumpy executive assistant had to look up momentarily from her on-screen crossword puzzle to lead him in, the meeting could now start. The hardwood, ornate door closed with a thud behind her. Of course, officially, this meeting never occurred. Fritzy was not taking any chances of being accused of making an illegal in-kind campaign contribution. Not only did he imagine Richards as a vessel to help advance his Aryan race supremacy agenda, he saw practical business advantages, largely in increasing his radio and television station holdings. The current FCC was stingy in its aggregation rules, and Fritzy desperately wanted to expand his European presence, then consolidate with his US operations, and continue to grow his online presence.

His business plan could increase the value of his empire by $2 to 3 billion. One of his cases trying to throw out or significantly weaken the aggregation rules was pending before the DC Circuit court, and undoubtedly would end up at the Supreme Court. But having Richards gave him extra options. A change in administration leads to a change at the FCC and maybe a change in rules. A change at the Department of Justice which was prosecuting the case against NewsFirst could lead to dropping the case and, as a last resort, a change in the composition of the Supreme Court leads to a more favorable, business friendly court if the first two options failed. So, really, investing the $200 million in dark money to help prop up Richards was a pretty good investment with a possible 10 to 15 times return.

Richards, of course, was the first to speak. "So when do we launch?"

"We have the basic infrastructure built," answered Clark. "We've been waiting for a window you could jump through and make a big splash. This is it." Richards looked puzzled. "This, Drake, this Ebola crisis. Lots and lots of people are scared. We helped make sure of that. We've been stoking this on social media and chat rooms online for months, and have covered Ebola every week on our broadcasts. A natural enemy to fear – a deadly disease – combined with people a lot of our constituents already don't like – people coming to our country from Africa. You follow?" Richards tucked his tongue against his left inner cheek, tilted his large head to the left, then right. Fritzy and Clark both understood the light bulb had not yet come on, so Fritzy jumped in.

"You're going to a hold a press conference tomorrow. You're great at the mike and in front of the cameras. You'll announce a presser today and let suspense build around what you're going to say. Some will assume it's about whether "Pitch Me" is coming back next year. You've seen the media reports around that?"

"Sure, of course. Some assholes leaked my negotiations with the producers about whether I'd be willing to renew." Clark smirked.

"I'm that asshole. We planted the story to build buzz around your press conference." Clark didn't bother to correct him that the story was actually that the network was ready to dump him.

"Is that why O'Day didn't want me on? I called him a few times and he didn't jump at having me on like usual."

"That's why." Fritzy was on that. "Plus we were wicked busy getting him credentialed at the White House. I told him hold you away for a few days. Our correspondents knew this thing was brewing and we figured it was only a matter of time before there was a big White House event, telling everyone not to panic. Helps to have a guy on the inside of the administration." Fritzy paused a moment, proud of himself. "So you'll be on O'Day tomorrow night. The presser will be in your lobby tomorrow afternoon at two. Your media lady is ready to send the announcement and it's all set up – except for what you'll be announcing. You tell your wife you're going to run?"

"Nah. Not yet. I'll tell her tonight and tell her to wear one of those runway model dresses she's been buying. Something sexy right?"

"Sexy is fine but not distracting. Make sure you get most of the camera time." Fritzy chimed in. "This story is about you, about what you're going to say, not what designer your wife is wearing."

"Not a problem. We'll make a big entrance, and I'll make my announcement. Who else you want there? Any of the kids?"

"No," Clark, thinking not those idiots, jumped in, "not for this. Not yet. And Steffi won't join you on O'Day. There's plenty of time to flash her and get her fans on board. Just not yet." Richards pursed his lips and nodded his head forward and back. He wiped his mouth.

"So, what's my pitch?" Fritzy swiveled his head to Clark, who took a standard size mailing envelope out of his jacket pocket. The envelope had three index cards in it; they both knew Richards wasn't a reader and no matter what they told him to say, he was too undisciplined to follow. But three points, no more than 50 words, even he should be able to deliver that.

Card 1: Ebola is a deadly, incurable disease that will kill millions of Americans.

Card 2: This administration can't protect you; they've done nothing; they have no cure, no plan, nothing.

Card 3: I will shut down all flights from Africa until there is a cure for Ebola and we are all safe! As President, I will always protect us!

The press conference email and faxes went out 10 minutes after the meeting ended. Called for 2pm October 27, 2014 in the lobby just outside the security desk in Richards' building, in view of the elevators.

At press time the next day, as usual, Richards was running a purposeful 20 minutes late, letting the suspense build. He had one of his junior executives make sure the lectern had his huge book promotional boards surrounding it -- 2011's "Pitch Me" and 2013's "The Perfect Pitch." If Richards had his way he'd make it a book sell and sign also, but he knew these media bums wouldn't pay for copies. Richards for years promoted his books as #1 best sellers, which neither was, and had threatened to sue his ghost writer several times if he ever said anything negative about him, his family, his show, or his books. His assistant called up – again ⌐ that the press was getting restless. He expressed his anger to Steffi that only 9 reporters showed – 9 – for a Drake Richards press conference. Of course he knew there would be over 20 people there since he made all of his employees and a few people from his PR firm come (they preferred to be called media consultants). Eight of the reporters worked the style and TV beats for outlets like Entertainment Tonight and TMZ. The lone CNN reporter present was working their experimental weekend segment on pop culture, and doing odds-and-ends like famous New York real estate stories. She recognized Brian Cannon, a politics reporter from NewsFirst, and walked over to him while they waited.

"Brian, hi. Kim Donet from CNN. What brings you here? Fan of the show or you live in the building?"

"Hey, Kim. Hi. I loved your segments on the history of the Upper West Side. Really good stuff. Glad you're getting to grow over there. You thinking about getting out of game shows and soap operas altogether?"

"Only every minute of every day. Goddamn degree in journalism from Columbia and I'm covering this idiot, aging, has-been? I hope the network cancels his sorry ass show, honestly."

"You sound like a woman with a grudge." Brian unexpectedly struck a chord. Kim looked around, then leaned in.

"Yeah, I guess I am. Look, not for repeating, but last time I was on his set for a piece, which was the last time I was on the set, he thought I was on set as a piece – for him. The MF grabbed me and asked how..." She made a puking face. "Gross. I can't even repeat it. I mean, he's like my grandpa's age. The pig."

"Oh, man, I'm sorry. I didn't know." Brian was sincere.

"Yeah. Worst kept secret in New York. Guy's a gross womanizer. He's settled like a half dozen suits, all with iron clad NDA's he's somehow kept under the radar. Honestly, there's some chatter that your tabloid has been doing catch and kills with his accusers, but no one has anything solid enough to report out on that." She let that stew for a few seconds, and seemed convinced Brian did not know. "And you know he threatens to sue anyone who does a negative story on him, and sued several journalists for libel just for claiming he was not really a billionaire. The networks defend but the reporter gets tied up in litigation for years while the network has to bench him or her because being a defendant makes you look like you're not objective. So even when you win the lawsuit, you've lost a bunch of work. We all thought the last executive producer at his show would go public but she never did."

Brian looked puzzled. "What, you never wondered how a director from a game show ends up at your network running a major weekend news block?" By the look on his face, Kim could tell Brian never had thought much about it, and when he did he just chalked it up to Richards' relationship with O'Day. Then again, Brian was pretty sure NewsFirst had a collection of NDA's for their own on-air talent in their lawyers' safe, so the concept was not foreign to him. Brian cleared his throat.

"So, look, I'm here because we think Richards is announcing a run for a pretty high office. You may have a scoop on your hands. Keep it for yourself. Get a camera crew over here – you should go live with it out front as soon as this is over. Maybe it will help get you out of reporting on brownstones and flower gardens and into some real news." Kim appeared surprised and appreciative. She smiled and stepped a half step away, nodding her head in appreciation. She whispered "thank you. Owe you one."

She began texting the cameraman she usually worked with to get over to "Elektra East," the name of the building. As she did, the very large E on each side of the center elevator's glossy burgundy reflective wrap started to part. Never the gentleman, Richards stepped out of the cab ahead of Steffi. As TMZ would report it, he was sporting a fresh coat of make-up, plenty of hair spray, and a defiant look as he furled his unibrow and strode slowly, almost angrily to the awaiting lectern. The NY Times style section would note the standard dark blue suit, far too long even for his 6' 2" frame, long, shiny red, unpatterned tie, and the smart magenta YSL suit Steffi sported, which popped against the elevator foil and drew out her olive green eyes. Even now at 48, Steffi maintained the figure and skin tone she had at 35 when she was Russia's entrant into the Mrs. Universe pageant. That's where she and Richards met. He was the emcee of the pageant that year, in addition to being one of the executive producers. That night 13 years ago he pulled an envelope from his tuxedo pocket, and announced Mrs. Universe 2003 as Stefanvia Skrypnika – even though the name on the card was Leonette Mmballa from Sri Lanka. The only other people who knew what he had done at the time were the head judge, the co-executive producer, and the show's main sponsor, Afdavil Dakrespitka. No one ever bothered to correct the mistake– not in Russia, not anywhere. Later that night, he shared the news with Stefanvia, now his wife Steffi, when he propositioned her. The SOB that he is, he still has the 2003 "and the winner is" card locked in his office. Dakrespitka kept the other copy, in case he ever needed a favor from Richards.

Kim turned her iPhone recorder on as soon as Richards grabbed each side of the lectern. He looked around, mostly down at, the assembled audience. "I have a brief statement. I will not be taking any questions. If you have any questions you can call into Joe O'Day's show at 8pm tonight." He removed the envelope from his pocket He cleared his throat. Card 1.

"My name as everyone knows is Drake Richards. For the last 15 years I have been the most famous man in America and the most successful television host ever. Ever! I totally and completely love this country, as does my beautiful wife Steffi who you see here behind me." Clark was starting to taste vomit in his throat while watching the live feed that only NewsFirst was carrying. He wondered, could Richards screw up a scripted announcement? "This great country has allowed me to build massive wealth, beyond the dreams of any contestant on my great and awesome show Pitch Me. Thanks to this great country I am a self-made billionaire." He paused for dramatic effect, surveying the small crowd.

Clark shouted "Stick to the cards" at his TV.

"You are all scared of Ebola. It is a totally major, deadly, uncurable disease that will kill millions of Americans."

Card 2: "This administration can't protect you. They've done nothing. This President", he leaned disrespectfully into the word president. "You saw his pitiful press conference. He has no cure, no plan, no nothing. In fact, to be totally honest, he won't do anything because the truth is he was born in Africa and will never turn against his homeland." Richards paused; Clark and Fritzy smiled.

Card 3: "In order to protect this great country that I love so totally and completely, today I announce that I am running for President of the United States. And believe me, when I am president, the first thing I will do is shut down all flights from Africa into our country until we can figure out what the hell is going on with this Ebola. Only I can keep you safe – and I will!" And with that, after lingering for a few seconds as the sole live camera zoomed in for his trademark "I look so smart" pursed lips and furled eyebrows, he turned, grabbed Steffi's left hand, and walked into the waiting, open elevator doors that his frumpy assistant made sure was perfectly timed for him, on threat of being fired if she screwed up the staging.

As Brian had the cameraman pivot to him for the "you just witnessed" follow up, Clark smiled. "Son of a bitch," he shouted, "he actually pulled it off." Clark's phone vibrated, with Fritzy's name lighting it up. Kim ran out the front doors, and started a live feed, breaking news on CNN from outside Elektra East.

| 10 |

Chapter 10: Soaking up the spotlight

At 8:00pm, the opening splashes began to run, clips showing O'Day interviewing current and former presidents and world leaders, ending with a clip of him from Iraq while embedded with a forward platoon during Desert Storm. The fact that most of those visuals were shot when Joe was with NBC News and then Fox didn't bother Fritzy. Joe loved how rugged he thought they portrayed him. Less than three years ago, Joe signed on with the then fledgling but brash cable news network. He said he made the jump to help lead a brave new frontier in news gathering and reporting. Others repeated whispers that O'Day was forced out for "behavior incompatible" with his most recent employer's reshaping of its image. When he moved over, a huge chunk of his on average 3 million loyal viewers followed him, leaving a huge hole in the prime time slot he'd vacated. Richards had been a featured guest on O'Day's Fox show several times, and made periodic call-ins as well.

As soon as the introduction concluded, O'Day was center screen in front of the stark background of multiple news screens. Square jaw, graying hair, dark blue suit, starched white shirt and red power tie, Joe exuded a confidence that exceeded his intelligence. But he knew one thing very well – how to draw his kind of viewers. They were a huge slice of white middle America. Basically, an average age of 58 coupled with a high school diploma. Their average annual income hovered at $42,000 per year, with a four-member average household. For all of their talk of traditional values, most were divorced or on their second marriage. As for race, many were white and others whiter. And they were mostly angry and pessimistic. Many had lost manufacturing jobs to foreigners and to too high operating costs due to stupid environmental rules. Their mines had closed or cut their shifts back due to so-called "workplace safety" rules. They firmly believed their own glory days and that America's best years were in the rearview mirror. And, thanks to incessant NewsFirst and internet messaging, they had an enemy, someone to blame for their worsened situations – the others. Blacks who succeeded only because of affirmative action; immigrants who illegally swam across the Rio Grande or burrowed under border fences to steal their jobs and sell drugs to their children; Middle Easterners with their tech skills and convenience stores; Asians with their superior math and science abilities.

O'Day tried to make himself appear to be one of his adoring fans, and largely he was; a middle aged white guy who never finished college, with an ex-wife and a prior encounter with opioid addiction. Of course, O'Day's income exceeded what any of his followers would make by a large multiple, but he'd managed to make that irrelevant. He was savvy enough to know the demographic he could best hone for his brand of instigation. They were people who carried a chip on their collective shoulders, naturally aggrieved. They and their children bore the burden of never-ending wars in Iraq and Afghanistan, because getting hired by the armed forces was a hell of a lot easier than finding work in a coal town or at a plant that sat rusting and closed. Most would never accept that they'd lost their jobs as the result of automation and technologies. But, they found solace in having someone to blame. They could relate with his dropping out of college, and admired O'Day for enlisting in service of his country.

O'Day often acknowledged he was an agitator, not a journalist. This allowed him to push grievances and fact-free conspiracy theories. Why do the boring research and present any evidence if his followers would believe him just because he said it? He had long ago lost any interest in being factually correct. Emotion trumped reason, so why do the heavy lifting? For him, the harder and louder he pushed his point of view, the more right it made him. He also reveled in having become something of a cult-like leader on the internet, especially in darker, angrier websites and chat rooms. Joe would sometimes purposefully be photographed at a coffee shop sporting a "F*CK PC" ballcap, his way of clearly expressing his disdain for the liberals, the woke and the politically correct. His world view made him kindred spirits with Richards, to whom any business setback was due to someone else getting pushed ahead of him out of societal guilt, not on the merits.

The glinting of camera 1 drew his stare. "Tonight, we are honored to have for the entire hour exclusively Drake Richards, the leading contender to be our next President of these United States. And as an extra special treat for our millions of viewers, tonight we are also introducing another new innovation. You can send questions in for our very special guest on our website, NewFirst.online. That's our online site, NewsFirst.online." Of course, O'Day, his producer and Richards knew the only questions that would be asked would be the ones that Richards had agreed to in advance, but the eager viewers wouldn't need to know that, as those who did not need help navigating the internet flocked to the web presence. "Drake. I have to ask you," Joe leaned in towards his guest, "I get that Bursan has done nothing to protect us from this incredibly lethal Ebola crisis. We've been on that story here at News-First for a long time now. Millions of Americans are scared out of their minds, and rightfully so. But, do you really think he's done such a terrible job with this plague because he was born in Africa?"

The scripted opening. They both knew that Richards had started toying with the idea of a run for president a few years earlier– no lower office would be worthy of him - but no one in the mainstream media took him seriously. He published a couple of full page adds at socially explosive moments to draw attention to himself. His accountant had figured out how to expense those adds, but his account executives at "Pitch Me" cringed each time he did. Not getting any major media coverage for anything other than his own show pissed him off.

So in 2011, he decided to stick his face into this fledgling internet conspiracy theory that Bursan was actually born in Niger. The baseless idea had gotten a small amount of traction on some fringe web sites but nothing in the mainstream media. But when Richards, then one of the most popular game show hosts on TV, did an interview on O'Day's then most highly viewed prime time "news" show while he was at Fox, he repeated this hateful rumor about the President of the United States, saying "you know, Joe, I'm not saying it's true. But a lot of people are saying this. So I sent a team of investigators to his home country and we're gonna have some very explosive things to expose, I promise you that. And I'll be back on your show with the evidence, which will be totally damming." Of course, Richards had come up with nothing. Still, this nothing-burger, nut-job theory now had major media outlets covering the absence of any evidence. That made a non-story into a story, and millions more people heard about it. Some chose to believe it while some put the burden on the President to disprove it.

Tonight, as an announced candidate, Richards went for it even more aggressively. "Joe, and I'm being totally honest here, as you know, we've had investigators looking at this very closely. Very closely. Since we, you know, when you asked me about it like a while ago. And you know how terrible the records are over there and so much corruption. So much corruption. We can't have this and it's not right, it's a sham, a total crime and conspiracy for this to happen in our great country. A lot of people are saying that one of his buddies burned down the grass shack poor excuse for a records building where his birth certificate was. Maybe it was Idi Amin; we can't know for sure – not yet." The reference to the former brutal dictator of Uganda who was exiled in 1979 and died in 2003 was another tested fear and hate button that Richards was told to press. This notwithstanding that Kampala, Uganda, where

Amin's last ruling palace had stood, was almost 2,700 miles away from Maradi, Niger where Bursan's parents were married.

The conspiracy theories of Bursan not being an American citizen grew out of his admission that his parents were married on December 17, 1963 in Niger after she was pregnant with him. But actual documents showed unequivocally that they left Niger on January 2, 1964 for Atlanta, seven months before he was born – in Atlanta, as his birth certificate clearly stated. As Bursan had explained many times, his parents wanted to be married in his dad's ancestral home, but as an American citizen his mother was refused the right to marry in Niger for several months, and she was pregnant by the time the license was granted, just weeks before the scheduled end of her service commitment in the Peace Corps. To those who bore Bursan ill-will because he was black, this was the perfect storm -- a white woman marrying a black African, having a baby out of wedlock, and allowing his father to become an American citizen by marriage and parentage. The hate-mongers who wanted to keep him from being elected President and then worked non-stop to undermine his legitimacy in the minds of as many who would listen, including Richards, kept up this assault on his citizenship and back story.

But none would doubt that Richards' adopting the conspiracy in 2011 gave it more legs. Some websites on what once were the outer fringes of the internet were now gaining currency and clicks. They also posted two allegedly authentic documents. One crumpled, slightly charred piece of paper looked like a birth certificate for a boy born in October 1963 in Maradi, Niger given the name Ohwalla Ma-deo, the name of Bursan's Nigerian grandfather; and the other, a supposed death certificate of a baby boy who was born in Atlanta on July 22, 1964, Bursan's birth date, and given the birth name John Lewis. The conspiracy went on that to claim that the real John Lewis baby born on July 22, 1964 in Atlanta to parents named Burnam died at 9 months. As for the Bursans, they stole his identity and paid off his grieving parents with money they needed for the funeral.

Richards could not keep this many details in his head, including that Niger and Nigeria were different countries with a shared border, but he knew and had promoted the basic theory. "But a lot of people have been worried about this and its totally, maybe we have to see, could be true, and we have people looking very closely into it and we expect to have more answers soon, very soon. And of course, we all know how terrible the records are in Atlanta, so much corruption there too."

The questions box on the website blew up, as did the phone number for the show posted on the same site. O'Day and Richards pretended to read listener questions, and went ahead with 48 more minutes of Bursan bashing, excluding the oh-so-necessary commercial interruptions. They could barely wait to finish the show and get the overnight ratings. The other topics they covered were how many more people were on welfare under Bursan, how many jobs were lost because of what a disaster NAFTA was, how the US was losing the trade war with China, and, Clark's favorite, all the illegals coming in through Mexico to steal your jobs and sell your children drugs. This stew compromised the hot button topics that Clark planned to make centerpieces of Richards' campaign. He needed O'Day to keep the total number of topics to five, praying Richards could keep track and just remember to say words like "disaster, awful, losing." He did. For the next 18 months, these would be Richards' go to topics.

| 11 |

Chapter 11: July 2016: The Richards Revolution

Can people still be shocked? In the age of the internet and 24-hour news cycles, where virtually nothing is private? When anyone can say anything from anywhere and reach a large audience with few facts? Where incredible violence can be captured on body cams, TV cameras, and video capable drones? The question remained to be answered. What was about to unfold would be a good test.

In July 2016, Richards stood back stage on the opening day of his party's nominating convention, assured by his incredible and improbable run of primary victories over 16 mostly career politician opponents, that he would receive the 1,237 delegates needed to capture the GOP's presidential nomination. He was about to become the race-baiting face of what was once called the Party of Lincoln. Political pundits on every major station except NewsFirst had spent months talking dismissively about Richards' publicity stunt of a run, how it was really just a PR campaign for some new show or business deal he was cooking up. It had to be.

In fact, news execs were so sure that Richards had no chance, they never thought to balance the air time he was receiving against any of the major, established candidates. He was awful policy but good TV.

By June 2016, with the nomination all but sewn up, a couple of news integrity non-profit groups estimated that Richards' campaign had received between $600 million and $800 million in free media, a staggering amount that no other campaign could possibly withstand. How long would it take, if ever, for major news outlets to reflect on the role they played in the Richards revolution?

By the numbers, 81% of his voters were white, 74% over 50 years old, and 63% had a high school diploma as the highest degree of education. Although most of the convention delegates were college grads, they had to follow the will of the voters, at least 200 of whom Clark made sure were sprinkled in amongst the delegates, just to make sure no one got some crazy idea about casting the wrong votes. The rest of the crowd on the floor were party operatives and press, along with event security. Politico reported that there were more black security guards than delegates.

Sporadic boos could be heard as a few delegates in states he had won attempted to vote for someone else, anyone else, on the first ballot. Those disloyal delegates were quickly surrounded by Richards supporters, wearing menacing glares. But the outcome was sealed.

Political insiders and party loyalists saw this as a prelude to a McGovern or Mondale type shellacking in the general election, notwithstanding that at least a dozen states were solidly for anyone running with this party's nomination. The PAC and Congressional reelection committees started shifting big money to down-ballot races, hoping to secure the House and Senate to offset having Richards at the top of the ticket.

Peering out from the left side back stage, Richards smiled as he viewed the sea of red "Richards Revolution" and "Richards Rebels" hats, tee shirts and buttons, many waving Confederate Flags. What a great business deal he fell into. He had negotiated for 35% royalties on all of the convention merchandise, and would be able to offload a few thousand of his books at sign and sells. While most candidates about to become their party's nominee waited in their hotel suites for the floor vote, didn't make an appearance at the convention until making their humble-sounding acceptance speech, Richards, without doubt, was not most politicians. He would be set up in the lobby, surrounded by Secret Service agents, hawking books and merchandise like a carnival barker. Dignity was not in his lexicon; profit and winning were.

The call of states was purposefully done out of order, so that his home state of New York could "cast its 162 delegates for the next President of the United States, Drake Richards," and in that moment formally secure his nomination. As soon as the state party chair finished speaking, hundreds of red, white and blue balloons dropped from the rafters, and Bob Seger's "Against the Wind" began blaring from the amped up audio system. Within minutes, emails would start flying from Capitol Records (an irony), demanding they stop playing the song without first obtaining the label's express permission and consent.

This would not be the first or last time Richards' team would get unauthorized use of protected media demand letters. He didn't care. Each time he received one he'd leak it to the press, which invariably played a clip of him surrounded by adoring fans as the music he was not supposed to use blared in the background. He may have been a social Neanderthal and ethically vacuous, but he remained a brilliant marketer.

Backstage, Steffi and Richards' two favorite children stood nearby. He kept checking his watch, knowing he would be forced to wait a few more minutes until the call of states was completed. His cell phone rang, as did Clark's. Richards' call was from O'Day, congratulating him and confirming their interview for 8pm, live from the convention center. "Yup. Got it." and flipped his phone closed. The call to Clark was from Fritzy on a burner phone, for a shared congratulations.

None of Richards' siblings called to say they were happy for him or proud of him. In fact, not once since he announced his run did they reach out. His two sisters and brother were still very angry about how he had manipulated their father into putting him in charge of his large estate, which he quickly depleted chasing bad deals. Yet somehow, he simultaneously was making big money on good deals. Several lawyers and accountants had tried to unravel the legal pretzel Richards has used to insulate himself from liability, but to no avail.

The senior campaign staffers' phones were blowing up with calls of offers to support the campaign; PAC's, Section 501(c)(4)s and 501(c)(6)s —dark money donors, companies formed in states like Delaware and Wyoming. Big, big dollar support was coming, and very little had to be made public. Current election finance law allowed huge amounts of "soft" money to remain hidden in the shadows. Some money had already been flowing in once Richards hit 1,000 committed delegates, others were now jumping on the Richards freight train. Richards held grudges his whole life, but never said no to money. He also made a mental note to call his personal lawyer when he got home to respond to Steffi's request to restructure their pre-nup.

As soon as Wyoming cast its delegates, the nomination on the first ballot was concluded. Richards had 1,516 delegates coming into the convention, more than he needed and enough to scare off any real challenge to get to a second ballot or a brokered convention. With Mike from Fort Worth, Texas manning camera 1, Richards was ready to make his way past a stage strewn with balloons, in front of his adoring fans, and a few hundred "Never Richards" t-shirt wearing detractors who now would be silenced by party unity. While "Pitch Me" never had anything near this number of cameras, he'd had more viewers for his show than were tuned in live right now. Regardless, he stood ready to soak in this moment he knew he so totally deserved.

Richards was now the nominee, an improbable twist on a wild ride. He pulled his jacket down, cleared his throat, and an intern pulled back the curtain. Pandemonium exploded as Mike's camera lens led him in. Mike always knew when to pan in, when to pan out. Queen's "We Will Rock You" filled the air, a subtle, yet unauthorized, shout out to his native borough. At the lectern, set up to look more like a pulpit, he surveyed the adoring crowd, sporting his now too familiar look, I am tough because my jaw is clenched, I am smart because my eyes are narrowed. Prime time is now.

Yet two days earlier, Richards had stared into the teleprompter as he rehearsed his lines. During the campaign he swore that only losers needed that dreaded gizmo. Not anymore. His left pocket held Clark's three cards from his announcement two years earlier ago, another five cards were stashed in his right pocket for tonight. Clark had made a habit of giving him between three and a half-dozen cards for every major campaign event. Tonight was no different. With teleprompters casting almost life size words, Clark was almost comfortable with the cards remaining holstered. But, still, a winning habit had been formed, and it had worked incredibly well. There was no reason to stop now.

Richards pursed his lips and Mike zoomed in. Richards' soft, manicured hands grabbed each side of the lectern. He never admitted to being nervous, not even to himself. Nerves were for losers, he often screamed at show staff and his children. "Tonight, we take our country back. We have totally won and our country is ours again!" Screams and cheers erupted, most from the rabid supporters who knew who "we" are and that they were counted among them.

"These past eight years with Bursan in our White House have made us a joke around the world. Our borders are weak, and criminals are rushing in from Mexico and all those awful backwards countries down there." Even with a prompter in easy view, Richards could not be stopped from riffing. "The Latins, the Mexicans, the other illegals who are not born here, they are not part of our America. I will secure our border for all real Americans!" The timed heightened volume and pause allowed for another delirious round of chants of "Richards, Richards, Richards" from the adoring faithful, the "we" the "real Americans" on the floor here, rousing the millions watching at home. "Terrorists are flying in from the Middle East, Muslims who want to kill us. No one is watching, no one is protecting our America. But I will!" Another planned pause and more fervent clapping and hooting of his name.

"Disease, plague, Ebola running wild in Africa and is coming to kill us. No one is protecting us, but I will!" More cheers, more love pouring up from the crowd. "Our streets in America overrun by gangs, totally disgusting criminals, thugs, scaring good Americans, killing good

Americans. No one is protecting us – but I will!" With that he slammed his left fist down, turned left, then right, jaw clenched and face squinched into his tough guy look. "As your next President, I will protect you. No one else but me can do it. And I will!" With that, he turned and left, kicking a few balloons on the way to back stage. Mike panned to the crowd, as all other cameras did.

In the second largest suite at the official convention hotel, Fritzy and Joe O'Day were so excited they were actually hugging. "Four months, Joe. Four months and this son of a bitch may actually become the next President."

"Let's make it happen. Hey, we got him this far." They clinked their Waterford double old fashioned glasses from Fritzy's collection, filled higher than usual with a healthy pour of Jameson's Irish whiskey.

"Yes we did." Clark would join them in 10 minutes, his poured glass waiting on the coffee table.

| 12 |

Chapter 12: November 2016: The Election

CNN, MSNBC, FOX and NewsFirst all had their election desks and front line anchors primed for a long, grueling day-of exit polls, on location interviews with voters, talking heads, political experts and pundits who seemed to know how this election would end. For almost every day since the conventions coronated the major party candidates, virtually every recognized poll had Richards losing nationally by 3-4%, and by electoral math by a margin of 336 to 202, maybe a bit closer depending on Ohio. Only one Quinnipiac poll had Richards getting close to the 270 needed to become president, but not above 254. One pollster/pundit at Politico, Evan Robby, kept trying to cut through the "we all know what's going to happen" group think, as was Jason Corbin Hall, the documentary film maker and political activist. For weeks, Hall warned and Evan predicted, "Richards can win this."

Hall made his point very specific. "What scares me the most is not his race baiting, his massive ego, or the dog whistles to far-right wingnuts. We have millions of people in this country who lost their jobs to automation, good union jobs. My family has worked in that mill and in that mine for generations kind of jobs. And they are pissed off. They are angry at every politician, local, state and federal. They have seen courts approve of affirmative action and gay marriage and so many things that they grew up never thinking would happen. And for a lot of them, when they go into that voting booth and pull that lever or take a sharpie to the circle on that ballot, they will vote for Richards as a way of saying screw you to the establishment, screw you to everything that has been happening to them and to every politician they blame for letting it happen. Richards can win. Don't get complacent."

Because he was Jason Corbin Hall, he got plenty of TV time, mostly on more liberal leaning cable news stations, but even once on Fox, albeit at the 4pm news slot. He spent weeks and a lot of his own money on a get-out-the-vote drive throughout his home state of Ohio.

Evan Robby fumed on pundit panels when liberal hosts called him needlessly alarmist and reflexively contrarian. Joe O'Day saw an opportunity to have Evan on for a 10 minute segment where he walked through the map and predicted states Richards could take to get to 342 electoral votes. Evan basically parroted what had been the unspoken campaign strategy: concede New York, New Jersey, Massachusetts and California, but put every other state in play. The only part of Evan's map that drew an O'Day challenge was New York. Playing to his audience, O'Day predicted Richards would take his home state "by a landslide."

How election night unfolded left many jaws dropped, and a few commentators in tears. The electoral math predictions at 6, 7, 8, 9 and even 10pm, with Theresa Janson winning easily, all started shifting at 11pm. She could no longer hide behind a rust belt firewall. There were audible "OMG" moments on cable as the votes poured in and results were starting to be called. Overseas, the Hang Seng, Nikkei and DAX stock markets started to tank. In the US, S&P and Dow futures started showing predictions of a 10% drop at the market opening .

At 2:45am, Wednesday, November 9, 2016, Theresa Janson made "the call" to Richards. The concession was short, painfully delivered, but gloatingly received. No class, none at all, is what Theresa told her husband after hanging up. It didn't matter. In the end, she had squandered a lead and lost. While the ultimate margin of victory for

Richards came down to less than 50,000 votes in four states, out of over 140,000,000 votes cast nationwide, it didn't matter. A win was a win was a win.

Richards assembled Steffi and their two children along with his three others from prior marriages. They defiantly headed to the ball-room, filled with his most rabid supporters who could afford the exclusive celebration ticket, and the high dollar donors, most of whom were late to the revolution. Richards' senior campaign staff, led by Clark, had already gathered. Fritzy stayed in his suite, texting with O'Day and a couple of his consultants and executives about how to best exploit this gold mine.

Clark's best speech writer had composed only one speech, proclaiming victory. Richards forbade a concession speech. It would bring bad luck he screamed. In the elevator, Clark handed him the envelope with three index cards. Even though the speech was now being cued on the prompter, Clark knew the president-elect would need to follow the campaign ritual of having a few cards each with a few words written on them. Mike from Fort Worth was at camera 3, the close-in camera that would carry the speech live to the nation and in the ballroom to the worn out media pool surrounded by cheering and elation.

The Richards family kicked and threw balloons, danced around in the confetti, as they headed center stage. His eldest son had invited a young woman he picked up in the hotel bar to come on stage with him. "Best pick up line, EVER!" he later texted a frat buddy who wanted to know who she was and how she got there. "I said, hey, want to meet my dad, the next president of the United States?" Tired, bleary-eyed but pulsing adrenalin, the Richards family defiantly strode across the stage like prize stallions at the state fair; all except his seven year-old son. He could barely keep his eyes open, as Steffi dragged him with her. They fanned out around the lectern, Richards, as always, at center stage.

Card 1: "I just received a concession call from my opponent. I proudly claim my massive victory as your next President." Of course, no graceful acknowledgement of a hard fought race.

Card 2: "Together we will restore our great country, the real America of our parents and grandparents. The America we all loved and the rest of the world respected." Richards was never a "we" fan, so he extemporized. "I am the leader you need, that this totally great and awesome country has long needed."

Card 3: Richards looked at this short list of thank yous, to his wife, his children, the voters, his campaign staff. For a split second, he considered this a moment of humility and appreciation. Like gas, the feeling passed. He raised both arms to a Nixon-like V: "I won. I am your president!" He stood and soaked in the applause that ensued, glowing and accepted what, in his narrow mind, he, and he alone, had accomplished.

Ricky looked up from his laptop at his desk at the Ministry of Health in Bangui, the capital city of the Central African Republic, to see a flurry of text alerts on his smart phone. He had been there for a month working on a containment and cure operation for a suspected outbreak of monkeypox. The WHO had issued an alert concerning 26 acknowledged cases of monkeypox in Central Africa in the early fall of 2016. The international agency advised that "Epidemiological investigations are currently on-going to evaluate the magnitude of the outbreak." Ricky had helped lead the international response team, whose work had now concluded. He was finishing his notes, but once he read the texts, he clicked open Sky News' website, which reported the proclamation of victory by Drake Richards.

Ricky was non-political, but had worked with enough American government officials and had enough friends in the US to know Richards was feared as an isolationist at best when it came to world health issues. His nearby lab partner, Jacques Riav, was vocal. "What an ass. He will set back our global health work by decades if he has his way. Protectionist. Denies the need for international cooperation." Ricky shrugged his shoulders, not knowing if he should or how to react while Jacques began shouting what he assumed were curses in French, some of which he'd heard, some of which were new to him.

His flight from Bangui to Beijing would leave in four hours. He needed to concentrate on finishing up his notes for the White House International Pandemic Task Force, which he was now concerned could become extinct. Ricky was looking forward to a few days with his parents, but not the 26 hours of flying it would take to get home.

| 13 |

Chapter 13: August 2018: Ricky at 34

On August 11, 2018, Ricky was about to acknowledge, not really celebrate, his 34th birthday. His mother, Mae, had just ended their video chat with a not-so subtle reminder that even for him, life's clock kept ticking, and maybe it's time to think about starting a family.

He had nearly finished packing his few travel items for a trip to London to reunite with Professor Dorchester. There, he would begin studying a potential new outbreak of Middle East respiratory syndrome coronavirus (MERS-CoV). Ricky was now affiliated with the British National Institute for Health and Care Excellence, which operated under the umbrella of the National Health Service. It had been a year since Richards disbanded the White House pandemic response team, and now Ricky's O Visa was about to expire. Even an esteemed scientist like Ricky could be impacted by the whims of an administration not focused on global health alliances.

A friend from California, Jeanne D'Onet, who held a PhD in immunology from Berkley, had texted him the day Richards shuttered that team: "no more US PRT. hope won't bite in butt."

Many colleagues, especially those in the US, wished him luck, success and future collaborations.

During the past few months, Ricky had been reading up on anecdotal, third party reports of patients in Saudi Arabia who suffered from acute respiratory symptoms that were non-responsive to traditional immunotherapies. But these were one-off cases lacking any real pattern. So nothing hit the scientific radar in any meaningful way. But Professor Dorchester well knew what Ricky easily surmised -- whatever reporting was being shared with the WHO out of the Arabian peninsula to this point was, in Dorchester's words, "less than complete and likely inaccurate". As scheduled, Ricky met Dorchester at the Public Health England Birmingham laboratory, and shared the little that they both thus far knew and guessed.

Days after his reunion with Professor Dorchester, on August 22, 2018, in accordance with the International Health Regulations (IHR) multilateral accord, the UK notified WHO about a laboratory-confirmed MERS-CoV infection. According to the report, an octogenarian male from the Kingdom of Saudi Arabia had fallen sick. He had flown from Riyadh to London then drove around Great Britain and Northern Ireland. He had no history of interacting with sick patients in Saudi Arabia or the UK, but had direct contact with camels prior to travelling.

Once symptoms appeared, his underlying chronic medical conditions made things worse. He was isolated and treated in an infectious disease facility in Liverpool for MERS-CoV. Concerned about animal to human transmission and the patient having travelled while infected, the medical team immediately sought contact tracing and international cooperation in accordance with international protocols. Authorities contacted the passengers who had sat near him on his flight to Heathrow along with the entire flight crew. They were asked about their own health and were furnished with information about the unknown infection.

A while later, the WHO issued an advisory that "MERS-CoV is a zoonotic virus that has repeatedly entered the human population via direct or indirect contact with infected dromedary camels, mainly in the Arabian Peninsula. Human-to-human transmission has been limited, but can be amplified in health care settings when infection prevention and control procedures are not adequate. To date, there is no evidence of sustained human-to-human transmission anywhere in the world. Currently, there is no vaccine or MERS-specific treatment available." The WHO went on to warn that people with certain underlying illness such as diabetes, renal failure, chronic lung disease, and those who are immunocompromised, could be at high risk of severe disease from a MERS-CoV infection. They were warned to avoid close contact with animals, particularly camels.

The Saudi patient was allowed to leave Liverpool to return home as soon as his symptoms disappeared and his fever was gone. He died three weeks later in Riyadh. The doctors in Saudi Arabia listed kidney failure as the cause of death, not MERS-CoV. Dr. C learned of the case as part of his infectious disease studies. Unfortunately, due to the Richards administration's guidelines limiting international cooperation, he was barred from flying to the UK or Saudi Arabia to further investigate. The CDC found itself similarly handcuffed. There was no longer a coordinated governmental effort to keep an eye on diseases germinating around the globe.

Dr. C begged the CDC head to let him brief the President and seek a travel waiver. A senior advisor who lost a coin toss brought the matter to Richards' attention on Air Force One, on the way to a rally and golf fundraiser in Ohio. Richards bent the aide's ears back and blasted him. "Are you fucking kidding me? We're about to sell $10 billion of the most beautiful weapons to the Saudis, and my son's company is negotiating a major real estate deal with them. You think we want to start a panic right now and blame them for something that kills camels? Idiot!" The aide was fired before the plane landed. Dr. C and the CDC never received any written response to their travel and study request, and but did get a resounding "hell no" on briefing Richards.

Ricky spent Labor Day weekend in Birmingham at the home of his professor. He planned to return to China to resume his research on avian influenza A(H7N9) after his contract with the British NHS expired at the end of November. However, on November 27, he received an interesting call from Jeanne D'Onet. She asked if Ricky would take a WebEx meeting with a growing biotech company in the Boston area, the Brain Belt as they liked to call it, which was doing "some really innovative and cutting edge work." Jeanne knew Ricky was wrapping up in London from their periodic texts, and made clear she had not yet joined the company, but was taking a hard look at it. Ricky agreed. The next day Ricky was on the video conference platform with Derek Chris, CEO of CNOVation, his sister, Melissa, the CFO, and Hernan Diego, the CIO.

The team briefly explained their work. Actually, it sounded more like a summary of what Ricky already read on the "About Us" section of their website. Derek asked Ricky to fly to Boston to talk about potentially joining them, and promised more details about their work in a more secure environment. Ricky hadn't seen Jeanne or been in Boston in several years, but explained that his parents were expecting to see him, which sounded lame when he heard himself say the words out loud. "Can I come in 10 days?"

Derek understood where Ricky was coming from. "Listen, I totally get it. You've been on the road a long time, and you made a family commitment. If we can derail you here for just 2 days, 48 hours, I promise it will be a worthwhile side trip, and we'll send you straight off to China." Ricky was hard-pressed to say no to Jeanne and he was curious, so he agreed. Within minutes, first class seats on British Airways, departing in two days, hit his email, along with a business class flight on China Airlines leaving two days later. "First class, sweet," Ricky heard himself saying to no one in particular.

| 14 |

Chapter 14: That was weird

Ricky's flight to Boston landed on December 1 on time, but was held away from the gate for several minutes. Everyone else in first class was on their smart phones, computers or iPads, so Ricky fired up his laptop. He had fallen asleep and forgot to charge his smart phone, so he plugged it in to his back up battery as they waited. Nothing on Logan's twitter feed, nothing on the departure arrival info except that the flight was listed as landed. Because the pilot had not yet given the "welcome to Boston" speech or turned off the fasten seat belts sign, the flight attendants were not allowed to unbuckle from their jump seats.

After a few minutes, the passenger in 3A, on the window, with whom Ricky had made sporadic, polite conversation on the flight over, tapped him on the shoulder and pointed out the window. They could both see Air Force One beginning to taxi away from the terminal. Simultaneously, they both googled "President Richards Boston", and saw he had held a rally at the nearby Worcester Art Museum (Steffi picked the venue; he couldn't care less about art), and then grabbed a round of golf at an exclusive country club. "That was weird. Guess we can't dock until he takes off." Ricky nodded his head, just as the captain began his welcome speech and explained the hold. An odd happenstance that Ricky was headed to the same city Richards had just vacated.

After deplaning at the international terminal, Ricky waited patiently with his fellow first class flyers on line to clear customs. When he approached the TSA agent, he maintained his normal routine at any international airport. Chinese passport out and open to his picture, customs form fully completed, maintain eye contact with the agent. "Purpose of travel to the United States today?"

"Business."

"What kind of business?"

"I have a meeting at a biotech company in Brookline."

"You're Chinese?" For whatever reason, the agent looked down at the passport photo then at Ricky several times.

"Yes sir."

"You have been to a lot of countries the past few years." This interaction was taking longer that prior times he had entered the US, and he did not much care for the tone of the agent. Ricky noticed the coffee mug near the front of the forward facing window, low enough to be below line of sight for anyone on any other side of the booth. The mug bore a spiral snake with the words "Don't Tread on Me." He remained calm and polite, which was easy for him anyway.

"Yes, sir. I have. I am a research scientist, and I often go to different locations to study infectious diseases."

"Are you a doctor?"

"A research scientist. I do not treat individual patients." Amid the conversation, two people in different lines, white Americans, had cleared their usually perfunctory interviews. In spite of how much time he'd spent in the US, Ricky felt like an unwelcomed foreigner.

"Please wait here sir." The agent slid his window closed and placed a call. Within a minute, another TSA agent appeared at the kiosk. The two chatted on the other side of the glass, which the booth agent lowered so they could talk. With a nod, the more senior agent walked around and asked Ricky to gather his carry-on items and accompany him. Ricky knew asking if anything was wrong was a waste of time at this juncture. The more senior agent, A. Simons by his ID tag, led Ricky to a windowless gray room, and politely asked him to please take a seat at the cheap, veneer-topped table, in one of the three well-worn blue chairs. Having caught up on all the technical journals on the flight over, he pulled a novel that he'd picked up at Heathrow out of his worn out backpack.

After 45 minutes, Agent Simons entered with another gentlemen, this one sporting a Homeland Security badge, not TSA. Smiling, he introduced himself as Alfred Doland, Homeland Security, and extended to shake Ricky's hand. "Dr. Tsang. We apologize for the wait, but we do have a few questions we need to ask." Ricky was aware that US – China tensions had been increasing with Richards as President. "I'm sure you understand." Ricky nodded. Both agents sat, one to each side, as the chairs screeched like dull chalk across on old fashioned blackboard. "Sir, can you tell me the name of the company you are here to meet with?"

"I'm not sure if I can tell you." Doland and Simons looked displeased and perplexed.

"Sir, the biotech company in Brookline. You told the customs officer … agent you were meeting with a biotech company in Brookline. You don't know the name?"

"Excuse me, Agent Doland for being imprecise. I meant no disrespect. I do know the name of the company I am meeting with. I am not sure I am liberty to disclose the name. Corporate secrets and concerns for leaks is what I was advised before I agreed to fly here and meet." Doland twisted his head at a 45 degree angle up and then down and then up to the other side.

"We know that a company chartered in Wyoming called NOW, LLC bought your ticket. We pulled your itinerary and checked your passport and any records on you at Interpol." His tone was brisk. "We know you are a Chinese citizen and that you travel a lot, but have no criminal record. So, sir," the voice inflection on sir was quite derisive, "what we need to know is the actual company behind the shell company that paid for your flight, and why you are then headed to China."

"Yes, of course. Sir, may I call the gentleman who invited me to come here to meet, and ask does he mind if I share the company name with you? I do not wish to prolong your inquiry or not answer your questions. If it were my information alone to share I would be more than happy to comply." Doland could not be sure if he was talking to a spy or a polite Chinese scientist. He just knew he was talking to a Chinese scientist who wouldn't tell him what he wanted to know, and that there was a ton of cyber warfare now raging between their countries.

"You may. Your cell phone will get poor reception in here. On purpose of course. Please, come use my office. For security reasons Agent Simons will need to stay with you in there." Interpol and the CIA had nothing in the "Adverse Information" section of the report he had printed on Tsang Yi DeeLu, but Doland was not going to be the guy who cleared a spy to enter the country. They walked together to Doland's office where, as expected, Ricky saw his luggage closed, but assumed it had been rifled through, given the large, yellow "Inspected" sticker. He felt a bit embarrassed that he could not recall if he had done his laundry before he left for Heathrow. Ricky checked his emails for the contact info of Derek Chris, and rang his cell.

A pleasant voice answered, "please hold for Derek." It is a busy man who has an assistant answer his private cell, but a courteous man who allows his first name to be used. After less than a minute the pleasant voice returned. "Good afternoon. May I tell Derek who is calling?"

"Yes, it is Ricky Tsang."

"Oh, Dr. Tsang, the car is on its way to Logan to meet you. Are you through customs and have your bags?"

"I am at customs but I have my bag. I have been asked by" he thought it better to say TSA "before I am cleared if I may state the name of the company I am meeting with."

"Yes sir. Hold please." The next voice Ricky heard was Derek.

"Hi Ricky. It's Derek. Sorry you've been detained. May I speak with the officer who is with you?" At the age of 43 but with more worldly experience than most twice his age, Derek knew that a Chinese scientist would likely be questioned upon arriving here in the current political environment. Ricky handed the phone to Agent Simons.

"Hi. Who's this?"

"Agent Simons, TSA. Who is this?"

"Hi Agent Simons. My name is Derek Chris. I am the CEO of a major government contractor research company out here in Brookline. If it's not too inconvenient, can I get you to hand the phone to the Homeland Security agent in charge of this ... detainment?" TSA never called these interrogations, just temporary, noncustodial detainments. Something to do with giving Miranda warnings. Simons simply scowled, and handed Ricky back his phone.

"Wait here." As if Ricky thought he was at liberty to go anywhere. He and Derek made small talk about how was the flight, the food any good, I hope you liked your seats and got some rest. Agent Doland quickly entered his office. A quick whisper, and Doland extended his left hand to Ricky, motioning for the phone.

"Alfred Doland, Homeland Security."

"Oh hi. Agent Doland. Derek Chris. CNOVation. I didn't think your TSA agent had clearance to get you what you needed. If you run DOD100417 through your system I think that should clear this up. I think we actually spoke a couple of months ago." Doland remembered. Derek Chris was personable, brilliant, and exceptionally well connected at the Defense Department.

"Sure." Doland went to his laptop and entered his password. Within a minute he had the confirmation he needed. He looked up, expressionless on the outside, not so happy about clearing another foreign scientist on the inside. He extended his left arm with Ricky's cell phone. "Dr. Tsang. You are free to go. Agent Simons, please escort Dr. Tsang to the main terminal." Ricky pressed the phone to his ear. It was Derek's assistant again.

"Hi Ricky. Derek had to go, but said he is glad that worked out without too much delay. There will be a driver waiting for you at baggage carousel 3. Have a good ride out." The line disconnected, and Agent Simons motioned this way, without speaking. In a few minutes, Ricky was approaching the meeting spot. He passed a few red hat wearing, sign toting older white people who were near the carousels, but did not seem to be waiting for luggage. A couple nudged each other and pointed to Ricky, like they knew who he was. Ricky noticed a large white poster that one man held at his side, with red, white and blue letters spelling out "Our country, our way." The last two letters were blocked by his jeans, but the message was clear. Ricky had used his detention time to catch up on local American news, and read that a crowd of about 50 or so rabid "Richards Rebels" came out to Logan to cheer him on as he returned to Air Force One. He'd even held an unscheduled press conference on the tarmac, with Logan used as a backdrop to rally support for his preferred candidates for Massachusetts governor and senator. Each man stood next to him. That photo op in front of Air Force One immediately anchored fund raising emails and letters.

Richards also promised a billion dollar, much needed improvement to this airport and the great city of Boston. Richards assured the crowd this project would only come if "his guys" are elected, and assured the crowd Logan would turn into a "totally disgusting, third world airport" if his guys lost. He then congratulated himself on how much money he'd raised today for these "real American heroes." He never considered how much air traffic delays and backups this extra 12 minutes was causing at this busy, Northeast corridor airport.

The bus for this group of supporters was going to pick them up outside the international terminal, strategically selected so they could stare down any foreigners coming in who did not belong here. Many were using the bathroom while they waited, others looking for outsiders who may be flying here to steal their jobs. On the ride over this group's organizer had offered a 5% discount for the "few remaining tickets" for the big tour coming in a few weeks: a trip to the US – Mexico border in Texas to yell at illegals storming the border in huge caravans (according to the Richards campaign). None of these fans knew, or really cared, that behind this tour company was a holding company controlled by an LLC owned by Richards.

As soon as he saw "Ricky" light up the iPad, he ended his observing and waived at his driver. The large, athletic black man approached Ricky, and without speaking took his roller bag. "This way, sir." Ricky followed the driver, and they passed the sign-carrying Richards supporter who had not broken his gaze at Ricky.

"Why don't you go back to Korea?" was verbally hurled at him. Audible enough to be heard, edgy enough to be hateful, but not loud enough to attract attention. Ricky had seen enough discrimination around the world not to pay heed to an ignorant sentiment, and had no interest in educating this person that there are, in fact, two Koreas. "And take your boy with you." Ricky and his driver kept walking. In five minutes they were in the car headed to Brookline.

| 15 |

Chapter 15: You're black again

Ricky was emailing with several of his colleagues as they drove away from Logan. He was pretty tired from the flight and the ensuing ordeal, but he was used to being tired before, during and after international travel. The driver had asked if he liked any particular type of music or wanted a news station; Ricky chose classical music. "Sir, I hope you don't mind me saying, but I thought that was totally uncalled for back there. That protester." Ricky nodded his head.

"What is your name?"

"Jesse."

"Jesse. I am Ricky, which you know since you had my name on your sign. I have been to many countries in my work, and I have seen many forms of discrimination. I am usually too busy to spend much time thinking about it. It has long concerned me that there are many who will judge us purely from outward appearance with no idea who we are as people."

"Amen sir."

"It seems your president was holding a gathering at the airport today and expressed his anger at North Korea. Perhaps the uninformed man near the exit was not aware there are two Koreas, one a staunch supporter of your country, the other a brutal dictatorship."

"Yeah, that's who Richards hates today. If you'd have flown into JFK last week the guy would have called you a Muslim. That was Richards' rant last week. Today it's North Korea. Next week it's gonna be illegal Mexicans. After that, who knows?" Jesse shook his head, looked at his passenger in the rear view mirror. "Ignorance is very popular here again sir. In America, I mean. So is outright hate. As a black man in Boston, sometimes it's really bad, sometimes it's not an issue. But if you don't mind me saying, these past few years with this president in particular, it's been worse than I've ever seen. I'm 55. Boston started changing for the better after all the civil rights marches and protests, and all that. Took a long time for things to get better. I was bused from my all black hood to a mostly white school and got my butt kicked almost every day until I got big enough to protect myself. But my daddy who's 84, he lived in Alabma until he joined the Army. He settled here after serving in Korea. With all he's been through, he says it's like the whole country is turning into the Deep South in the 50's and 60's." Ricky had enough context to understand the reference.

"We all thought... we hoped that with a black president for eight years we'd all get along so much better. Post-racial they called it." Jesse shook his head, tried to laugh, then cleared his throat. "My kids are in their 20s. Post-racial. I asked them four, five years ago when they were in high school what they thought that meant. They said Dr. King's dream had come true. You know? We'd all be judged on the content of our character, not the color of our skin. But, I gotta be honest, sir. Like I told my kids when they went off to college two years ago. Guess what? You're black again." Jesse shook his head. "It's like the haters went underground for eight years and were breeding like cockroaches, and came out stronger and meaner."

"Your country. The world really. There is so much fear, so much misunderstanding. I am a scientist. I work to cure diseases, viruses that invade the body. With the people I work with, we have managed to stop the spread of diseases that can destroy you from within. We can cure so many illnesses, but we have no vaccine to eradicate the hate of people like the gentleman at the airport."

"Color blinded, my daddy calls it. The color we wear on the outside blinds people to who you are on the inside." Ricky nodded.

"He is a very wise man, your father." They arrived at the three-story, gray smoked-glass building with the relatively modest "CNOVation" sign on the light green, concrete walkway out front.

"You enjoy your time in Boston, sir. I hope you don't mind me saying what was on my mind." Ricky stood on the sidewalk as Jesse handed him his roller bag from the trunk.

"Jesse. I also pray for the day your Dr. King dreamed of, when we look at each other and all we see is content and merit, not pigment or eye shape. In my faith, the path to enlightenment brings freedom and peace out from within. Intolerance and hate block that path."

"You invent an antidote for hate? You'd win the Nobel prize." They shook hands, and Ricky began his walk to the entrance.

| 16 |

Chapter 16: Nanobots and terabytes

Derek Chris himself greeted Ricky as he cleared the security desk. "If you don't mind, we'll do the nickel tour later. Right now we have the team in the main conference room." Ricky nodded.

"Of course." Derek's assistant, Amanda, took his roller bag.

"We'll store this in Derek's office. Is that okay?"

"Yes, thank you." She went off to a different elevator bank. Derek had Ricky follow him down the hall to a secure door that Derek un-locked by placing his picture ID with the RFID chip installed up close to the card reader. After passing through that door, 20 feet or so down the nondescript hallway they approached an elevator bank of two eleva-tors. Derek placed his hand on a fingerprint ID scanner, which turned red then green. The green metal, heavy doors parted. Derek again used his RFID card to operate the elevator to the "SB" floor. "Don't mind the cloak and dagger. Can't be too careful."

"Not to worry." Once they reached the sub-basement, Derek led them to a smoked-glass encased conference room, placing his right hand again on a fingerprint scanner. The door opened on its own. Ricky noticed a similar scanner near a larger set of doors down the hall to his left. Inside, two people sat around a large, chrome table equipped with multiple communication devices. The chairs were simple black leather thin backed seats with chrome arms that matched the table. There sat his good friend Jeanne, and Shimon Deitsch, an Israeli with a PhD in theoretical viral hemopathology from Oxford. Ricky remembered Shimon from an Ebola project they worked on a few years before. They all shook hands and hugged. As they did, Ricky noticed the sole artwork in the room, a poster of a yogi or a Sherpa on a mountainside, could be Asia, could be elsewhere. The sky was blue, wisps of high clouds surrounded the message, "Embrace the future with the soul of your past." The same as the company motto on its website.

"Now, that's my kind of team." Derek was very pleased how well his hoped-for team got on. Derek looked very much like what might be called a surfer dude, tall, tan, stringy brown blonde hair, blue eyes, athletic frame; someone you'd expect to be more at home on a boogie board than in a board room. In fact, he had surfed while he attended Cal Poly, then Stanford, then Berkley, which is where he met Jeanne.

"Okay, so now that everyone is here, I can explain why all the secrecy. Well, I can explain some of it anyway." Derek stood in front of a 68" LED screen at the front of the room. "Since you have signed your NDAs I can share with you parts of what we are doing at CNOVation and why we'd love for you each to join us. You will understand as we go why we cannot be completely transparent with you – yet." Derek kept looking at his guests and said "nano video 3" to the smart screen, which slowly illuminated and a glossy, slick video began to run.

A soft-toned woman began narrating. "Here at CNOVation, we believe we must embrace the future with the soul of our past. Science has always been about discovery, about pushing boundaries." She narrated as a blood doctor in a sterile lab performed a simple vein puncture procedure on a chimp, sorted the specimen through something that looked like a small hardware store paint shaker for frosted, glass vials, and, then ran a sample run through a special glistening silver machine. She continued as men and women peered through high powered microscopes, typing on a flat keypad.

The casual observer would see blood being drawn and analyzed, like in so many CSI-type TV shows trying to detect who had spilled drops at a crime scene. But Ricky, Jeanne and Shimon were focused on the advanced work of an electron cryo-microscopy, a technique of firing beams of electrons at proteins frozen in solution to reveal their genetic structures. Several times, they had wished that all of the labs they had worked in had access to Cryo-EM imaging tools. This technology had helped drive rapid advances in cell biology and related fields. But, they also understood reality. Many countries could barely afford clean needles without international assistance, much less hi-tech devices.

"You're gonna love this part. Watch." Derek could not contain his enthusiasm, even with his calm, cool demeanor. Tiny, moving robots, nanobots, were then injected into the cell field on the huge plasma screen. "You guys know the current limits even of Cryo imaging. Every currently in use microscope technique involves a compromise. If we use fluorescence microscopy, we can study cellular biology in real time, illuminate the target proteins and other cellular components. But this technique limits us to the physics of visible light, which can't distinguish between objects closer than 200 nanometers and therefore limits our study of organelles. Electron microscopes allow us to achieve much higher resolutions, but only function in a vacuum and so can't be used on live samples. We are about to ... well the goal anyway, and we are really, really close, is to deploy nanobots to get deep inside the cell structures live to analyze what right now we can only study in a vacuum." The three visitors nodded in agreement, Shimon's mouth slightly open in awe or desire – or both.

"Well, yeah, that would be way cool." Jeanne was the first to speak. "I mean, I know some folks from my old department at Berkley who've been trying to do this for a few years."

"And I'm pretty sure Israel is close, but I can't share any details" added Shimon. Ricky remained transfixed on the images on the screen, the video having been paused by Derek speaking.

"Applications? What applications are you looking at?" Ricky had been imagining this diagnostic tool for a year or so and just assumed it would be available at some point, so he spent the spare time he did have to think about how to harness it rather than how to obtain it. Derek shrugged his shoulders.

"Sorry, dude, even with the NDAs that's all I can share."

"DOD?" Ricky was pretty sure this was somehow a restriction placed by the US government.

"DOD, DHS, HHS, IP lawyers, board of directors, shareholders, blah blah, etc. etc." Derek took three iPads off the chrome desk and handed one to each. "These have your offers in them. We're asking for a two-year commitment from each of you. Technically, you'd start January 1. We figure you'd need time to do some wrap up on what you're doing now, gather whatever clothes you have up from wherever they are right now – or we can take you shopping when you get here. Go see friends, family, stuff like that. Take these pads with you and please, think about it. We have a dinner meeting set up for tonight at your hotel and can answer your questions then. Maybe, a couple of other members of the company officers and a few lawyers too." Derek looked back at the screen. "Maybe a couple of military guys. An undersecretary of something or other." He turned back to look at his guests. "Oh, and a senator. I think that's it. Not too intimate – 20 or so plus you - but you guys are crazy busy, and this stuff is ultra-top secret, so the whole gang's coming. Meantime, I can give you a tour of part of the lab. Leave the pads here. We can grab them after the tour and get you a snack if you're hungry. I hope you like tacos. That's today's specialty."

"Wait, hang on if you'd please." Ricky's mind was, as often, running at warp speed. "The nanobots. They would capture data and what, transmit or be uploaded at extraction?"

"Goal is we upload wirelessly while we retrieve them to get the best data dump."

Jeanne chimed in. "Yeah, a couple of my PhD students put out a theoretical dissertation on that last year." The three others at the same time said in unison, "Read it."

Ricky was not quite done. "But what's the memory capacity of the nanobots? You'd need, I'm not sure, 128 gig with ultrafast download time before the microcells are corrupted if you build them to transmit wirelessly, to avoid compromise of the bots before they are extracted."

Derek put his left hand on Ricky's shoulder, and stared him squarely in the eyes. "With you three here joining the team we already have? We'll get there. Hey, think fast, how long does it take a particle of light to cross a single molecule of hydrogen?" Shimon popped in.

"247 zeptoseconds, at least according to a team of German researchers. So, 247 trillionths of a billionth of a second." Jeanne recalled lecturing her graduate students that a zeptosecond is a trillionth of a billionth of a second. To emphasize how literally lightning fast that is, she'd go to the chalk board to write a decimal point followed by 20 zeroes then a 1.

"Listen, between us girls, the goal, if you guys join us..." Derek looked around, as if someone might be listening – which was always a possibility - so he pulled the three visitors in close so he could whisper "the goal is a terabyte upload in that 247 zeptoseconds."

Shimon now drooled with imagination for what that could mean. "Shee-it."

""Yup," added Derek, and with that, led them out towards the secure doors down the hallway to the left. "Clean rooms. We'll suit up before we go in." Jeanne, Shimon and Ricky were making calculations in their heads of the possibilities this could open up.

| 17 |

Chapter 17: Dinner and a show

By the time they were done eating tacos, the sweep team was in place at the hotel in advance of the dinner meeting. No amount of precaution was too much. The threat of government hacking and corporate espionage kept many of the dinner guests up at night.

When Derek first set the meeting, his contacts assured him they could keep the group to 10, excluding the sweep team that would first secure the room and then remain outside. Once Derek talked to the legal team, his side alone swelled to a dozen. When the Amtrak Acela train left Union Station in Washington, DC at 1245pm, DOD, DHS and HHS had added another 14, including 3 star General August Lind, in civilian wear. The general would be the government's lead liaison for the meeting. While the sweep team was making sure the room was secure, two DHS agents borrowed from the Boston field office were completing interviews with every hotel employee who might be involved in the food service that night. The room was set up for a cozy dinner for 30. The hotel general manager, experienced in meetings of senior government officials and high profile guests was familiar with outside advance teams doing security. She only needed to know the two additional rooms that were being held for the night would be charged at the federal government rate, as would the dinner service. This was not a political fund raiser.

After riding together to the hotel, Ricky, Jeanne and Shimon had three hours before the meeting to relax, study their offers, and check emails. Shimon used the down time, as he usually did, to swim. He made sure to get in as much exercise as he could, to keep his lean, 6 foot 3 inch frame as close to the shape he was in when he completed mandatory military service in the Israeli army at the age of 21. Jeanne took a quick 3 mile run, followed by a 20 minute meditation session using her favorite app. Ricky took a quick nap – he was too restless for anything longer. Then he went for a walk, listening on his earbuds to a concert his favorite Chinese pianist, Lang Lang, performed with American singer Katharine McPhee at the National Memorial Day Concert in Washington, D.C., in May 2009.

Lang Lang was about his age and, like him, was very well respected in China – he had played for billions of viewers at the 2008 Olympic Opening Ceremony in Beijing - and made many trips to America, but never forgot his Chinese roots. Ricky couldn't remember when he added this performance to his playlist, but it was a favorite. After his return to his room, he called his mother at 4:45pm local time, 5:45am for her, knowing she would be up preparing breakfast for his father. They spoke in Mandarin, which she scolded him ever so softly as not quite perfect, but good enough for a person who did not spend enough time at home. He asked to speak with his father, Tsang Wai, who was ecstatic that his son was considering a profitable position with what Ricky vaguely had to describe as a small, high tech company in Boston.

"All you have done, the travelling, the dangerous places you have gone. Saving the world with the touch of your hands, the power of your mind. It is wonderful what you have done, selfless, Tsang Yi." His father paused. "Ricky. This is a wonderful opportunity. Even Buddha himself recognized a right to rupa, a material existence, a form in the real world. It is time, Ricky, for you to engage your right to possessions; no one would ever challenge your accomplishments as a scientist or your selfless advancements as a Buddhist. You should accept this opportunity as an inevitable part of your journey."

This was the first time his father called him Ricky, even as they spoke in Mandarin. And how Western his father had become. Working for Renren, essentially China's Facebook, as a senior officer. Living in Beijing, in an even more immaculate home then the one in Shenzen. Employing a Chinese capitalist's reminder of the five aggregates of Buddhism; sensations (vedana), perceptions (samjna), psychic constructs (samskara), and consciousness (vijnana), all psychological processes, and how these may co-independently exist along with rupa. Many of the precepts were intertwined with his business philosophy of guanxi.

"Thank you, dear father. Go in peace."

"And you, my son."

| 18 |

Chapter 18: A monk and a military commander walk into Buckingham Palace …

As agreed, Ricky, Jeanne and Shimon gathered in the hotel lobby at 5:30pm, half an hour before the dinner meeting. Derek waved them over to where he was standing, and led them to a horseshoe shaped booth in a dark, rear corner of the bar. A distinguished, older gentlemen, silver hair, steely blue eyes, was nursing a club soda, reading the New York Times. The man and Derek shook hands, and Derek made the introductions. "Senator Sindel, my dream team." This was not the time or place to educate Derek about that maybe not being a nickname he'd want to keep, so the senator made a mental note to fill him in later. As planned, Ricky slid in to his left, then Jeanne. Derek slid in to his right, then Shimon. Derek then rattled off a short bio of the soon-to-be former senior Senator from Massachusetts who served for 24 years in Congress and was ending his 12 years in the Senate, the last four as chair of the Senate Intelligence Committee. "On January 6, the Senator will be joining us as a board member and advisor. It's been publicly announced, so I'm not breaching national security here." Derek let out a chuckle, and the Senator nodded, smiled. While the Senator had no particular expertise in viruses or robotics or public health issues, his $2 million a year contract was considered a steal for CNOVation. The senator intimately knew the inner workings of Washington and how to snag public funding for private research.

"Derek speaks very, very highly of each of you. You will get much more context about what we are hoping to do here over dinner. Of course, you can only get broad outlines." The Senator paused, "but let's wait for our final guest."

"Yes, thanks Senator. Meantime, who needs a drink?" Derek motioned the waiter over. Typical scientist orders - water with lime - for Jeanne and Ricky; but not for Shimon.

"Do you have Goldstar? In the lager?" The waiter nodded, his tightly packed dreadlocks barely moving.

"This week, we do. We had an Israeli trade delegation here last month, so we stocked up. Man, you brothers can drink some beer!" Shimon laughed and smiled broadly. "Bottle or glass?"

"Bottle. In Israel, who has time to pour?" They all laughed. "Please, bring one for each of my friends." The Senator stopped the waiter.

"You should bring me a Sam Adams also. I'm a Massachusetts politician. If the voters see me with a beer in my hand and it's not a Sam, there'll be hell to pay." They all laughed.

"And we have one more joining us, so an extra Goldstar for her."

"Of course, right away." The waiter winked at the Senator. "I voted for you first and every chance I had." As the waiter walked away, Anis Eljim arrived. Derek made the introductions of his Pakistani born associate general counsel, holder of a master's in physics from MIT and a law degree from Harvard. They talked a bit about their personal lives, such as they were, while enjoying ice cold bottles of Israel's most popular beer. Derek's assistant Amanda entered the bar and walked to their booth.

"They are assembling. I'll finish up in here."

"Thanks, Amanda. Ok, let's go."

Shimon grabbed Ricky's still half full beer. "Never waste a drop of Negev water."

From just 30 minutes of being able to relax and socialize, Derek could imagine his team coming together. Of course, for each of them, 30 minutes of downtime and calm, idle chatter was like a week for most people.

Two tall men in black suits, white shirts and black ties were slowly patrolling outside ballroom C. Anyone who walked by would likely assume they were limo drivers waiting to pick up their rides, or extras for a *Men in Black* movie. Of course, at 6pm on a Wednesday night, anyone who had been in a nearby ballroom for a convention or trade association meeting was either at the bar the group had just left, in their room getting ready for a fine, expense account dinner in one of Boston's top restaurants, checking the emails that had filtered in, or engaged in activity that they hoped would not show up on the hotel bill or security cameras.

The thick carpet changed patterns inside the dining room. It was exactly 6pm and everyone Derek expected was already inside. Small gathering indeed thought Ricky. Senator Edward "Teddy" Sindel walked directly to General Lind. "August."

"Teddy." Their warm enthusiasm for seeing each other outside of an oversight hearing or Gang of 8 secure briefing was evident. "You know Abigail Rainey?"

They shook hands, double cupped. "Major."

"Senator." At 48, Major Rainey had already made quite the name for herself. First in her graduating class from the Naval Academy at Annapolis at the age of 20, two tours in the early stages of Operation Desert Storm, detailed to the CIA for projects after 9/11 that remained classified. She was well known as a rising leader at the Pentagon after having served as a trusted advisor to the Vice Chairman of the Joint Chiefs of Staff in President Bursan's last 2 years in office. But her avid supporters knew she'd have to keep a lower profile in the Richards administration, since anyone who loyally served and openly spoke favorably of Bursan was going nowhere with him. "Mr. Chris." They shook hands, not for the first time.

"Derek, please. Let me introduce the dream team of scientific brilliance." Sindel looked at Lind and shrugged, mouthing "I'll fill him in later." After they all exchanged courtesies and each met the remainder of the attendees, they took their assigned seats at the index cards with only first names in front of the plated salads, not even listing their well-earned ranks and titles. Not even an "Hon." As protocol dictated, General Lind spoke first.

"I thank each of you for being here. I must remind you that, under the Patriot Act, everything we are about to discuss is classified. And while we cannot yet get into everything that we may ultimately discuss, the work each of you has done and clearances you each have will allow me to be detailed in some respects. I cannot overemphasize that this is the rarest of job interviews for our visiting scientists." Everyone laughed. "Usually it's the applicant who tells us everything about what they are up to, but because of the sensitivity and critical nature of the work we would like you to undertake, I have the requisite authorizations to share what you are about to learn. Again, remember, nothing leaves this room. Agreed?" Being positioned directly across from Ricky, Jeanne and Shimon, in that order, made it easier for him to look directly at each as they verbally affirmed their consent. General Lind turned his head to the left, looking at Senator Sindel who was at a 45 degree angle from him and the guests. "Senator?"

"Of course, General. And thank you again for traveling up for this. With your permission, may I begin?"

"Yes, Senator, and thank you." A well-practiced politician, the Senator knew how and when to make eye contact with everyone in the room. He rose to speak, always thinking more clearly on his feet than sitting on his butt.

"CNOVation has been working under a contract with the Department of Defense for advanced virologic research. It is a joint venture also with Health and Human Services. You each have a well-documented history in the cure and containment of viruses that have the potential to spread quickly and lethally. The vast majority, well as of right now all reported diseases, have been naturally created and mutated by species contact. Sometimes human, sometimes animals or birds, etc. But here we are in 2018. The threat to our national security we fear the most is laboratory-created, easily transmissible diseases, biological weapons if I may put a fine point on it."

Senator Sindel looked around to emphasize a point on which everyone agreed, and of which all were aware. "We are not talking about toxins like sarin or other poisons that require point of contact exposure. You are likely aware of past, publicly reported attempts to deploy poisons and nerve agents that have been in narrow, typically single victim undertakings. Well over 90% of reported white powder incidents have turned out to be flour or baking soda – thank God. But we are talking here about agents that can be spread by coughing, sneezing or other human-to-human exposure. Two months ago, the Intelligence Committee released a redacted version of a joint task force report and investigation on the new frontiers of biological weapons. A copy of that report is on the iPads you were given at CNOVation." He noticed Ricky, Shimon and Jeanne look down, remembering that they had not brought the iPads – they did not expect to need them.

General Lind chimed in. "The devices have been collected from your rooms. Apologies, but a necessary step. They are here to be returned to you at dinner. Senator?"

"Yes, thank you, General. Along with the redacted publicly available report, we have just loaded an encrypted version of the report on your devices." Derek jumped in.

"That report is classified as the General and Senator explained. The encryption is two factor authentication, so even if the iPad gets stolen no one can access it. Plus it's got an 18 hour key in it, so the access is automatically impossible after noon tomorrow. You'll each get a unique password, and then you'll need a second password for the TFA. Each of your devices keys to a different cell phone, as an extra layer of security. Of course, your access is contingent upon signing the employment contract." Shimon was impressed.

"You guys are not screwing around."

"No, Mr. Deitsch, we are not." The general's look was his classic, no BS glare. "Major Rainey?"

"Yes, thank you sir. As the General and Senator have been addressing, there is heightened tension in many parts the world, not much of which is anything new. We have the usual state actors that we track; North Korea, Iran, Russia, China - no disrespect Dr. Tsang – as well as nonstate actors like Al-Qaeda, Hezbollah. We do not believe that China is currently interested in war grade biologics, or that any of the other countries or NGO's we are monitoring are presently capable of developing and delivering such a system. For whatever you think about Al-Qaeda and Hezbollah as highly effective internet recruiters, they are still pretty much in the 20th century mindset for physical destruction - strap on a vest bomb or set a roadside IED. And they lack the technical expertise and the bandwidth to pose a cyber threat. Then there are some smaller, fringe groups that have been pursuing dirty bombs but they have pretty much blown up on everyone who tried to build one, and even the jihadis have gotten tired of such poor results. With that said, we have reasons to believe that there are collaborations going on to develop war grade biotoxins that mimic a SARS type disease in symptom and progression and, worst of all, in transmissibility. You scientists know that the types of diseases you study and cure have an unpredictable spread pattern in a natural state. Imagine a laboratory created toxin that can be injected in a cow in Ireland and kill thousands of people in Boston."

"Thankfully," chimed in Senator Sindel, "as the Major and General indicated, no one has perfected a disease like that, at least not yet."

"Yes, sir, thankfully. However, as you will see in the classified portions of the reports, we have reason to believe that there are NGO's with dark money from one or more countries that are collaborating together and getting far too close to a contagious, lethal, readily transmissible biologic. Derek?"

"Right, thanks. And so that's where CNOVation comes in. We have an unusual dual mission; beat the bad guys to the development and deployment of such an agent by creating a vaccine against what we think they are still trying to develop." Ricky surveyed the table; military, civilian, Pentagon, Homeland Security, Health and Human Services, former Senator, private corporation. From his work on the White House Ebola Response Task Force and with the WHO, he was aware of these types of intragovernmental arrangements and intergovernmental cooperatives, but not with private industry so heavily involved. Shimon was similarly curious, but intrigue of this nature was not part of Jeanne's analytics.

Ricky asked, "Sirs, madam, will there be questions allowed?"

The General responded. "Of course, Dr. Tsang – within limits."

"Sir, thank you. Of course. If I am to understand, our work would be to create the weapon and then figure out how to treat people who are exposed to it as well as to counteract it?"

"Well, we believe with your incredible talents, you'd do both simultaneously."

"Thank you, General. But even to do this, we must create the biologic? Otherwise how would we know if the cure or antidote or neutralizing agent or whatever it might be actually works?" General Lind looked to the Senator, who appreciated that a member of the Pentagon and career military officer could not possibly answer that question, no matter how secure the meeting was. Senator Sindel spoke, still standing.

"Ricky, yes, you are right. You'd have to create it to destroy it. But, one way or another, someone is going to create one or maybe a few of these disaster scenarios. Simply put, we need to be able to defuse these bombs before anyone successfully builds them." Shimon then chimed in.

"I am no politician – I served in the military in Israel as all my brothers and sisters did, but never the Knesset – my father did."

"Oh, yes, Shimon. I worked with your father Guri several times in my time in the House. He was a terrific man; he would have been a wonderful prime minister one day if not..."

"Thank you, Senator, yes if not for the bombing that killed him and several diplomats visiting Gaza. And I must believe that part of my background played a role in my being selected for this ... project. My field, as I'm sure you each know, is hemopathology, so I study diseases and disorders afflicting blood cells. See a disease, find a cure. Imagine a disease, imagine a cure. But Ricky here -- not only is he an incredible virologist – maybe, maybe the best in the world, but he is also considered a leading bioethicist. Me? No. Like I said, see a disease, find a cure. But even me, I have to ask." Ricky interrupted him.

"With apologies to my friend. It would be part of our mission, if you will, that we create a potentially lethal agent, so lethal that it should never be allowed to exist. And then we must discern how to defeat it. Our employer would be a private company, funded to some extent by the American government, overseen in part by the American military. I recognize your system of government is quite different from my homeland of China and Shimon's in Israel. But, and I mean no disrespect, but my training requires that I ask not only can we do this, but should we. So, the obvious ethical imperative here is how would we keep the very weapon we are creating out of the hands of the American military, and avoid its use in warfare? That is what I believe Shimon was inquiring, and I would have asked the same. So I have."

For the first time in the meeting, Anis Eljim spoke. "We have looked at this very, very closely from CNOVation's standpoint. We are not solely a defense contractor; we also have purely civilian projects. So, the concern arises from 18 U.S. Code §175, which states, and I am quoting now, "Whoever knowingly develops, produces, stockpiles, transfers, acquires, retains, or possesses any biological agent, toxin, or delivery system for use as a weapon, or knowingly assists a foreign state or any organization to do so, or attempts, threatens, or conspires to do the same, shall be fined under this title or imprisoned for life or any term of years, or both.""

Anis emphasized the "for use as" by louder volume and slower pace. "Our lawyers have concluded that yes, it would be illegal if we were to create an agent or toxin for use as a weapon; our defense contract, as is standard, prohibits us from violation of this or any other federal law.

And under no circumstances would anyone at CNOVation ever be allowed to illegally develop anything for use as an agent of warfare."

The General added "And of course, treaties and UN resolutions prohibit the US and all member nations from creating and deploying any such bioagent."

Shimon finished Ricky's Goldstar. "Due respect, Ricky and me – we're not asking about going to jail. Although it's good to eliminate that fear. But, if I may be so bold - we're asking about burning in Hell." Shimon turned to his colleague. "Sorry, my friend. I am Jewish; I was taught to believe that sinners spend eternity trapped in some kind of Hell. I know you're Buddhist but am ignorant on where your soul would go if you helped create such a weapon."

"It's alright Shimon. But, yes, this is clearly a question of bioethics."

General Lind stood up, which drew all eyes to him, as it was meant to do. "First, I must state unequivocally that the United States military has no, zero, interest in creating a war grade bioagent, or ever, ever using one. This dilemma keeps me twisted up like a pretzel. Should we create something so terrible that if anyone knew we had it we would be sanctioned and vilified by our allies, yet feared and envied by every dictator and autocrat? Even knowing if we did so, it would only be so we can know how to counteract it to protect our citizens and prevent the senseless murder of millions and millions of innocent people here and perhaps around the world? An age-old question, really. Does the end justify the means?" The General paced a bit, for effect, as if addressing a combat battalion about to be deployed to Kuwait or Afghanistan or Iraq or other places he had led troops in the theater of war. "In other words, can we still be the good guys if we are doing what the bad guys are doing, no matter the reason?"

He stopped, standing behind Derek and Ricky. "Let me tell you a story. Please, indulge an old war horse." He began to walk around again. "In March of 1991, we were well into Operation Desert Storm – the major fighting was over pretty quickly, but the years of rebuilding were still ahead. You may be too young to remember the crazy scenes of Iraqi troops surrendering to CNN reporters." General Lind laughed, mostly to himself.

"That's where I met then Navy Ensign Rainey. Well she was a newbie, wet behind the ears, all education but no experience, couldn't wait to be a fighter pilot. She was on the low end of the totem pole with a fighter wing positioned for aircraft launch from Saudi Arabia, part of my command under the joint deployment. Anyway, with all the shit that was going on then, I get an invitation from my command level counterpart from the UK for a small group meeting with the Venerable Geshe Kelsang Gyatso Rinpoche, the Founder of Modern Kadampa Buddhism. Geshe-la I believe you would call him. Had no idea who he was then. My counterpart from the Royal Air Force, Group Captain ... Major do you remember his full name?"

"Yes, sir. Group Captain Anthony Seaver."

"Thank you, Major. Group Captain Seaver asked me to come, so of course I said yes - after clearing it with my boss, General Norman Schwarzkopf. I know, I know. I was as confounded about the invite then as you are in hearing about it now. I thought, what in the name of Jesus H Christ does a Buddhist monk want to talk to me about when we are ass deep in a conflict in Iraq? Pardon my language, of course. But General Schwarzkopf asked me the same thing. But as a courtesy, he told me to go. Anyway, Geshe-la was residing in London at the time. I later learned that he'd been the resident teacher at the Manjushri Centre in the UK for a dozen or so years by then. So we get the orders signed, and assigned a noncombat C-2a Greyhound to take us on the first leg off the aircraft carrier, with a crew of 4, including one Ensign Rainey."

"So we learn on the long flights over that Geshe-la had asked for a very private audience with Princess Diana of England, out of his concern for the plight of Buddhists in the Middle East in general, but in Syria, Lebanon, Iraq and Iran in particular, and what the effect of this military operation and any ensuing rebuilding might be on them. The Princess was well known to have a soft spot for humanitarian issues like this, even if it only impacted a small percentage of the UK popula-

tion. The Queen at that time had approved of Diana having building relationships with Buddhists in her portfolio. The Queen was also aware,
that as small as Buddhism was in Great Britain and the Middle East, it
was just as big in Asia, and the UK was entering into very large trading partnerships with several Asian countries with World War II very
much in the rear view of history." The General stopped, took a couple
of sips of water, then continued.

"I promise, almost done. So we cable General Schwarzkopf, who answers, basically, don't screw this up, we need the British forces. He no-
tifies the State Department, who of course lose their shit over a major
meeting, even a private one, with no diplomatic advance work. When
we finally get to Buckingham Palace for the meeting, even though no
press was alerted, they sneak us in through a food delivery entrance.
We do our best to bow and curtsy like we are told. Geshe-la makes his
point about the fate of such a small minority population in such a large
and diverse culture. He was vague enough that he could have been talking about Buddhists in the UK or the Middle East or black people in
Japan, but was clearly aware of our mission in Iraq. State gave me a
few words to say, noncommittal, respectful, have to see how things develop. And then he just looked me straight in the eyes and said, 'Major,
you are from a country that is very formidable and strong. Buddhists
in the Middle East are small in number, but strong in spirit, yes. And
while we do not hate, I am not naïve that there are many in that part of
the world who would do us harm, just for the religion we practice. You
cannot truly appreciate the lengths some can go to do you harm, unless you fully understand your own frailties.' I have never forgotten that
moment or that meeting or that day. Neither has Rainey. We know, my
friends, as Americans that there are those in many parts of the world
who would harm just because of our free and democratic society, and
unless we fully and completely come to grips with what our weaknesses
are, we will never be truly safe. Right now, we are vulnerable to toxins
being deployed against us, and we know there are forces of evil that are
trying to assemble and unleash such an awful weapon. We have to push

the outer edges of this out of self-preservation, and if the best way to do it is to create the damn thing just so we can destroy it, then so be it."

General Lind had made his point, quite convincingly. Shimon had his doubts about the whole story. It sounded like the opening to a joke – a monk and a military commander walk into Buckingham Palace to meet a Princess. Even with a witness to the whole event sitting in this very room, Shimon had his doubts. Did Lind make up a story about a renowned Buddhist monk to sell Ricky on the ethics of the challenge at hand? But, wow, what a whopper if it wasn't true. Still, Shimon fully appreciated the plight of a small minority surrounded by those who hate and would kill them. After all, he was Israeli. Plus, the incredible challenge placed in front of him – who could turn that down? The money was quite impressive also.

Ricky was not quite convinced, but his concerns were somewhat lessened. He had heard of such a meeting, never confirmed, of Geshe-la with the Princess. He had read that when the Queen of England addressed a special joint session of the American Congress in 1991, in referring specifically to the Iraqi invasion of Kuwait and the international response, she did say "Together, we are doing our best to reestablish peace and civil order in the region, and to help those members of ethnic and religious minorities who continue to suffer through no fault of their own. If we succeed, our military success will have achieved its true objective." He also knew that Princess Diana and Prince Charles had in fact visited the Bulguksa Buddhist temple in Gyeongju, South Korea in November 1992. Despite their own internal turbulence, the British Royal Family had expressed true concern through the years for Buddhists as an oppressed people in countries where they were in such small minorities, not just the United Kingdom.

To sign on with CNOVation, Ricky would require confirmation that whatever they may create in the lab would stay in the lab, and never actually be used against anyone. And he really, really wanted to read the unredacted report.

Jeanne had decided to join CNOVation before she asked Ricky to fly over, so didn't really need any convincing.

Derek signaled the two sweep team members guarding the door, who opened them to let the wait staff bring dinner in. Shimon caught the eye of one, held the empty Goldstar up, and pointed to himself, Ricky, Jeanne, Derek, the Senator, the General and the Major. Within minutes, salads were being eaten, and more beers consumed.

| 19 |

Chapter 19: All Aboaaaarrrd!

Dinner began to break up at 8pm. The government officials who were relegated to staying at other lower hotels left together and shared rides. The outside lawyers, except Marc Hale, also began to leave. They all shook hands with the visitors, the company representatives, the General and Major. Each expressed hope that the scientists would join and how they looked forward to working together. The group from DC would make as much of a night of it as they could, with 7:15am Amtrak tickets in their pockets, and 3pm meetings back in DC. After they left, Derek asked the wait staff to move a couple of chairs to opposite sides of one of the tables, where the plates and silverware had already been cleared. Then Lind, Rainey, Sindel, Ricky, Shimon, Jeanne, Marc and Anis sat back down next to each other. Shimon positioned himself next to Rainey, finished his third Goldstar and asked, "So, this is now when we get what you call the rest of the story?"

"Kind of." Derek waited until the nine were alone and the doors again closed. "By the way, our general counsel, Nancy Lauren, feels awful about missing this meeting. She had to be in DC today, of all days, on some ... well an unavoidable matter. It has to do with this project. General?"

"So, everything you heard is already known to the government folks who just left. Trying to contain intel about any type of project with military and civilian involvement is a major pain in the ass in the best of circumstances. I won't bore you about Washington politics and turf wars. We don't have anywhere near enough time." Sindel interrupted.

"Sorry, August. And some of this we did not share earlier because we did not want you unintentionally feeling awkward or giving a negative signal to any of our administration friends. General."

"Correct. You're all too busy with real life work to know or care that the current HHS Administrator, who was not here, is under a lot of fire in DC for jetting around the world with his wife on taxpayer dollars and installing an expensive shower and sauna in his office. His deputy who was here is an exceptional, career public servant. If the current administrator was to get fired, we'd carry the deputy on our shoulders to a confirmation hearing. But we all know that's not how this President operates. Let's just say this president hasn't built a track record of appointing the best people. Senator?"

"Right. If you follow American politics at all these days, you know that Richards has been installing his lackies in many key government posts. His ego is almost as all-consuming as his paranoia. Frankly one reason I probably lost my seat is because I had the audacity to take him on and open an investigation into his family's business dealings with two countries – Russia and Saudi Arabia. As I'm sure you can imagine the possibility of a President's family being compromised or influenced by any foreign government, friend or foe, is an incredible national security headache. I did what I thought was right, and now I'm a private citizen." The Senator let out a long melancholy sigh. "Anyway, thankfully, he hasn't infected the Pentagon, HHS or CDC – yet. We fear his supposed lead candidate for HHS is a big dollar campaign donor who happens to be a major investor in a biotech company in Texas." All eyes shifted to Derek.

"Which is where we come in. CNOVation is not the oldest or the biggest company with government contracts, but we are the best at secrecy and information control. Knowledge is particularly powerful in the DC ecosystem. Hernan, our CIO, is as good at what he does as you are at your work. He's not here in person because he's been up in a room with some of his cyber team jamming any listening devices that may be trying to eavesdrop." Shimon jumped in.

"So all the James Bond, top secret, kill you if we tell you stuff, that wasn't just theater for us? You're not really worried about us spilling anything confidential. You're worried about having a mole on the team, so to speak, if you get a new set of eyes on you?" The General nodded his head

"That is one of a hundred possibilities. Richards couldn't care less about the work we're doing. Honestly, I'm not sure he even knows what CDC stands for. But government expenditures are part of a mostly public process, and we have always structured our most sensitive outlays in line items we can use that won't garner too much unwanted attention." The Senator continued.

"My successor in the Senate is a Richards loyalist. That's how he beat me in Massachusetts. Turned out unprecedented numbers of older, white, middle class folks, many of who'd lost their jobs to automation here. They somehow made the Brain Belt into a negative, saying all we've done is replaced hard working Americans with Indians and foreigners who stole their jobs. They filled people's minds with easy punch lines, and all the work we've done and the governor here has done with job retraining … anyway. You saw Richards here stumping for his pick for governor? There's a special election in February. He might get that guy elected. So, if his choices for HHS and governor get in, we expect an ugly power play to break out once - not if – word of this project gets in the wrong hands." Derek cleared his throat.

"Let me put a finer point on this. If the Texas guy gets HHS, he'll want the project at his former company. That guy raised crazy amounts of dark money for Richards, and has been pushing for a Silicon Valley type area outside Austin. We also hear Richards is promising the guy he's hawking for governor here the vice presidency in his second term, but only if he plays ball on moving a bunch of Boston area projects to Texas. We'd be swept up in that. We have plenty of allies on the Hill – that's where Nancy has been all week – but if this kind of fight breaks out, all kinds of leaks will start. These guys play dirty. Then the actual work we're doing becomes the victim of a messy public fight over a US company creating deadly poisons. None of these people have the intellectual bandwidth to understand that this is not the kind of work you want to spread sunshine on."

The General continued. "Look, this is all political inside baseball that has nothing to do with your actual work. We think we have figured out how to keep this work under wraps for two years, which is both the length of your contracts and takes us past the next election cycle. We think ... are pretty comfortable that we can run out the clock on the wrong people getting the wrong information for two years. So, not to put too much pressure on your team..." Shimon interrupted again.

"No. Pressure? Hey guys, come join us. You will be creating the deadliest toxins in the world, finding a vaccine for them, and making sure no one finds out. PS – you only have two years to do it, and your biggest enemies might be the people you report to. How can that be considered pressure?" Senator Sindel and General Lind looked at him with surprise and disappointment, but before either could speak he added, "Are you fucking kidding me? I love this! I'm in! If I could tell my brother in the Mossad, he'd be in too." He swigged the last of his beer. They all laughed, even Ricky.

Jeanne added, "Count me in, too. Experience of a lifetime. Ricky?" All eyes shifted to him. Ricky had never been nearly as expressive as Shimon, or as quick to a decision as Jeanne. It was his training, his upbringing. But he also never shied away from a challenge. In spite of all the incredible work he had done around the world, and the literal and figurative landmines he had learned to navigate, none had been as intricate as this.

"Shimon, I believe your Talmud says, 'Who is the wise person? The one who foresees the consequences.'" He paused, for dramatic effect, something he had not been known to do before. "It is better knowing the road we travel before we begin the journey. Plus, I like Boston, and we get the chance to help save the world from unimaginable harm. You can count on me." Ricky also thought that while his mom will miss him, his dad would be proud that he is getting his feet wet in the private sector. Hands were shaken, backs slapped, and even a bit of applause.

They made small talk for a few more minutes. Shimon turned his attention to Abigail Rainey. "Swim?"

"You asking me if I do swim or if I'd like to go swim?"

"Both." He smiled, as did she.

"I was co-captain of the swim team at Annapolis."

"Okay."

"The men's swim team."

"Okay."

"In 1988."

"Okay, I know. You are older than me so I must be a gentleman and not beat you up and down the pool too many times." She gave him the look of challenge accepted.

"5am too early?" Shimon smiled, flashed his you can trust me, disarming look.

"Of course not. You brought a suit?"

"I never stay at a hotel with a heated indoor pool without one."

The rest of the table conversation was breaking up. At 8:45pm, everyone said good night, and Shimon, Jeanne and Ricky were given their iPads. Derek reminded them. "Remember, you need to sign your employment contract and NDAs then get the second password to access the full report. Your first level encryption passwords are on these cards I'll give you. When you sign the contracts you'll get a text to the device with the cell number to call for the second password. It's automated with voice ID so you won't be waking anyone up. I'll meet each of you back at CNOVation at 9am for coffee and a debrief. A car will be waiting for you at 8:30am out front. Ricky, we'll get you to Logan in plenty of time for your flight home. This, my friends, will be the experience of a lifetime."

| 20 |

Chapter 20: March 2019: Insurrection

Late in the afternoon on Friday, March 22, 2019, Richards was finishing receiving his post golf massage, when his travelling personal valet entered this secluded section of the executive clubhouse at his favorite South Florida private club. "I am so sorry to bother you, Mr. President." Richards didn't move; whatever the valet had to say could wait until Sheila was finished.

"Keep going. What is it?" As he often did when trifled with any of his responsibilities of being the leader of the free world, Richards was and sounded pissed.

"You have a call, sir."

"Okay, Ted." His name was actually Stuart, but no one corrected this man. "Hand me the damn phone."

"Yes, sir, it's a secure call, sir." Richards was on his stomach so he could not see that Stuart was looking at Sheila.

"Jesus, you're worried about a masseuse stealing state secrets? Hold the phone to my ear!"

"Of course, sir." So Stuart stood there, only a towel separating him from the leader of the free world, while he clicked the phone on, and held it to Richards' ear. Awkward could not begin to describe how Stuart felt, as he pressed the phone to Richards' upward facing ear. "You have the President."

"Put the damn call on speaker." Stuart looked at Sheila.

"I am finished, Mr. President. As always, it is a pleasure to see you." With that, she left the room. Richards didn't bother to sit up. Once the door closing was audibly heard, Clark began.

"Sir, it's JB. Sorry to interrupt, but we have a situation in Pittsburgh."

"Pittsburgh? Pennsylvania voted for me. What's the problem?"

"Sir, there was a trial held outside Pittsburgh. A white police officer shot and killed an unarmed black teenager during a traffic stop last summer. The trial lasted four days. The officer was acquitted on all charges a couple of hours ago. The mayor and governor are worried about protests, much worse than what they had last summer after a video of the shooting went viral on the internet. Crowds have been gathering since the jury started deliberating, and weekend protests are usually the worst, even this time of year."

"Mayor and governor – they our guys?"

"Governor is ours – he won when you did. Not the mayor."

"Did the governor endorse me when he ran?"

"Strongly, sir. He's always said that your support really helped him win."

"Is the mayor black?"

"Yes. It's Pittsburgh."

"Okay, so what does my friend the governor want?"

"Governor Larry Donell. Wants some muscle from us. He's gonna call up the Pennsylvania National Guard, but he's worried that might not be enough."

"Ok tell him I'm signing an Executive Order to do that." Richards couldn't be bothered with details like it being governors can call up their own state's National Guard, but he knew about signing Executive Orders – he'd signed 137 already, mostly to reverse changes implemented by Bursan.

"Yes, sir. I will. He was ... we were thinking maybe go a bit bigger."
Now Clark had Richards' attention, so he sat up, too quickly for his
valet's preference, who had to grab the towel off the floor and try to
get Richards to wrap himself back in it. Richards waived him off, sitting there is his years long ago passed state of natural glory. "We have
a meeting with the Governor and your attorney general tomorrow
morning in the Oval. We can discuss the details then."

"Fine with me. Just not too early. We don't land until about 11pm."

"Yes sir. We set it for 9am."

"Great. I'll be there by 10. Just give me the headlines when I arrive."
Clark would not dream of involving this President in the substantive
discussions that would have to be held to get approval for the actions
Clark and Donell wanted.

By 8am the next morning, Donell, Attorney General Milo Thaddeus
Farraday, and White House counsel Max Gold were in Clark's chief of
staff office, the one that has just a 4 foot corridor and 1 door separating Clark from the Oval. For as much power as Clark wielded, and as
little non-photo op time Richards spent in the working portions of the
White House, Clark should have just switched offices. They made idle
conversation while they waited for Clark to return from another meeting.

Farraday was a blue blood. His family traced its roots to 1607 in
Jamestown, Virginia, claiming themselves to be direct descendants of
one of the men who arrived from England on the Godspeed, handpicked by King James I himself. Farraday attended Groton, an old-line
prep school, Yale University and Harvard Law School. His family ties
got him into the exclusive Skull and Bones society at Yale, and he often
dined at the males-only Porcellian Club while at Harvard. According to
his many, many detractors, he never worked an honest day in his life.
The great, great great grandson of slave owners, many of his relatives
still referred to the Civil War as the War of Northern Aggression. Farraday made most of his money as a partner in the big Park Avenue law
firm his grandfather founded. On occasion he handled a Richards real
estate deal, always careful to make sure the other side was paying his

firm's fees as part of whatever deal they negotiated. Ending his legal career as Attorney General of the United States seemed a fitting cap for an American royal, as he regarded himself.

Gold was Farraday's polar opposite. Born in the Jewish slums in Brooklyn after World War II, Max barely graduated from high school. His parents were first generation Americans. They ran a small shop in the schmatta district of New York City, but wanted him to be the first in the family go to college and law school. Max wasn't interested in all that studying – he assumed his destiny was to take over the rag store his parents called a garment shop. One day, a friend of his from the synagogue introduced him to an ethically challenged lawyer on the Lower East Side named Vin. Max was able to pick up a few bucks here and there in the 1980's as a process server and helping Vin with evictions. Vin told Max to forget about the rag business and get a law degree. Vin even helped Max pay for his formal education by teaching him how to run small swindles, the rackets he called it. Vin's favorite was a scam he ran on unsuspecting immigrants, promising to help get their family members visas to come to the US or citizenship to stay here for $250, and then blaming government red tape when the papers failed to arrive. He never forgot Vin saying, "kid, this is the easiest money a lawyer can ever make, but it helps to actually have the degree. Kapish?" Max squeaked through college and went to night law school, which he barely graduated in 1992. He often told his favorite joke, "what do you call the person who graduates last in his law school class? A lawyer." He took over Vin's office and practice after Vin got a 3 to 5 year federal prison sentence for racketeering under something called the RICO statute.

From then on, Max's practice was mostly "ambulance chasing" and divorces. One day he had the great fortune, in his mind, of handling the second divorce of a guy named Drake Richards. Max was cheap, as was Richards. While Richards generally despised Jews, he preferred having them as his lawyers and accountants. Max did a very good, aggressive and inexpensive job on the divorce. As a reward, Richards would periodically throw him some low level work like evictions and tenant law suits.

To be sure, it was not out of loyalty. Richards hired Max because his rates were a fraction of what Wall Street and Park Ave lawyers were charging, and Richards could string out paying him. When Richards' first White House counsel had to resign under an ethics investigation, Richards picked Max, who was elated to serve. Oh, how he wished his parents could have lived to see this -- their son, the lowest ranked law school graduate now the lead lawyer for the White House. Clearly, Max didn't spend his government salary, the highest he ever earned on the books, on clothes or lodging.

While in DC, he stayed at a local Chabad, having long ago befriended the rabbi in charge of this mixed use building – religion and housing all in one. He had to pay fair value for his housing and meals, and to keep kosher while within the building, which he did. But where else in DC could he safely stay for $50 a night with meals?

Farraday could not help but exhibit disdain for Max anytime he had to be in the same room. Today was no different. Max was wearing a tattered green striped, brownish sports jacket over a fading white shirt and some kind of salvation store tie. Farraday leaned away in his Saville row, three-piece perfectly tailored medium gray suit, vest perfectly buttoned, French cuff, white shirt, medium starch, Hermes tie. Farraday could not help but wonder if he had anything in his donation bin that Max could use if he dropped 35, maybe 40 pounds. Not only were his legal talents inferior, and his sense of style and decorum pitiful, Max could not even seem to manage a hair brush or razor correctly.

Clark stormed in, checking his watch as he did, tossing folders at his assistant to take care of. "Okay, I've got Treasury in 20. Larry, you've met the AG and White House counsel?"

"Yes, JB. We have introduced ourselves."

"Great. So let's get right to it."

Chapter 21: Pleased to meet you, try to guess my name

Governor Donell laid out what he hoped to accomplish. Make Mayor Pete Jones look weak, show himself as strong. Quash all protests in his streets, deter anyone who might want to rise up elsewhere in the state. Pennsylvania was not the center of racial tensions in America, but it could set an example for other liberally run, out of control cities around the country. "And God willing," he added, "let the thugs behind those masks know that we mean business, and this shit about advocating violence against police has got to end." Farraday waited until he was done.

"Governor, I agree with everything you are suggesting. But what is the federal government's role here?" That's when Clark jumped back in.

"Insurrection Act of 1807." Farraday and Gold were both confused. Farraday because he knew what the act was, Gold because he didn't.

"JB, Governor, due respect, that Act hasn't been invoked in a civilian setting since Bush 41 used it for the LA riots of 1992 after the Rodney King thing." Clark went on.

"But before that Eisenhower sent the 101st Airborne Division to enforce the desegregation of public schools in Little Rock, Arkansas. Kennedy also used it to enforce desegregation. Bush 43 used it to respond to Hurricane Katrina. Look, I'm not a lawyer in this, you guys are. But I think all Richards has to do is issue a warning to the rioters to leave the streets, and if they don't he can send in federal troops to keep the peace. Milo, Max, I need legal opinions on this, so we can move forward." Max nodded his head, a consummate yes man.

"Sure, we can do that." Farraday was willing but not as convinced.

"Hold on. What troops are we … you sending?" Clark smirked.

"That's the best part. With your guidance, only if it's legal of course, we will borrow federal agents from ICE and Homeland Security, Bureau of Prisons if we need to. Deputize them as a federal response strike force. Call them whatever you think we should. We're thinking 50, 60 troops storming Pittsburgh in addition to the National Guard should put this thing down in maybe two days."

"And so we are going to have news crew following these federal officers around, asking all kinds of questions about what ICE and DHS and BOP is doing policing the streets of a major American city? Don't get me wrong, I'm all for the concept. It's the execution and fall out I'm worried about."

"You're the AG. You tell me?" Farraday stood to stretch his legs, even though the office itself was not that big. He knew he was the smartest person in the room, but this was not his usual type of legal analysis. All of a sudden, Max began humming, bopping his head, tapping his fingers on his tattered slacks. Clark, Donell and Farraday were not amused. Farraday snapped at him, having been embarrassed by his public and private behavior on several prior occasions, well aware of his reputation of not paying attention in even high level meetings, but knowing he could not get rid of him.

"You want to stay with us? Can you do that?" Max nodded.

"Never left. Sympathy for the Devil. Rolling Stones." Now Clark was pissed.

"Max, what the f…"

He had an awful singing voice, but tried with his still thick Brooklyn accent anyway. "Pleased to meet you, hope you guess my name. Woot woo, woot woo." He paused for effect. "You said we deputize agents from different agencies. That means when they hit Pittsburgh, they're not ICE or whatever, they are a ... federal peacekeeping force. So tell them to take their off official ID off, just give them name tags that say federal agent or security. Shouldn't matter. But without names or ID, gives the press less to chase down. Try to guess my name!" Donell, who had stayed silent intentionally, felt now he could contribute, as the second most media savvy person in the room.

"And helps change the story. Media will chase their own tails about who these guys are as much as why the hell they're putting down a civilian uprising." Clark agreed.

"And they'll know in advance why they are there. Richards will just come out and tell everybody ahead of time. We are doing this if you don't get off our streets. So the story shifts from why they're there to who they are." Clark looked down at his watch. "Love it. Milo, Max, make it happen. Memos on my desk in three hours. Governor, we'll meet with the President at lunch instead of 10. He won't mind. Susie will set you up where you can wait." And with that, he pushed himself out from behind his desk, and grabbed the files from a waiting Susan, barked at her to let Richards' staff secretary know they'd be meeting for lunch instead, and to set the Governor up in a comfortable room. Susan then asked the Governor to follow her to the Mural room. Max and Milo then each left, having nothing to really to say to each other.

By noon, Farraday had a lower level attorney deliver a blue folder to the Chief of Staff's office, containing a 15 page memo with the following executive summary:

> Broad authority for use of federal agents to quell a riot and keep the peace:

> The Insurrection Act of 1807, 10 U.S.C. §§ 331-335, provides, *inter alia*, "That in all cases of insurrection, or obstruction to the laws ... the President of the United States [may] call forth the militia for the purpose of suppressing such insurrection, or of causing the laws to be duly executed, [and may] employ, for the same purposes, such part of the land or naval force of the United

States, as shall be judged necessary, having first observed all the pre-requisites of the law in that respect."

The predicate step is for the President to first issue a proclamation ordering the insurgents to disperse within a limited time. 10 U.S.C. § 334.4. If the situation does not resolve itself, the President may issue an executive order to send in troops.

The memo detailed in general terms what prior administrations deemed insurrections, and concluded that because the federal government no longer has a standing militia, the President was empowered to deputize federal agents to suppress an insurrection. Farraday added a section to the memo himself about the roots of this power being in the Federalist Papers, a stretch to most legal scholars, but having some historical support. There were historical writings evidencing that the Act was considered to be a product of a strange plan hatched by Aaron Burr to gather up an army to invade Mexico under the false claim of being at war with Spain, and then keep any land they seized for himself. Burr's plot lost its historical significance after he shot and killed Alexander Hamilton in a duel.

The only legal limitation the AG noted was that the mission should be curtailed to a "reasonable proximity" to a federal building, like a courthouse or a post office, to avoid any possible question on the use of "peace keeping federal agents" on the streets of an American city, particularly should the officials in charge "decline an offer of federal assistance."

Shortly after the AG's extensive and well detailed memo arrived, Max had an associate White House counsel deliver his three-page letter. While short on any historical context, Max agreed the President had this power to send in federal agents to Pittsburgh to put down a "lawless, violent uprising," concluded that there was no established legal precedent requiring the agents be identified by name. Therefore, as Commander in Chief, the President had broad, sweeping power over the "manner and means" of sending in federal officers.

Clark read both memos before he had the Governor brought to him at 12:15pm. He explained lunch would be in the residence, and walked him through the Oval. "I'll get you the photo op before you leave today." They proceeded through the open air, columned walkway between the West Wing and the Executive Residence, passing the Rose Garden. Clark had no doubt Donell was contemplating how he would decorate the Oval Office and what events he would host in the Rose Garden after his run in 2024, whether Richards wins or loses next year.

They entered the residence at 12:20 pm. Richards was not yet ready for their noon meeting, which Clark expected. The butler sat them at their round dining table, the fine crystal water glasses already filled, bone china ready for serving each course, shining silverware splayed perfectly. They asked for soft drinks, which were brought, along with Richards' diet cola. He had made it clear not to let his drink sit too long, because if the ice was allowed to melt it watered down the flavor. The butler then wheeled in a side table with a crystal bowl of a mixed green salad and large pieces of chocolate cake. Richards entered as the salads were plated. Both stood, Donell extended his arm to vigorously shake.

"Mr. President." Clark softly mouthed. "Larry Donell."

"Larry. So great you're here and we can help you. You scratched my back to help me win Pennsylvania last time, and I'm sure you'll be totally 100% with me next year." Richards started drinking his diet cola, and eating his salad. He started talking again, even with lettuce and tomato still in his large mouth. "It's burgers today. Hope you don't mind. Real treat is that chocolate cake. Look at those pieces. Best damn chocolate cake you'll ever have." Richards swallowed, wiped his lips. "So tell me, Larry, what's your pitch?" Richards never stopped using his game show tag line, even as president.

Donell repeated what had been discussed in Clark's office earlier, why a strong public show of strength could help both of them in Pennsylvania and Richards around the country for their reelection campaigns next year. Clark endorsed the idea, and said he had run it through the AG and White House counsel.

"Okay, we'll do it. Strong, totally strong show of force. Probably Antifa anyway. We need to do that." Clark starting eating his burger – medium rare as he preferred it, and when he finished a sizeable bite he added, "what's the timing?""We'll have you address the press at 4pm today in the briefing room. It's on your schedule. Donell will stand next to you, along with the AG. You will announce this as a peacekeeping mission, meant to protect the law-abiding citizens of Pittsburgh and Pennsylvania from lawless thugs who are robbing and looting."

"Sure. Fine. Put it on the prompter. You have the cards?" Clark slid an official White House engraved envelop across to the commander in chief, with three index cards inside. "Larry, we'll stop at the Oval on the way. Take some photos, let some press in. No questions til the press conference." Richards pivoted to look at Clark. "You'll have our buddy from NewsFirst in the press room with my softball?"

"I'll take care of it. Call on her first."

"Her? What happened to that guy, Jim or something?"

"Mark Tauben. He went back to Fox."

"Too bad. He was a pretty good golfer. Who's the girl?"

"Analise Simmins. You'll love her." Clark was grinning, smirking.

"How come?" Clark picked up his burger, looked at it longingly, then answered.

"She's black. Very light skinned, but black. You call on her, she loves your answer. She'll do live reporting from the site when the troops get there. Media can't call this a racial thing. Will help make the story about law and order." Clark took a big bite. Richards slugged down some more diet cola.

"Larry, wait til you try that cake." They finished their meal mostly silent, Clark receiving and returning three texts as they dug into their dessert. By 1:10, they were done. Clark and Donell walked back to the West Wing. Clark reminded Richards.

"Mr. President. Oval at 3:45. Briefing room at 4." He waved as they left, a large piece of cake still sloshing around in Richards' mouth.

| 22 |

Chapter 22: March 2019: MERS is still simmering

Ricky was finishing his lunch at his desk at 1:10 p.m. on Saturday, March 23, 2019. Derek had been fairly insistent that none of his Principals work more than half a day on the weekend - at the office anyway. Derek changed the nickname for Ricky, Jeanne and Shimon after being told why "dream team" conjured up bad memories for many people of a famous double homicide trial from the 1990's. CNOVation had installed state of the art security access devices that logged all entrances and exits, which Derek let be known he checked to make sure the Principals complied. So Ricky wrapped up a half-day at the office, then did his grocery shopping on the way home. At 6 pm he placed a video call to his parents. Ricky was growing uneasy with his mother's respiratory distress. She was still experiencing difficulty breathing since his last Saturday call. She had promised to see Dr. Tzen, the specialist Ricky recommended in Beijing, who in turn assured him he would get her test results to him right away.

During their call, Mae mentioned that she had received a lovely get well card from Li and Shia Yung. Ricky paused as he tried to place the names. Mae helped him. "Son, you attended academy with their lovely daughter, Caihong. Such a pretty girl." Caihong? Caihong, Ricky thought. At 12 years old he had not really been noticing girls, but her name was vaguely familiar to him. "They say she is very successful now. And still single. And you are about the same age." Mae peered into her son's eyes for some reaction, but none was forthcoming.

"Mother, I am concerned about your slow recovery. I am going to move up my trip home and come as soon as I can. But, please, do see Dr. Tzen very soon. He will see you right away."

"I will, my son. We are very excited to see you. Your father wishes to speak with you now." And with that Ricky and his father spoke for a few minutes, nothing in particular, other than Tsang Wai assuring Ricky that mother would see Dr. Tzen on Monday.

After disconnecting, Ricky kept thinking about MERS. Cases were still on the rise around the world, some in China, but most in Saudi Arabia. He cared as a son and worried as a researcher because of the unusually high fatality rate -- over 34% -- that came with MERS. He did not know if his mother had it but he could not rule it out with what little facts he had to go on. Another bleak possibility was a strain of the severe acute diarrhea syndrome coronavirus (SADS-CoV) outbreak that began in China and had been traced to bats. He would not have known of this possibility absent the details his father discretely supplied but that his mother omitted out of modesty. Ricky knew Mae occasionally would walk with a friend through a local exotic market where bats hung for sale, even though she never bought or ate bat. Still, SADS-CoV had also devastated livestock such as pigs. And even though his mother rarely ate pork, Ricky knew well that China often under-reported diseases that could hurt its exports.

One of the Chinese government's stated goals for 2025 was to slash US pork imports from just over $1.3 billion to $600 million. Getting there meant continued rapid expansion and consumption of home-grown hogs, a task that would be complicated if this livestock was considered disease ridden.

Derek had OK'd Ricky moving up his planned trip home by a few weeks. If Ricky was lucky, his mother would recover before he arrived, and he could bring back to the lab a few of her cultures and some from local pig farmers for further study. Getting the proper authorizations to travel with medical transport equipment and lab specimens took tremendous efforts. General Lind had to intervene and get the State Department involved. But they got it worked out.

Ricky went in Monday morning to meet with Guri from the medtech department, who had assembled the specially encased travel bag, which the State Department had precleared with the airline and Chinese customs. The dual layered, polycarbonate plastic specimen vials would be properly preserved to both withstand the 22 hour flight home and not be contagious if they somehow broke within the James Bond-esque travel bag. Although designed to look like a plain old Samsonite carry-on, this bag was lined with a specially coated, freeze wrap interior. The bag would be warm to the outside touch and 56 degrees below zero inside the vial compartment. All Ricky had to do was activate the freezing element once the vials were placed inside. Of course, he knew he would draw odd looks on the flights home and back, since he was required to have biohazard stickers placed on both sides of the travel bag.

Ricky met with his team and updated Derek on all of his projects before he left at 2pm. When he returned to his apartment, he packed for his flight, which would depart at 9pm that evening. With a few hours to kill, he turned on CNN to see what was happening "here at home and around the world," at least according to this station. It was just shy of 4pm, and the White House correspondent stationed near the front gate on the lawn was talking about the press conference that was supposed to begin "any time now," at which point they would cut live to the briefing room. The DC weather had turned overcast and windy, so, according to the correspondent, Richards didn't want to be outdoors, especially after playing golf in 80 degree temperatures in Florida a day earlier. The reporters knew the Pennsylvania Governor had been in the White House all day, and there was speculation it could be about a major infrastructure project Richards had promised in 2016 during his campaigning in the Keystone State. A few "talking heads" had speculated it could have something to do with the Pittsburgh verdict of acquittal for the white police officer, but the expert pundits, former assistant US Attorneys, were quite self-assured that the federal government would have no role in the protests that had been on going. All who were asked doubted very seriously that this President, his Attorney General or this Administration would be announcing a federal civil rights investigation into the officer involved shooting.

Ricky checked his emails and read a few Google alerts while waiting for the press conference's start. He double checked his suitcase, flight itinerary, and set up a ride share pick up for 4:30. Finally, at 4:11 p.m., the CNN anchor announced they were now cutting away to the James S. Brady Press Briefing Room. The cameras showed the left side door open, with Richards followed by Donell and Farraday ascending to the podium. Richards held three index cards in his left hand, and approached the lectern. He exhaled audibly directly into the mike, and, as he almost always did, grabbed both sides of the lectern, and exposed his jaw clenched, the I am smart and in control look.

Card 1: "As you know, a jury in Pittsburgh lawfully acquitted a police officer yesterday. The legal process was totally followed."

Card 2: "Roving groups of thugs and criminals have taken over the streets of Pittsburgh, breaking windows, robbing stores, setting fires, causing chaos for law abiding citizens. I met today with Governor Donell," he pointed to the governor so he could make his head nod of deference, "and have assured him that this awful, disgusting lawlessness will not be tolerated. Not by me." He then made sure to look directly into the center camera, manned by Mike from Fort Worth as it had been during his entire administration when he addressed the press or the nation.

Card 3: "This is my warning to these rioters and Mayor Pete Jones, who has been totally weak. If you can't protect the streets of your great city, I will. My attorney general and I have decided, at the governor's request, to invoke the Insurrection Act. Mayor Jones, you have a day to get your streets under control. If not, if these crooks and thugs are not off the streets in 24 hours, I will sign an executive order to send in federal troops to restore law and order." The card said peace-keeping federal law enforcement officers, but close enough thought Clark, as he watched from the back of the room, out of view of the press. Arms shot up; questions began being shouted. Richards, as cued, called on the attractive, young black reporter in the third row. "Yes, you."

Up she stood. "Mr. President. Analise Simmins. NewsFirst. Sir, are you at all concerned that this move may be seen by the public as a white president sending in federal troops to stop lawful protests by Black Americans? Our reporting is that over 90% of the protesters are black. Are there any racist elements here, sir?" Richards worked to maintain his me smart and in charge look.

"Miss Simpson. There is totally no racism here. I am the least racist person in this room. This is about controlling thugs and criminals who are running freely around American streets, making damage, looting. Who knows, maybe raping young women? You never know, they are bad, bad dudes. This is about restoring law and order. Period." She seemed convinced enough to sit back down. Clark waved as he told Richards he would, signaling it was time for him to leave. "Ok, I have to go. You will hear from the Governor and our Attorney General now." And with that, he bounded out through the door he had entered.

Ricky shook his head in disappointment. He had travelled enough to know this was not a typical thing in the US. Sure, in a major Chinese city, a public and well publicized show of force would be expected with the type of violence that Richards had described. But China had not called itself a free and open democracy for over 240 years or a bastion of free speech.

Jesse texted him that he was outside, which the ride app had already notified him. He appreciated that Ricky made a habit of asking for him whenever he needed car service. Ricky looked forward to their chats, getting updates on how his family was faring. Once in the car, Ricky ignored his Google feed to chat with Jesse.

"Pittsburgh is gonna explode Ricky."

"How do you mean?"

"I mean, the black community there can't stand Richards or this governor, and they love Mayor Pete. They rioted for four days when that boy was shot and all the videos went around on the internet. The cop flat out murdered that boy. The state's white attorney general took that case over because he wants to run for governor when Donell runs for senate or whatever other office he's thinking of. The cop got to move that trial to the next county over, he says, to avoid a tainted jury pool. Tainted? They meant darkened. So, right next door they get about the whitest county they can, a suburb of Pittsburgh they kept calling it. It's where all the rich white folks ran once the steel mills started closing. So they end up with one black lady on the jury, who now we're finding out dated a cop in college and had a nephew accidentally killed by some gang bangers." Jesse was nearly shouting he was so emotionally wrought.

Ricky had been interested in race relations and religious discrimination his entire life, and tried to keep up with these goings on in the US as best he could. But he knew this was another major flashpoint. "Jesse, do you think this will be like Ferguson?" Ricky knew Ferguson, Missouri had a similar incident in 2014 – unarmed black teenager shot and killed by a white police office. The local county grand jury decided not to bring criminal charges; riots in the streets lasted for about three weeks. Massive destruction to streets, homes, businesses and police property. All of that happened while Bursan was President, and he tried to bring calm and restraint through words and a federal investigation, never through a show of force.

"Like Ferguson? Ricky, this is gonna make Ferguson look like a Thanksgiving Day parade. My community is sick and tired of being sick and tired about police violence. Richards is pouring gas on this fire, and it's gonna explode. A lot of innocent people are gonna get hurt. Don't get me wrong. We have plenty of good cops, good police chiefs and good mayors; Mayor Pete is one and so is his police chief. Hell, I got two cousins on the job around Boston. They'll get it under control, but they gotta let the people protest and get it out of their systems." Jesse's raw emotion was evident, his frustration, even anger. "But this racist? I'm sorry if I'm saying too much."

"No, really it is fine."

"This racist in the White House. He's gonna send federal storm troopers who don't know sh..." Jesse caught himself and then continued. "Uniformed thugs from DC who don't know anything about the community. It's a powder keg and there's gonna be a lot of people getting hurt when it explodes."

Ricky was not good at consoling people. He felt the desire to, he just never could come up with the right words. "We can pray for the young man and his family, and for the good people there, and hope for the best." Jesse was tearing up as they arrived at Logan, but didn't want his passenger to notice.

"Pray for my kids too, if you don't mind. That could be one of them one day, shot dead on the street in broad daylight, and nobody held accountable. No justice." He stayed head and eyes ahead, then wiped his eyes under his glasses before he exited the car to get Ricky's bags from the trunk. They shook hands, and Jesse wished him a good flight.

As expected, Ricky drew several odd stares with the biohazard markings on his case, and pretty much no one wanted to stand next to him and his scary looking bag on the security line. Once he cleared TSA and was at his departure gate, he checked his Google feed. Pittsburgh was heating up. People were screaming about militarized federal troops being dispatched to an American city to shut down lawful protests. Mayor Pete issued a statement and held a press conference calling on the president to stay out of this local matter. Ricky would have plenty of time to read all about it on his long flight home.

| 23 |

Chapter 23: Sweet steamed buns

By the time Ricky landed in Beijing, his mother had been transported to a local hospital. He would meet his father and Dr. Tzen then. As a precaution, they brought her to an isolation ward in Beijing Ditan Hospital. Ricky was well aware that, even still a Chinese national, his role as a medical researcher would be severely restricted and closely monitored. The United States had closed its National Science Foundation office in Beijing in 2018, along with other offices in foreign cities. Both the NIH and the CDC had been forced to reduce their staff in Beijing. In addition to what Ricky had read, his father had informed him that growing tensions between the US and China and harsh rhetoric from Richards led China to be even more circumspect about what medical and scientific information it would share with US partners, and even the WHO.

Dr. Tzen advised Tsang Wai and Ricky that he was concerned about the progression of the illness and Mae not responding to the prescribed drug regimen. The testing was inconclusive. Some of her symptoms were consistent with each of MERS, SADS and SARS. She had headaches, discomfort, body aches, chills, a sore throat and shortness of breath. The hospital would also be best for Mae's pneumonia and hypoxia.

The fact that Tsang Wai had not become symptomatic also inclined Dr. Tzen to believe that Mae had a flu, which was generally less contagious than a coronavirus, especially in close quarters. And, of course, there had been very little public reporting of a new novel coronavirus in China so no testing was yet available. Dr. Tzen knew he had to choose his words carefully, even with Ricky, which saddened him. To Dr. Tzen's superiors, Ricky was an American now, so the information sharing restrictions in effect across Chinese health agencies were applicable here. He would wait until they had left the hospital to speak more freely.

Even still, this was his mother, so Ricky had received permissions to scrub in and put on the biomed suit, specially used for the isolation ward. The royal blue suit was embossed with large, red lettering ???? on the back, Chinese for biohazard. Ricky slipped on the airtight goggles, a mask with oxygen tube, then the thick plastic gloves. Only then did he enter the room with Dr. Tzen. Tsang Wai would not be allowed in, but could watch and listen on the 26" monitor hanging in the special waiting room.

Ricky held his mother's hand, and exchanged a few words. She was clearly tired, the byproduct of shortness of breath and medications. He looked at her chart and recognized the regimen as a traditional antibiotic and an experimental antiviral. Thankfully, she had not needed to be intubated or placed on a respirator, which gave Ricky and Dr. Tzen hope that she would recover quickly.

Before they left her room, Ricky announced to his listening father that he and Dr. Tzen would need a few minutes to gather the samples of her tissue and blood that Ricky would be testing for further analysis. Dr. Tzen would need to be with him while he gathered the samples and placed them in the biomedical transport bag. Ricky left the bag at the hospital for inspection as required by the agreement the State Department had reached.

After the hospital visit ended, the three men went to lunch. Ricky continued to ask questions, knowing his friend and mentor could only go so far in what he could say. "How long can you stay?"

"I will fly back after mother has gone home."

"You should rest from your flight. I will meet you at my lab tomorrow morning." Dr. Tzen was not scheduled to work that day, but in this circumstance he was happy to do so. Plus, outside of the heavily monitored isolation ward, he might have a bit more leeway in helping Ricky help him solve this medical mystery. Tsang Wai thanked Dr. Tzen for all of his help as they left. The restaurant was less than a mile from the apartment, so even with the roller bag, father and son decided to walk home. They spoke very little on the way, neither having much affection for idle chatter about how the flight was or whether it would snow.

"Mother will be fine, father. I will not allow her not to be."

"There is only so much we can control, my son. But I can think of no one, no one, I would rather have at her side, and mine." Ricky had never seen his father cry; this came very close.

Once back at the apartment, now so quiet, unable to sleep and jet lagged from the long flight, Ricky turned on the TV in his room. He clicked back and forth between the news channels carrying the state run Xinhua News Agency and the China News Service. Both were broadcasting unflattering images of Richards and the protests in the streets of Pittsburgh. Smashed store windows and cars being set on fire filled the screens. The news presenters commented derisively on how the American president could not control the streets of his country.

He then checked the online versions of China's main state run newspapers, the People's Daily, Beijing Daily, Guangming Daily and the Liberation Daily. Again, he found multiple reports castigating Richards, but nothing helpful on his mother's possible disease. Ricky looked at his emails. Derek, Jeanne and Shimon all wished his mother well, offering any help they could provide. Lying in bed, still unable to sleep or shut down his mind, he surfed the portions of the Renren social media feed he could access without an account. He found a lot of comments on how Richards was fueling racial unrest in America, and how China's

President was a far smarter and more effective leader. This was China's hoped for reaction to the news reporting he had watched and read.

Knowing he needed sleep, Ricky opened his meditation app, the one Jeanne had shared with him, and listened to calming piano music until he fell asleep.

At 5:45am local time Wednesday, he could hear his father moving around in the kitchen, making himself a pot of tea. He stretched, brushed his teeth, and went in. He knew his father was in unfamiliar territory fixing his own breakfast of steamed stuffed buns. These two men stared at the steamer, unsure how to heat these dough buns filled with sweetened bean paste. Ricky had become pretty adept at a breakfast of toast with jam and using a microwave for left overs, but this contraption was outside his skill set. They two men laughed at their shared weak spot. "Father, I'll shower and run down to the market and bring us back some properly prepared steamed buns." Tsang Wai nodded appreciatively, and began to read his morning paper. Ricky knew how important routine was to his father, as for most Chinese.

Ricky grabbed a face mask, ever present in most Chinese cities, and strapped it on. The smell of the market place and the bustle even at 6:15am brought back good memories. As short a childhood as Ricky had, the time he'd spent with his parents, especially his mother, in true Chinese traditions made him smile, even something as simple as strolling by stores smelling for the best stuffed buns. Ricky made his way to a nearby vendor, placed his order in Mandarin, and walked back to the apartment with their warm breakfast.

The 15 minutes he then spent with his father was time he would always cherish. They spoke as adult men of the careers they pursued, the challenges they faced. His father shared stories Ricky had never heard of his rise in power and prestige. He was proud, never boastful, except when he spoke of how he would tell colleagues of the work his son was doing, saving lives all over the world. Ricky described in very limited fashion the work he now engaged in, the intrigue and seeming senselessness of American politics. By 7 am, Tsang Wai needed to head to work, and Ricky to Dr. Tzen's lab. In the elevator down, the last thing father told son was, "Your mother never smiles so much as anytime she speaks to you or speaks of you." It was Ricky's turn to well up a tear.

"You will see smiles for many more years then."

As Ricky entered the nearest Beijing subway station, he put his disposable surgical mask back on, as the majority of the commuters had. Wearing protective masks in public areas such as malls, train and buses had been commonplace for many Chinese since 2003, after the first major SARS outbreak. Ricky could not help but notice while in America that many Asians still wore masks in public and many Americans looked at them oddly, even joked about it. Ricky saw nothing humorous about a simple yet effective public health measure.

After arriving at the lab, Dr. Tzen introduced the Chinese security officer who would monitor Ricky's activities. The doctor then shared with Ricky the high definition photos of the culture slides he had examined from both his parents, and the diagnostics he had run. The picture quality was decent, which made Ricky think about the advanced imaging project he had been immersed in back in Boston. As they agreed the day before, the two scientists spoke in sterile technical terms. They assumed the security officer would prepare as close to a verbatim report as he could without understanding much of the discussion.

Ricky had been given clearance to run a few tests himself, limited by the diagnostic equipment available in this lab. Ricky knew that since 2004, China's version of the CDC had been operating a national pneumonia surveillance system. The system had been designed to allow timely detection of novel respiratory pathogens, such as SARS. Ricky had interfaced with scientists from the Chinese CDC many times during his career. But he was also painfully aware that China, in recent years, had been decreasing its funding of this system, which undercut the effectiveness and reliability of its pneumonia of unknown etiology (PUE) database. Dr. Tzen was allowed to access the PUE and to share findings with Ricky, which took the entire morning. Everything they found was inconclusive. Ricky knew when he got the cultures home he could run more advanced tests and access the WHO database, but not all of the PUE data would likely be there.

Ricky thanked Dr. Tzen and headed back to the subway, masked and ready to see his mother. Dr. Tzen could not go today, but Ricky had his signed forms allowing him to enter at 1pm. He assumed he would also be accompanied by a Chinese security officer. He texted his father at work, "reviewed labs; nothing conclusive; headed to see mother," in Mandarin of course. His father texted back "Thank you. I will meet you at hospital at 4pm."

| 24 |

Chapter 24: That's Richards in Pittsburgh, not Putin in Moscow

Ricky signed in to Ditan Hospital at 1:40pm. As instructed, he waited at the entrance desk. As he had suspected, a security officer in the same drab, olive military uniform as this morning introduced himself as his escort for the afternoon. The desk receptionist then paged a nurse, who came out and explained that his mother was resting, and asked that he wait in the family waiting room until the attending doctor could accompany him to see her. "Of course." The nurse led Ricky and his escort to the main family room, where the 42" HD TV was set to Xinhua News Agency, the volume off. The third story contained images of large men in black uniforms wearing tactical gear, no ID badges, chasing rioters through dark streets, large buildings silhouetted in the background. The reporter who had been on screen in a small box disappeared as the station rerolled tape of unarmed civilians being dragged into large, unmarked black Suburbans, the images played and replayed on the screen. Ricky tried to make small talk with his military escort. "Putin appears to be cracking down again." The officer heard him, and looked up, but did not speak. Ricky looked around for a remote control to raise the volume. He could not hide his surprise, almost disgust as the news reporter's box reappeared on the screen, the words "images from Pittsburgh USA care of ITV" flashed above her. When the station switched to a female news anchor who began describing the highly successful steps China had been taking to free itself of dependence on American pork, the officer looked up.

"That was your American President, Richards, arresting protesters in an American city. But, yes, it does look like Putin putting down opposition forces in Moscow." The officer had a wry, derisive smile, knowing Ricky was not an American citizen, but had come from and would go back there after this trip. Ricky felt sick being associated with this type of conduct. Ricky was well aware of the Chinese government's 1989 bloody crackdown on student-led protests in Tiananmen Square. Although he was only five years old when it happened, he had read a lot about it when he started his work with Professor Dorchester. But no one in authority in China had spoken of that dark event for years, and no state run TV station, newspaper or website was about to draw any comparisons between what was unfolding in Pittsburgh and what had happened in Tiananmen Square.

Ricky looked down at his phone, and checked his limited, internet accessible sites for more information. He viewed seeing essentially the same footage about federal storm troopers surrounding a major American city, arresting civilian protesters and rioters alike, making some mention of small scale looting, and a large scale, unidentified, masked federal police presence. Those stories all mentioned the protests were about white police mistreatment of black citizens. Ricky knew most Chinese citizens would not understand the difference between local policing and the use of a federal force in the US, but they knew about black and white.

After the pork story, the Chinese station had a panel discussing the racial tension and unrest being fomented by the American President, with parallels drawn to Richards' anti-Chinese agenda. They interspersed scenes of the federal troops with snips of his inflammatory rhetoric against China. Two panelists agreed that Chinese Americans should be fearful that he would wage a similar campaign against them to squash any opposition to his anti-Chinese posture. State media was careful to depict all this as part of a Richards' agenda and actions, not America's philosophy. China played the long game and knew not to alienate trading and business partners it would need for many years, long after Richards would be gone. The reporting also made no reference to possible US censorship, given that China was not exactly a bastion of free expression. Instead, it played a few selective clips of prominent American journalists and civil rights leaders decrying this brazen assault on American freedom.

At 2:30 pm, the staff doctor came in to talk to Ricky. He advised that his mother's breathing had become shallow, and she had been put on a ventilator. He assured Ricky this was purely preventive, that her overall organ functions were fine, and her brain activity was in an acceptable range. They were continuing the traditional antibiotic and giving her a slightly higher dose of the experimental antiviral. Yes, Dr. Tzen had been consulted, no, they did not expect this to be necessary for more than 48 hours. She remained weak and would not be very responsive. Ricky could suit up and see her now. He knew that between putting on and removing the gear he would have about an hour with his mother before his father arrived, which would be fine given her need to rest and his need to alert his father to what he would be seeing once he entered. The military escort would be taken to the same private observation room, with an open line pumped in to Ricky's microphone and earpiece.

Ricky mostly sat at his mother's bedside, held her gloved hand in his. He carefully observed the air move in and away through the ventilator, and watched her vital signs on the health monitor made by a tech company in Shenzhen. Ricky was familiar with this device. It monitored her heart rate, blood pressure, body temperature, blood oxygenation and carbon dioxide levels. Having used these machines in prior research, he also knew these had wireless capacities. He would ask Dr. Tzen to have her levels simultaneously sent to his smart phone or laptop.

After an hour, he signaled for the nurse to let him out so he could prepare to meet his father. When he arrived in the lobby, he saw his father in conversation with and being comforted by Dr. Tzen. When Ricky approached, his colleague explained that he wanted to be personally present to check Mae today, given the change in treatment protocol. Both men assured Tsang Wai that the ventilator was not to be taken as a sign of severe disease, just a precaution. Dr. Tzen would go in first, draw some blood and take a few swabs for further testing. After a few minutes, father and son could join him. The security officer remained in the observation room. The doctor assured Ricky he would ask for remote transmission of all recorded vital signs to him, but getting permission could take some effort. He understood.

Dr. Tzen left Mae's room at 6pm. Ricky and Tsang Wai stayed until 8, the latest they were allowed. Mae's condition was about the same throughout the period. Dr. Tzen had texted Ricky at 6:15pm that he would be monitoring his mother's vital signs remotely, would receive an alert if anything compromising showed up, and immediately share that information. Ricky's request for direct transmission was being "reviewed." Ricky read the text when he and his father retrieved their phones, clothes and possessions in the changing area. On the walk home, they stopped for dough buns filled with sweetened bean paste for tomorrow's breakfast, and dough buns filled with minced pork for dinner, even though neither was of a mind to eat.

As they walked home, the clash between protestors and federal agents in Pittsburgh escalated, inflamed by outside agitators who had traveled to the area to raise hell, make things worse, and blame the other side. Clark and Richards were succeeding in driving an agenda that had nothing to do with restoring peace and promoting racial justice, but was all about using force to suppress minority dissent. If cooler heads did not prevail, the United States was edging up to its own Tiananmen Square.

| 25 |

Chapter 25: Like Christmas, everyday

Clark sat in his office watching another night of Pittsburgh's streets packed with confrontation and tension. He reveled in the chaos, even the bloodshed. He made multiple media appearances, calling the mayor weak, pitiful, unable to protect his own citizens. Earlier in the day, Richards had threatened to impose martial law in all of Alleghany County.

Clark could not decide which he enjoyed more: watching badge-less federal agents pouring out of large black vehicles in full riot gear, indelicately sweeping the streets near the Pittsburgh federal courthouse, or the liberals crying on TV and the internet about an excessive and unprecedented use of force. At 8:01 pm, he flipped to O'Day on NewsFirst. The breaking news chyron screamed "Thugs, gangsters and criminals wreak havoc for a 6th day in Pittsburgh." O'Day's first guest that night would be a constitutional law scholar who would bloviate that Richards was absolutely obligated to restore law and order to this fine American city. Next came a junior congressman from Texas who would argue the only mistake Richards had made thus far was not already declaring martial law.

Clark's happiness was interrupted by a secure message on his non-government burner phone. The encrypted message was from Ulf Knutsson, confirming the meeting of The Leaders for next week, just outside Paris, where Clark's public schedule had him going as part of the advance work for the summer's upcoming G20 summit. Anyone who intercepted the message, which was possible, would see "G2 adv Lyon?" While Lyon was also an advance team meeting location, other messages had established The Leaders meeting for after-hours in Le Musée De La Grande Guerre, the Museum of the Great War in Meaux, France. This location was chosen for irony and because a trusted contact assured late night access and complete confidentiality. It was just under an hour drive from Paris. Knutsson and Deng Xu-Pei knew that not even Richards was crazy enough to recommend their countries be allowed to attend the G20 summit. They remembered the flak Richards caught at the 2018 G7 summit in Quebec when he insisted Russia be readmitted to the club.

Clark sent an encrypted "how Pburg look?" text back. Within seconds, he received

"Like Christmas, every day." He closed his phone, and prepared for his morning meetings with representatives of the Treasury Department. He would task them with imposing sanctions on the EU if it would not open up free and fair trade with Knutsson's and Deng's countries.

As Clark packed his briefcase to head home, Ricky and Tsang Wai stood in the semi-circular portico of the front entrance to Ditan Hospital, waiting for Mae to be wheeled to the waiting car to be taken home. All were overjoyed that her struggle ended successfully even if mystifyingly. Dr. Tzen assured them that with a few days bed rest and finishing the regimen of antibiotics and antivirals, she would be soon able to resume all activities, even shopping. They also understood she was in quarantine for four more days and could not leave the apartment. Ricky called Derek to check in, who expressed thanks that Mae was well enough to go home. Again, he told Ricky to take all the time he needed.

Given the access, although limited, that Ricky had to Dr. Tzen's lab, and his desire to see his mother regain near full strength, he decided to stay until the following weekend. With his father taking a few days off to tend to Mae, Ricky obtained Derek's and local Chinese permission to travel to Shenzen to help analyze a recent human outbreak of cowpox and monkeypox viruses that infected several Chinese nationals. In exchange for permission, Ricky would share all test results with China's medical community. He also would give his professional input on modifying the smallpox vaccine being used to combat this outbreak. That exercise in back scratching enabled Ricky to get permissions to bring back a broader variety of cultures to help figure out what had in fact infected his mother, and, he suspected, others. He knew his mother's case could not be a universe of one.

By Saturday, whatever had infected Mae had been resolved to Dr. Tzen's satisfaction. She was now well enough to walk around her apartment. She could even go outside on Monday. Ricky returned from Shenzen on Sunday. On Monday, he made a grocery shopping trip for his mother after his father left for work. He would not let her exert herself. He clutched her shopping list and his father's note for the rice wine he should pick up. Mae looked forward to making a meal of fish, mushroom, water chestnuts, bamboo and tofu. She made sure to remind Ricky how to pick out the freshest fish and vegetables, as she rode down the elevator with him to walk him to the front door for some fresh air. They stood out front for a few minutes. As Mae waved to return to the apartment, Clark was arriving at his clandestine meeting in Meaux.

Not all of The Principles were attending, given security and publicity concerns – not that they were as concerned about being seen together in 2019 as they were in 2014. Clark still wanted to keep a known distance from the group. His eyes were fixed on Richards' 2020 reelection campaign. While Richards' most ardent supporters would be fine with this alliance, swing-voters might be turned-off.

After greetings exchanged, and as steaks were served, Knutsson spoke. "We have several candidates we want Richards to meet with during the G20 meetings."

"From which countries?"

"Austria, Germany, Poland, Iceland, Lithuania." Clark considered the list as he chewed his medium rare T-bone steak.

"Germany is a G20 country. You can't win there. Or in Poland. At least not now."

"We know. But just images of Richards standing with Ichben and Zyntizky sends a strong signal in the countries we can win now. We think Germany could be in play in 6 to maybe 10 years, Poland about the same." Clark still could rarely be surprised, but even his eyebrows went up.

"We take Poland and Germany, we run the table in Central Europe." Deng decided to weigh in.

"Elections." He scoffed, snarled. "When will you learn that not knowing how an election will turn out before hand is unnecessary drama." Knutsson and Clark waited to see if Deng was joking or serious, and once he smirked, they laughed. The rest of the discussion was about logistics – how, when and who Richards would meet. Clark knew Richards wouldn't care, as long as the cameras were rolling and clicking. If social media caught fire with him at the center of every story, he'd meet with anyone, especially if they had something to offer him.

| 26 |

Chapter 26: June 2019: G20? Jee-sus!

In late June 2019, representatives from the European Union and 19 other countries - Argentina, Australia, Brazil, Canada, China, France, Germany, India, Indonesia, Italy, Japan, Mexico, Republic of Korea, Republic of South Africa, Russia, Saudi Arabia, Turkey, United Kingdom, and the United States – gathered in Osaka, Japan, to discuss global trade and security, women's empowerment, human rights, and the climate crisis. As expected, security was exceptionally tight.

The Leaders wanted to get their photo-ops with Richards, hoping that would help their election chances. The Kansai Promotion Council for the 2019 G20 Osaka Summit established the G20 Osaka Summit Accommodation Center for media representatives to gather and stay. Journalists from around the world were staying there, not at any of the more secure meeting sites. Clark decided that the best way to get his people in was as press. He had an unexpectedly easy time getting media credentials for the European candidates that Richards would do his grab and grin with. Free press – what a joke, Clark thought.

A declared non-believer in climate science, Richards planned on skipping the day-long meetings dedicated to this topic. Instead, he opted to tour Universal Studios Japan with Steffi and their teenage child who had come with them. Of course, this visit created security headaches for Japanese and US security officials, but, of course, Richards didn't care. Many of the mainstream media outlets opted to stay at the central meetings, so just a handful of people with official Media Badges travelled to the park. As Clark had planned it, five "journalists" on the bus were actuality members of The Leaders; each was or shortly would be a candidate for high ranking office.

Richards unwittingly stopped 50 feet in front, in long lens camera view of the Banana Cabana game. Successful players won large plush toys from the popular American animated movie, *Despicable Me.* Richards was going to hold one of his impromptu press conferences. He started a rant against the "terrible, totally destructive trade wars with China," and, another one of his pet peeves, "the totally unAmerican failure of so many countries like Germany and France to contribute to the costs of preserving peace around the world, which is so totally unfair to America."

Irony was too strenuous a mental exercise for Richards. He failed to realize how being surrounded by an international security force protecting him and his family may, perhaps, be the wrong time to rail against who should bear the costs of security around the world. Clark had decided there was no need to arm Richards with index cards today. This would only be a few of his greatest hits followed by questions and more importantly, photos and handshakes that would be seen around the world.

As planned, Richards took questions from the five "journalists," ranging from "What should European voters do now to stop being overrun by illegal immigrants who are really invaders trying to destroy their country?" to "Is Europe doing enough to reverse years of damage done to white people?"

While whatever nonsensical word salad spewed from his mouth could hardly be organized into logical sentences – subject, verb, object – Richards' failure to reject the premise of any of the questions could not be ignored. And, why would he?

Richards invited these "brave journalists" in to shake their hands, to the dismay of his security team. And then it happened. Richards stood shoulder to shoulder with these five strongman-wannabees, two of whom had already declared their candidacies, and three others who soon would. The pictures ran across TV, print and digital platforms. Le Monde of France and Der Spiegel of Germany, upon discovering these five were politicians hiding behind media credentials, ran the picture with headlines that blared, "The Insane 6."

Katie Numoff, the Minority Leader of the Senate, and not part of the G20 entourage, sat behind her desk in the Dirksen Senate Office Building. She was watching the coverage of Richards' unexpected detour. A savvy, gristly political force, she knew what Richards was up to, and suspected Clark was behind it. Washington insiders long suspected that Clark had been playing footsie with the very types of people she now saw standing in solidarity with the leader of the free world. Richards had made no secret of his affinity for racists, but always couched it in terms of "real Americans." Her cell phone rang, not usual for 7:15am. The ID lit up as SOH, her code for Samantha Elysson, Speaker of the House, the highest ranking member of her party. "Morning, Sam."

"Morning, Katie."

"Any point in us doing a presser or putting out another joint statement of condemnation of this idiot?" Tiredness and distress were evident in their voices. Ever an optimist, Sam always tried to find consolation in humor, which had many times failed even for her since January 20, 2017.

"Yeah, how's this. Just two words – G20? Jee-sus!" Katie did chuckle, appreciating Sam's efforts. Through the numerous battles they fought as powerful, successful women, they had forged a bond like sisters.

"If we put more public emphasis on this, they'll just keep running the images of him with those other five radicals."

"I know, but if we don't, the press hounds us for days with, do you want to comment on the Insane 6. Look, with most of Congress gone for the 4th of July recess, and most of the regular press either in Japan or on vacation, we're going to have a bunch of newbies and junior correspondents. So, is it even worth it right now?"

Both sighed, realizing they would have to address this straight up once to avoid having to keep addressing it. They agreed that, rather than use the Senate Radio-Television Gallery, it would be best to meet in the middle and have the historic, picturesque Statuary Hall as the setting. "9 am?"

"Sure. Katie, can your folks set it up? I'll bring you coffee."

"Deal."

"Thanks, Katie. Hey, by the way, how's your mom doing?"

"Thankfully, she's much better. Surgery went fine. No complications."

"That's great. Really, Tell her I'm expecting one of her awesome pumpkin banana breads as soon as she's able to get back in the kitchen."

"Deal. See you at 9, Sam."

With that, each of their on-site deputy press secretaries sent out a media text alert, to notify the press of the joint press conference to be held in 90 minutes.

| 27 |

Chapter 27: I mean, doesn't the picture say it all?

At 9:02 am, the Speaker of the House of Representatives and the Minority Leader of the Senate stood behind a mahogany lectern with the white and blue seal of the United States Congress prominently displayed. Together, they prepared to deliver short statements under the TV-famous and tourist must-see dome of Statuary Hall, on the House's side of the Capitol Building. This site served as a familiar backdrop for many press conferences, and was famous for its ornate statues.

Seven reporters for network news and cable outlets CNN, NBC, ABC, CBS, Fox, NewsFirst, and ITV gathered. There would be enough press coverage, even with the lower tier reporters filling in for the better known names and faces covering the G20 meetings.

"Good morning. In case you don't recognize us, my name is Samantha Elysson. I am the Speaker of the House. Next to me is Katie Numoff, the Senate Minority Leader. Congress has been trying to do its important work for the hard working people of this country, while the President of the United States has been playing games at an amusement park. Yesterday, he purposefully skipped out on critical G20 meetings where leaders from around the world gathered to address the climate crisis facing our planet. He continues to exhibit his contempt for science and the real damage being done to our planet by pollution so he could win stuffed animals. This is yet another stark example of his inability and unwillingness to take his job seriously. If he just wants to do photo ops and win kewpie dolls, he should go back to hosting a game show. There is important business to be done in Japan, and it needs to be done now. Leader Numoff?"

"Thank you, Madam Speaker. I join my colleague in criticizing this President who continues to treat his office like a golden ticket to travel the world at taxpayer expense. Day after day, he exhibits his lack of concern for the real problems facing our country. As all Americans get ready to celebrate the 4th of July, our freedom and independence, you need to remind all of our leaders that you sent them to Washington to do the hard work required to improve your lives, not throw darts at water balloons or shoot water cannons at clown's mouths. We will now take a few questions."

Katie pointed at the first reporter they would let speak.

"Thank you. Kim Donet, CNN. Do you have any concerns about the pictures of President Richards with several far right wing leaders from multiple European countries who falsely passed themselves off as journalists to get into the G20?" Katie took the questions first, as she and Sam had agreed.

"Wow, well, that's a lot to unpack so let me try to address that. The pictures we have seen are disturbing. We have very strong allies in Europe, whose legitimately elected leaders were at the very meetings Richards … the President skipped out on. One major purpose of the summit is to forge and strengthen our relationships with countries we rely on and who rely on us. So, yes, it was very disturbing to see an American President grinning and cavorting with fascists."

"Let me add," Sam jumped in, "that it has long been a US tradition that we support the duly elected officials of our major trade and defense partners around the world. We don't go mucking in their elections to advance our personal agendas. The oath we have sworn to is to advance American interests, not far-right racist agendas." Sam then pointed to the next reporter. "Yes, Joe."

"Thank you Madam Speaker. Joe Lennon, CBS. Le Monde and Der Spiegel ran pictures with headlines calling this group The Insane 6. Do you agree with that characterization?"

"I am in no position to tell media outlets from free and open democracies how to cover politics, any more than I would tell the American press how to write their stories." Katie jumped in.

"Joe, I'm sure you will remember certain media-type outlets here referring to the Speaker of the House and me as the Laverne and Shirley of Washington when I became minority leader." Most of the journalists laughed. "So, is it a colorful description? Sure. But the real issue is why Richards skipped important meetings in the first place and why he met with them at all. Again, what we know about these other ... gentlemen is that whatever they stand for is not what America stands for, and should not be glorified by a US President, especially not as we prepare to celebrate the birth of our great nation and our hard earned freedom." The next reporter didn't wait to be called on, a typical example of their in your face style.

"Analise Simmins, NewsFirst. Are you calling the President of the United States a racist?" Katie responded.

"I don't think either of us said that."

"Well, you seem to be implying that he is flirting with racists." It was Sam's turn.

"Flirting? This isn't flirting. When a US President goes out of his way to pose for photos with people who have publicly expressed such vile views as these people have, that's not flirting. That's dating, getting married and having kids. Did we call the President a racist? No. Do we condemn in the strongest possible terms his meeting and posing with devout racists? Yes. I mean, don't the pictures say it all?" Katie jumped in, holding up the 8 x11" blown up photo up she had brought with her, of the Insane 6 with a game booth sign circled in red.

"Look. It says Despicable right here. Right here, over our President's shoulder. Draw your own conclusions. Thank you all. Enjoy your 4th of July."

In his hotel suite half way across the world, Richards turned to Clark. "Fire whoever the hell it was that staged those pictures. Made me look like a damned idiot."

Clark nodded his head. "Already did." He was lying, but Richards wouldn't know. The rest of the summit consisted of important meetings of serious people working on vital issues, and dinner parties. Clark and his senior staff attended the meetings. Richards went to the dinner parties.

| 28 |

Chapter 28: The untamed mind

Ricky and his team had continued their work through the summer and into the fall. They studied diseases from around the world, with an eye toward anything looking remotely like what had infected his mother. They found no indication of new man-made toxins or bioagents, certainly nothing highly transmissible. With Derek's permission, the Principals had lent their expertise to continuing efforts to find effective vaccines for the ever mutating strains of Ebola. He allowed them to consult with both Johnson & Johnson and Merck, which were searching for a preventive for the current strain of Ebola. The results looked promising.

Derek had explained to his board that they should consider this a good faith investment. One day, CNOVation would develop a vaccine that would be way beyond their production capacities, and would need a manufacturing partner to bring it to market. It also allowed his team to poke around the equipment and processes these two drug giants were using, to see if they needed or wanted any new diagnostic toys. CNOVation and the Principals signed off on NDA's in which they agreed not to disclose or seek commercial use of any developments, data, etc. etc.

On a mid-November Saturday morning, Ricky sat in his apartment and waited to place his weekly video call with his parents. He turned to reading his advance copy of a recent article by his colleagues, Peter Piot, Heidi J. Larson and others titled *Immunization: vital progress, unfinished agenda,* to be published on *Nature.com,* https://rdcu.be/cdjsy. He was especially taken by this part of the opening Abstract:

> *Although scientific progress opens exciting perspectives in terms of new vaccines, the pathway from discovery to sustainable implementation can be long and difficult, from the financing, development and licensing to programme implementation and public acceptance. Immunization is one of the best investments in health and should remain a priority for research, industry, public health and society.*

An all too familiar theme to Ricky. In his time living in America, he had grown surprisingly aware of the anti-vaxxers, a loose, unaffiliated group of people who objected to taking any vaccines. Ricky expected the Food and Drug Administration would soon be approving an Ebola vaccine (rVSV-ZEBOV) developed by Merck and a partner. This would be the first FDA-approved vaccine for Ebola. It would be used to combat the Zaire ebolavirus, a deadly and widely circulating strain.

Fortunately, there was still virtually no US domestic exposure to any strain of Ebola. Yet fear pervaded. Ricky had discussed this phenomenon with his father – how many Americans feared a disease while refusing to take preventive measures. Tsang Wai described this dilemma of public acceptance as "the culture of America". Ricky's father continued, "here in China, when a new disease is detected, scientists run to the labs to find a cure. Public leaders advise of sensible steps to be taken to minimize exposure, and when the vaccine is available, where to go to receive your shot. In America, when a disease is detected, politicians race to the microphones to blame another country for the disease and alarm people about its effects. When American health ministries advise people to take precautions, some bristle at this as curtailment of their freedoms. When a vaccine is finally available, these same politicians question both why it took so long and whether it is truly safe. It has become quite popular in American culture to turn science into a political issue. You would never see this at home." Ricky expressed his consternation.

"You are right. Since I have been in the US, I have observed leading figures who seem more interested in scaring people than protecting them."

"As you no doubt know, Geshe-la often says all fear comes from the untamed mind. Americans seem more interested in exploiting fear and even wallowing in it than in disciplining the mind by educating themselves about it. Chinese prefer to solve problems logically."

"Guanxi does not work on Americans?"

"Quite the opposite my son. You have many there who have mastered but perverted the intended reason for building personal trust and strong interpersonal relationships – the philosophy is designed to promote happiness and safety, never meant to sow fear and discord. I know you have never opened a Renren account. If you did, you would see so much less divisive chatter here than on American social media platforms." As a medical scientist, Ricky spent little time contemplating matters of social science, but could not ignore how this predicament of irrational fear could interfere with taking steps necessary to avoid the spread of a disease or the delivery of a vaccine. He recalled how the current US president rose to the highest office in the land by preying on people's justified concerns about Ebola, rather than helping to calm them. The untamed mind; the enemy of rational thought. "You should speak with your mother now. She is most anxious to hear your voice."

Mae accepted Tsang Wai's smart phone in her hand, and turned the phone camera to her. Still very traditional, they believed that the father should first speak without the mother in the frame, even though this technology was thousands of years newer than the tradition. Ricky then had a lovely conversation, blushing as he often did from his mother's pride in him, her continued thanks for helping to cure her, and her excitement of his upcoming trip home. They would welcome in 2020 together, a new year and a new decade of unlimited promise, unaware how awful a year it would become.

| 29 |

Chapter 29: 2020 arrives:
Happy New Year (not really)

Given how hectic the first half of 2019 turned out to be, Derek adopted a policy requiring the Principals to be away from the office for at least seven consecutive days annually. Derek explained, "we pay you too much for any of you to burn out." Ricky, Shimon and Jeanne co-ordinated their schedules. Given the distance each would travel, they ended up leaving close to Christmas Day.

Derek told Ricky to take 10 days, considering the long flight to Beijing. Ricky agreed, looking forward to a relaxing trip home to see his parents. His family had not adopted the Western style New Year's Eve celebration. So, December 31 would be a quiet dinner at his parents' home while hundreds of thousands of Beijinger's gathered at massive Western style parties all over the city to drink and dance the night away. Mae had told Ricky she would prepare her traditional Lunar New Year's Eve dinner of Chinese mud carp, a dish meant to bring good fortune, They all expected they would not be together for the Lunar New Year. Mae had also mentioned possibly inviting some guests for that dinner - Li and Shia Yung and their lovely daughter Caihong – if she could get away from her very important work. Mae wished to thank them for their concern during her illness. Ricky deferred to his mother's preference.

Dr. Tzen stopped by for dinner on December 28, and assured Ricky his mother had fully recovered. Ricky reiterated what he had written in an email a few months earlier, that all the testing they had performed at CNOVation provided no specific answers, but also raised no new concerns about infectious disease. His email dovetailed with the observations of the NIH and or CDC. While no one enjoyed the mystery, all agreed to celebrate the end result.

Early on the morning of December 31, Ricky made his daily check for news from the World Health Organization. He read that the WHO's office in China had picked up a media statement by the Wuhan Municipal Health Commission advising of several cases of "viral pneumonia" in Wuhan. Ricky then turned on the TV in his room, and clicked back and forth between state run Xinhua News Agency and the China News Service. In the 10 minutes he watched, he saw only a 15 second story on the pneumonia. He viewed the online versions of China's main state run newspapers, the People's Daily, Beijing Daily, Guangming Daily and the Liberation Daily. Each carried the Wuhan commission statement verbatim, nothing more.

Ricky could not access CNN's international web site. His parents did not live in a diplomatic compound or in an apartment block that the government permitted to have that kind of influence from the outside world. Ricky knew that censorship was a big part of Chinese life. His father probably had access at his Renren office. But this reporting did not raise enough concern with him to make a trip to his father's office or ruin his planned day off. And a field trip to Wuhan made no sense, as it was more than 1,100 kilometers away. Reports of a small spread of viral pneumonia in China in late December was not newsworthy.

During breakfast, Mae told Ricky that the Yungs were not able to come. Shia's mother had taken ill and the family decided to stay with her in Xiamen in Fujian province, a full day's drive from Beijing. Ricky inquired of her illness, for scientific purposes but also out of personal concern for her parents' friends. Mae related that she was simply experiencing the ailments of a 93 year old woman. But perhaps Ricky could contact Caihong by email or text. Mae would be sure to get her contact information.

Starting in the late afternoon, in bars and hotels away from their apartment building, parties raged on to welcome 2020 – what a year all the revelers agreed this would be, full of hope and promise. Inside, Ricky greatly enjoyed their quiet dinner. It was actually quite fun. In fact, the entire trip had been refreshing, a sorely needed break. Ricky's large corporate salary and business class flights warmed his father's heart. Just seeing him and hearing his stories was all his mother needed. Now, if only he could meet a nice girl and get married, she gingerly expressed.

The flight back to Boston in his comfy pod was as pleasant as these things went. He actually slept most of the way, something he normally could not do, and the food was pretty good. When Ricky arrived at Logan midday on January 3, 2020, no one pulled him aside at customs. This did not go unnoticed.

By 6am on January 5, Ricky sat at his office desk, invigorated and ready to tackle the coming challenges. Jeanne and Shimon would be back soon as well. He caught up on the internal corporate bulletins on his 42" ultra-high def second screen, including the completion of the upgrades to the already austere lab. While was he away, the company added an additional layer of concrete reinforcements laced with conductive metals so as not to interfere with their internet speed or secure communications. The latter would now be conducted in an upgraded communications room. More powerful HEPA filters had been installed to guard against any bacteria escaping. Ricky's version of the memo, given his level of security clearance, also noted other upgrades. The corridor's exterior glass was now bullet proof, and the entire floor on which the lab sat had been bomb proofed. No wonder Derek seemed overly eager they be gone for so long.

Ricky's tea pot whistled. He got up to steep his morning tea through the new filter, both of which his mother had given him, and which he also declared on his customs form.

While the tea settled, he checked his advisories and saw that late yesterday, the WHO had tweeted out about a "cluster of pneumonia cases" in Wuhan and that investigations to identify the cause were now underway. No deaths had been reported. Ricky sipped his tea, thinking about what this might mean. He emailed his WHO contacts and offered support, then went back to reading his team updates from the 10 days he was away. He reviewed their data, checked their analytics. As promised, Derek updated the Principals daily while they were away, and there was "nothing to report."

In a few hours, his Google alert popped up with another WHO advisory, which he clicked to and read. The WHO issued its first "Disease Outbreak News" report, providing more details about the Wuhan cluster and the Chinese national health authority's stated response measures. The WHO did not sound any alarms, and advised that "WHO's recommendations on public health measures and surveillance of influenza and severe acute respiratory infections still apply". He thought about reaching out to his contacts in the Chinese health ministry to see if there was more he could or should know, but since he was in the "private space," he knew that would be inappropriate. If China wanted outside help, they would have to seek it. While he pondered, Shimon texted him from Israel. "You following Wuhan outbreak?"

Ricky texted back a simple "yes."

"should we worry?"

"not yet."

"K see ya 2morrow flight leaves in hour."

"Safe travels. Jeanne here."

On January 6th, Ricky met with Shimon and Jeanne and caught up on their trips. The group also reviewed their teams' tests and analyses on the biotoxins they had been studying since mid-October. They knew their work was potentially dangerous but welcomed the absence of red flags. They would have little to report to Derek and General Lind at tomorrow's video conference.

Ricky then assembled a full team meeting to re-review all open projects, which Derek attended. Their work continued.

The January 7 meeting went smoothly. The General and Major Rainey wished them all a very happy new year, and repeated the no news is good news mantra.

On January 10, with his morning tea, Ricky's alert directed him to read the new WHO advisory about Wuhan: "Global Coordination Mechanism for Research and Development to prevent and respond to epidemics held its first teleconference on the novel coronavirus, as did the Scientific Advisory Group of the research and development (R&D) Blueprint, a global strategy and preparedness plan that allows the rapid activation of research and development activities during epidemics."

Epidemics, novel coronavirus. Ricky's eyes hovered over those words, his brain started racing. Shimon strode into Ricky's office, holding and partly spilling an unlidded, hot black coffee while looking down at his smart phone. "Shit."

"Yes. Not good."

"They're saying epidemic. We know what that means."

Jeanne walked in, also looking down at her smart phone and holding a cup of hot black coffee, but at least with the lid still on. "Crap."

"Yeah," snorted Shimon, "I already diagnosed that." Jeanne punched his arm, and they all sat at Ricky's round work desk. They started reading twitter feeds and looking for any other public reporting when Derek walked in, his smart phone in his hand as well.

"I assume this is not good."

"Join us," waved Shimon. "This could be a shit show, scientifically speaking."

"What's next?" Derek asked. Ricky repeated the WHO process that all of them were familiar with in varying degrees. The consultations, exchanges of information, taking a steady if not conservative approach to public dissemination so as to inform but not alarm, also trying to be sensitive to the politics of the reporting nations.

"I believe it could be a day or so before the WHO confirms the nature of the disease we are looking at. They have already said novel but we do not yet know if it is a new strain of something we have seen or something very different. They would also prefer to not get out ahead of the Chinese Ministry of Health…"

"But your guys hold bad news tighter than almost any other country. Sorry," Shimon calmed down, "didn't mean to personalize it. I know if it was you running that Ministry, you'd already have everything you know up on the internet – that is, if you could get internet access to post it." Shimon smirked. Ricky refused to take the bait.

Derek twisted in his chair.

"I'll call Lind. He's probably already way ahead of us on this. But if this is what you seem to be thinking, we may have to change directions. And fast." Shimon cautioned Derek not to expect the US military would have much more information.

"Again, and with no disrespect to Ricky, China is just really slow to report. They would say cautious. And I doubt seriously they are being more forthcoming with your government." All nodded their heads.

"Well," Derek flashed his surfer smile, "on a positive note, this gives us a chance to try out our new SCIF. Given how sensitive and proprietary our work is, our lawyers and the General suggested we build an advanced secure communications facility, so we did. It's pretty similar to what the senior military officials install at any major travel destination. It's not quite Camp David, but our Wi-Fi connection is way faster." Derek grinned again, trying to lighten the mood. "We made a bunch of other security changes during your break. Memos are on your secure drive." With that, Derek headed back to his office.

Ricky used the CNOVation scheduler platform to set up a meeting with his entire team for an hour from then, planning to use the time to find more information.

Derek had Amanda set up a SCIF call with the General and Major for 5pm the next day, January 11, and sent invites to the Principals. Within minutes of the invite, the General emailed him with just the word "Wuhan?" Derek wrote back "yes."

During Ricky's staff meeting, he explained the need to quickly catalog all of their work, back up any research and reports on their local drives and to the company's secure cloud, finish all reports, even if preliminary, because a substantial possibility existed of a major change in focus. Everyone did, no questions asked.

The Principals and Derek gathered at 4pm to prepare for the SCIF call. As they went over the gathered information, at 4:23 p.m. Boston time on January 11, the following WHO alert hit their twitter feeds:

BREAKING: WHO has received the genetic sequences for the novel #coronavirus (2019-nCoV) from the Chinese authorities. We expect them to be made publicly available as soon as possible.

Worse yet to Ricky, Shimon and Jeanne was that they had named it:

Shimon gave the first reaction. "Oh, shit." Ricky and Jeanne nodded. Derek asked, "how long until we have more info?" Ricky answered.

"As the alert indicates, we should soon have access to the genetic sequence of this COVID-19. It appears right now to be a new severe acute respiratory syndrome." They all looked at their phones. China in fact released the genetic sequence shortly after the WHO tweet. WHO started calling this a coronavirus 2, SARS-CoV-2. China then tweeted an update on the number of cases from the "novel coronavirus (nCoV) pneumonia outbreak," 41 cases, and noted its first death. Within minutes, other countries started to report their own, local clusters.

General Lind and Major Rainey opened the SCIF conference at exactly 5pm. Ricky, Shimon and Jeanne shared their preliminary impressions of the data that was available thus far. General Lind gave a verbal greenlight to pivot from their existing research on bioagents and shift all available resources to analyze COVID-19 as a possible man-made toxin. Ricky had his doubts about whether this was a manufactured agent, but having no scientific basis for his assumption, kept his doubts private. Not all thoughts were meant for sharing.

Before he ended the call, Ricky asked, "General, if I may. Once we fully identify the virus and can rule it out as a created agent, do we have latitude to work on a preventive vaccine?" General Lind smiled. If they were together in the same room, the General would have put his arm on Ricky's shoulder, as he often did as a sign of admiration. While the vast majority of the world would be shifting into panic mode, Ricky jumped ahead to formulate a response.

"Friend, I hope like hell this is not something created in a lab. And either way, if your team develops a vaccine for this, you can inject it in my arm on national television, and I'll fly your family here from Beijing to watch in person."

Derek chimed in. "And we'll put them up at the best hotel in DC. Yes, Ricky, we still have commercial exploitation rights of any discoveries that are not part of the government contract. Finding a vaccine for what looks right now to be a nasty virus is definitely within that scope, but only if we conclude it is naturally occurring." Ricky nodded.

The General added: "Before you go, I assume you need us to go out and secure live samples to test?"

"General Lind, I fear you will not need to go far. If this coronavirus acts as I fear it may, given the data we already have, the virus will find us. Our ... may I just say, I do not mean to sound critical of your government, but the American domestic and international preparedness efforts are not maximal." Ricky did not make the larger point, so Derek did.

"General, what Ricky is referring to, frankly, is both the current lack of a coordinated US inter-governmental response, and the president's war of words with China. You know, Ricky had been a key member of the White House Ebola Response Task Force. That task force had been part of a global health security and biodefense unit, responsible for pandemic preparedness. You know it well. President Bursan established it in 2015 in response to the Ebola epidemic." General Lind was scowling, shaking his head.

"Well aware. It was operating under the National Security Council. We liaised with it through DoD. Richards disbanded it. We've been in major shouting matches with Homeland Security for three years now. Even tried to resurrect it within the Pentagon but a bunch of ...," he bit his lower lip "a bunch of political hacks wouldn't even consider it. Why ... " he took a deep breath, let the popping veins in his neck settle, "anyway, nothing we can do about that but get back to work and hope that doesn't bite us all in the ass."

Derek nodded. The Principals all wished the General and Major well, and bounded out to get to work. Derek stayed. Once the secure door closed, the General remarked, "Never in my life have I seen a guy so excited by challenges that make most people shrink away. And I've been in war theaters all over the world, and four times in the Situation Room in the White House."

Derek added, "You know the saying, worth every cent? I can count on one hand how many people I can honestly say that about, and I've got a room full of some of the world's best scientists downstairs."

"Derek, I'm gonna have to answer a few questions about Ricky having just been in China when this shit storms breaks."

"Yeah, I know. That's paranoia."

"Paranoia is the electricity that powers Washington. I know that, Rainey knows that, you know that, all my professionals know that. But I have some high level Pentagon political appointees who get to read my reports, which of course include everywhere your team eats a sandwich, much less when they travel out of the country."

"Anything I can do to help?"

"Yeah. Pray I don't get fired or reassigned to Kazakhstan until we figure this damn thing out. We'll come up in about a week. Meantime, send secure updates as often as you can, at least every 12 hours." The General paused for dramatic effect. "Derek, solve this God damn thing will you?" Lind terminated the call.

| 30 |

Chapter 30: Let's hear it for the lawyers

Derek's assistant met him as soon as he left the SCIF. "They are ready for you." Derek walked to the elevator and rode up to the main floor conference room. Waiting for him were Senator Edward Sindel, general counsel Nancy Lauren, associate general counsel Anis Eljim, Derek's sister, Melissa Chris, Hernan Diego, the CIO, Marc Hale and three associates from CNOVation's lead outside law firm. The Senator started.

"Look, you have brilliant legal talent here and it's been a century since I practiced law. But a major first step is to make sure you have ironclad MOUs with any public or private entity you communicate with about this new COVID outbreak. Not just corporate espionage and trade secrets, but you possess military level information that cannot be shared." The lead outside law firm partner, Marc Hale, jumped in.

"The agreements we have are being updated. We expended the NDA components also." Nancy spoke up.

"For the non-lawyers in the room, it's all about having enforceable contracts. What we have right now protects the company's intellectual property, trade secrets and research when we share it with any US government agencies already under the MOU – memorandum of understanding.. We have a similar set of standard non-disclosure agreements – NDAs - for when we partner with any private biotech or other companies. Marc?"

"Correct, of course. You are covered on secrecy issues to avoid theft of any analyses you may run and any advances you might make and all other IP. But going forward, any data or theories you might share with any public, non-US entities like the WHO or foreign governments, those will require more detailed agreements and more intricate procedures. Honestly, it's already pretty hard to fully protect your IP when you share with non-US governmental agencies and NGO's outside the US. So, we are recommending that going forward, you not forward any data in any conference with any external party. Rather, only share information via screen, and do not transmit any data or permit downloading. The newest version of Microsoft Teams has the capacity to restrict external use of information, and our outside IT consultant is installing the upgrades now. And we suggest you have a senior lawyer at any video conference and even at any SCIF conference." Sina, the junior associate, then went around the conference table handing out the three- page "'CONFIDENTIAL ACTION PLAN'" she had last revised at 3:30am.

The Senator chimed in. "Derek, if you and Melissa think this is going too far, don't. It's a pretty smart, conservative move." Melissa jumped in.

"I have no qualms about what's been laid out. But, even if the WHO and the Chinese Health Ministry sign, and how do we enforce in China or Russia if they get our data but breach the contract?"

Marc responded. "Look, these contracts are strong, but that's just always going to be a risk of doing business with foreign governments. With the US entities, they'll most likely sign and those restrictions are already contemplated by your government contracts anyway. The new agreements mostly enhance procedures and stiffen your damages sections. The WHO? I mean, they are not an optimum target defendant, but they have no interest in getting publicly shamed for sharing information without permission. That would blow up the whole way they are designed to operate. Best advice I can give you? Be really, really judicious with anything you share with foreign governments and NGO's. Filter as much as possible through WHO and hope they follow their multinational confidentiality agreements." Derek nodded. Hernan Diego jumped in.

"I'll be the primary for any meetings with external parties. I'll oversee the data shares and monitor for any unauthorized downloads. We'll emphasize the importance of limited shares with our external parties. That will frankly be counter-intuitive to our scientists, but we'll make it work.

"Okay. Dinner has been ordered." Derek seemed relatively satisfied. "One more thing, though, Marc. We need a separate agreement with DoD to make absolutely clear we retain commercial exploitation rights on any vaccine we may discover for this COVID, once we rule out, if we do, that it is not a man-made biologic agent or toxin."

"Of course. A draft is in the packet." Sina then went around the table handing out thick packets in trifolds with the logo of Hale Firm, LLP on the cover.

| 31 |

Chapter 31: It's a China problem

The next SCIF conference was to be in 10 hours, at 9am on January 19. The meeting was set within minutes of WHO tweeting out the following at 10:45 pm local time on January 18, 2020:

> *According to the latest information received and @WHO analysis, there is evidence of limited human-to-human transmission of #nCOV. This is in line with experience with other respiratory illnesses and in particular with other coronavirus outbreaks.*

Ricky was still at his desk, busily poring over the genetic details of the virus as reported around the globe. A US military transport was quietly returning from Japan with live cultures from a confirmed patient. General Lind knew this, but had not yet been cleared to share it with Derek or Ricky.

By the morning, the General would be able to update the CNOVation team on this non-public data. He had been named a member of the newly formed corona virus task force (CVTF), established under the National Security Council. No meetings of the CVTF had been set, but Washington continued its love for acronyms. The heads of CDC, NIH and Richards' newly installed acting secretary of Health and Human Services would be members, with HHS the lead agency. Minutes before 10am, General Lind received an email confirming his ability to tell Derek's team they would soon have live cultures to study. But with one condition -- Ricky's team would do their work at CDC headquarters, and any analysis would become the property of the CVTF – not of CDC or NIH. "Here we go" the General said out loud, to himself. He saw the bureaucrats and spin control teams already circling, not having any idea what they were gathering around. Classic Clark.

A press conference would be held at some point soon announcing the CVTF. The big debate at 1600 Pennsylvania was whether Richards or anyone at the White House would be part of it. Richards despised smart scientists almost as much as he loved the limelight, so it would be a juggling act for Clark to get him to attend without dominating any press spray.

General Lind offered his updates at the opening of the SCIF conference. As of now, there would only be enough of a sample to thoroughly examine in one lab, and it would be at the CDC. The General spared the civilians the wrenching details of the screaming matches that had transpired to even get a task force pulled together and to include a private company, even a government contractor, with any access.

Derek, Marc Hale and Hernan Diego wanted to be certain of the ground rules. They agreed all data flowing from the culture examination would be government property, but CNOVation would be able to access the analysis, and still commercially exploit any serum if the disease were not a man-made biotoxin. The General verbally confirmed, and promised to follow with a DoD memo before the Principals left for Atlanta, the CDC's home. This greatly pleased Ricky, who welcomed the opportunity to work with his dear friend, Dr. C, and several of his former public health colleagues.

On January 22, while in Atlanta, Dr. C confirmed that the virus was indeed now present in the US. Patient Zero had tested positive on January 20. The virus bore genetic markings very similar to the sample that originated in Japan as well as the DNA composition released by China.

Ricky joined Dr. C on a secure call from CDC with several CVTF members, which Clark also attended. An in person CVTF meeting was set for January 28 at the White House. There, they would brief President Richards and the rest of the team. Daily updates would be required. Yet, most of what else they would learn would be from open sources until they had more patients and more cultures.

The Pentagon began considering implementing precautions such as limiting commercial travel of top officers. The NSC members of the task force weighed placing limits on international travel into the US.

Ricky's team returned to Boston on January 24. When they arrived, they updated Derek, Hernan and Marc Hale. They also shared their preliminary analysis about the nature of the virus, which was then still property of the US government. Ricky was already fairly sure he could rule out the virus as a man-made agent, but was not yet prepared to have CNOVation issue a formal finding.

As Ricky briefed Derek, Dr. C and Clark met in the Oval Office with Richards, who seemed uninterested. His attention, such as it was, focused on his upcoming trip to North Korea. Richards hoped to reach a deal on the destruction of North Korea's nuclear stockpile as a way to line himself up for a Nobel Prize. Richards asked, "How many cases?" Dr. C answered.

"So far, just one confirmed in the US; several hundred outside the US, right now mostly in China."

"So, we are getting hit with a China flu?" Dr. C called on his years of experience dealing with uninformed politicians and remained calm.

"Mr. President, this is a highly contagious virus, not a flu. We are still studying its transmissibility but we are very concerned about how it spreads. And, frankly speaking sir, we do not think it will help international cooperation to blame China for its origins."

"Well, if it came from China, it's a China problem. What else do I need to know?" Clark jumped in.

"Nothing more right now sir. We are setting up a task force meeting with you in a few days when we'll know more, and then do a press conference." Richards snapped his head in sudden attention.

"Press conference? About what?" Dr. C jumped in.

"Sir, from a public health perspective, we need to inform the public that this virus is here, and to recommend safety measures they should take. Simple things, but the sooner we inform the public the easier we can manage this." Richards was shaking his head horizontally the way a five-year old would protest the broccoli on his plate.

"No, no press conference. No way. This is a nothing, one sick guy. It'll go away on its own. It's flu season. And I've got a big, major trip coming up to Korea. Nope, no press."

On January 27, Ricky received a group email pushing the CVTF White House briefing back to January 30, due to "scheduling conflicts."

On January 29 at 9am, Ricky's team and Derek, along with Nancy Lauren and Herman, received a SCIF call from General Lind and Major Rainey, who were today joined by Dr. C. After pleasantries, General Lind updated them on the goings on in Washington. "The task force is being moved from NSC to the White House; they want more control over the ... they call it public messaging. Good news, though, Dr. Cooper is slated to head it up, although he will be reporting directly to the acting Secretary at HHS. Since we are briefing President Richards at 10am tomorrow, we'd like to have Ricky there in person. Dr. Cooper will be there and we think it will help ..." the General paused so as to not sound how he felt -- that Richards was not yet really paying attention -- "to ensure we have the White House fully behind this if we can get both private and public sector recommending a public statement. The press already has this story and they're working every source they can think of."

Derek gave the ok. "Absolutely, whatever you guys need." Dr. C smiled broadly.

"Ricky, it's great to be working with you again, other than of course considering these grave circumstances." Dr. C continued in his gravelly Brooklyn accent. "Mr. Chris you have a world class scientist there, and from what I hear the rest of your team is top flight. Ricky, we should meet beforehand with my team from NIH, and the CDC director will here also."

"It will be my honor" was all Ricky needed to say. The General jumped back in.

"I can't be there. Wish I could, but too much inside Washington political BS going on for me to attend in person. And with this at the White House now we can't make it look like it's a military operation. Public would go nuts. Major Rainey will be there, in her dress down civilian wear. Let's be clear - this is not a military operation, at least not yet."

| 32 |

Chapter 32: January 30, 2020: You helped make me President

On January 30, Ricky walked into the White House with Dr. C for the presidential briefing in the Oval Office. While this was not his first time in there, it was still incredibly awe inspiring. There were more people than seats, so Ricky stood behind one of the couches. Richards came in late, and dropped his large frame into his overstuffed chair behind the Resolute desk, as he always did for meetings where he needed to show that he was in charge – as if anyone would assume the President of the United States did not control an Oval Office meeting. After introductions, Dr. C explained the time line and possible spread patterns within the US, highlighting the handful of cases that were already here.

"Hang on. There's what, 10 maybe 15 cases here?"

"Correct, Mr. President. That we can confirm right now. As I'm sure you know, confirmed cases are different..."

"And this came from China?" As he asked, he stared at Ricky, who had not yet spoken.

"The first reported, confirmed cases originated in Wuhan province, yes sir."

"Alright. We'll close the borders to China. No flights or boats in. Cure the dozen or so people who are sick and we're done." Dr. C and the CDC head were clearly flustered, and Richards showed no curiosity at all. After three years with him as President, the career staff at many governmental agencies who remained had, to a large extent, just accepted his lack of intellectual curiosity. They mostly dealt with policy issues that moved money around in the economy. Richards had installed his own people, yes-men and loyalists really, to address what really mattered to him -- immigration policy and cutting taxes -- and they loved having the freedom to do as they pleased. Just then his senior policy advisor for immigration spoke up.

"Mr. President, that's a great idea. Shut down travel from China. Makes it even more important we keep a tight rein on the Mexican border." Richards nodded his head, displaying the face that he thought made him look smart and decisive.

"Yeah, that's great. Go hard line on China and the wimps who are crying about Mexico will have to shut up. Let's close the border with Mexico too." Ricky could no longer abide being silent.

"Mr. President, sir, if I might be heard. It is perfectly acceptable to adopt restrictions on travel from China as part of a comprehensive plan to contain the virus. Certainly, the less people potentially who bring the virus here, the better. But, sir if I might, we should consider adopting a multiprong, multi government, public private approach as we did with Ebola..."

Richards eyes popped wide open; his head swiveled at Ricky. He remembered. "Ebola. Ebola. I recognize you now. I saw you on TV a few years ago. With Bursan. On his Ebola strike team, whatever you called it."

"White House Ebola Response Task Force."

"Yeah, that was it. What's your name?"

"People call me Ricky sir."

"No, your real name." Richards bellowed.

"Tsang Yi DeeLu."

"Well, DeeLu, I have to thank you. You helped make me president." Richards let out a loud, ominous laugh. "That press conference you did with Bursan. About Ebola. That was my spring board, totally great job you did. Scared the crap out of people. That was my platform to run and win. Thanks DeeLu. And America thanks you for helping make me president." Ricky felt nauseous, never bothering to correct Richards that Tsang was actually his last name and DeeLu his mother's historical family surname.

"Look, fellas, go to the Map Room and plan out whatever you want to ask me for. But this is a virus, it's like the flu. It's flu season. Shut down travel from China, and don't scare the public." Clark's deputy chief of staff pointed them out, and led them to the Roosevelt Room which was already set up for the after-meeting.

Later that day, Richards tweeted out:

> *America is safe. No real virus threat here. We have it very well under control. We have very little problem in this country—five cases. And those people are all recovering successfully. we will have a very good ending. that I can assure you. USA is strong and safe!!! #ChinaFlu*

On January 31, Richards issued his China travel ban, restricting entry into the United States "of all aliens who were physically present within the People's Republic of China, excluding the Special Administrative Regions of Hong Kong and Macau, during the 14-day period preceding their entry or attempted entry into the United States." He made no other public statement on the ban, the virus, or the contemplated US response.

Two days later, as he walked out of the White House to board Marine One to begin his journey to North Korea, a reporter asked him about the travel ban and his overall response to the virus. "We totally shut it down coming in from China. We can't have thousands of foreigners bringing this flu. So we're going to see what happens, but we did shut it down, yes."

| 33 |

Chapter 33: March 2020: It's all fine, now find a vaccine

By mid-March 2020, the coronavirus was raging. In response, some mayors and governors started talking about what some considered severe steps – closing businesses and public schools. Many Americans began hording masks, toilet paper and over-stocking their refrigerators. Similar reactions were going on in Europe and parts of Asia. Some on the far right blamed China for releasing the "China flu", as Richards kept calling it. Members of the "Insane 6," who saw this as an event to be exploited for political gain, kept pushing this as worse than Ebola, all China's fault, a reason to distrust immigrants who carry diseases. Richards had appeared at the last four CVTF press conferences, interrupting Dr. C and other scientists when they were asked about how the US was responding. "It's all totally fine. We've got this under control. No reason to panic." When asked if he agreed with steps states like New York and California were taking to close businesses and schools and asking people to wear masks in public, he kept saying things like, "these radical liberal states are stepping on your freedoms. This will all just magically go away."

On March 19, Ricky sat in General Lind's office with Shimon, Jeanne, Derek, Marc Hale, Hernan, Major Rainey, Dr. C and two CDC scientists. They were prepping for their meeting with Clark and a few high ranking members of the HHS, NSC and DoD, in advance of a planned CVTF press conference at the White House. The General hoped to explain the intricate tap dance that would be necessary to convince this audience that this virus was both naturally occurring and a real public health threat. The General and Dr. C already had their hands full fending off rumors that this virus had been created in a lab in Wuhan and then released or escaped, as a few politicians, even a former head of British MI6, had publicly speculated. Some on the fringes of the media had been reporting this as man-made in a lab, and now more main stream outlets felt compelled to raise the question, while noting no evidence had surfaced to confirm the lab rumor. Richards had already started a battle with the WHO over its initial press releases about the virus, which really just gave him an opening to withdraw its US funding. Clark once joked that before 2020, Richards thought the WHO was a British rock band led by Pete Townshend and Roger Daltrey – and was not far off the mark. When an aide told Richards that the US had given the WHO over $500million in 2018, he screamed about hating their music.

Ricky made a point, as had Dr. C, of the need to change public messaging. Although US cases were under 1,000 per day, Richards' actions were dangerous and counterproductive in insisting it "is going away, and it will go away. And we're going to have a great victory." Ricky's team and Dr. C generated models showing a potential for explosive growth, replication, spread and mutation. Their estimates projected a total of 1 million cases in the US with daily infection rates up to 30,000 just by the end of April. Come Labor Day, they envisioned 3 to 4 million total US cases and 250,000 deaths if the virus was not taken seriously and contained.

Ricky also explained some of the science behind how new strains could already be self-generating, which in part convinced him this was a naturally occurring event, not lab created. General Lind agreed to a recommendation that deemed the outbreak to be a non-bioagent. The

General's sign-off would work its way up the Pentagon chain of command and, thankfully, did not require White House approval.

Before Clark and the HHS and DoD officials arrived, the General reminded the Principals and Dr. C to be careful in what they said. "These are not men and women who were selected for their love of science. They are Richards' loyalists," the General reminded them. The meeting went about as he'd expected. Clark asked mostly about how to avoid lock downs, keep people from panicking and keep the robust economy going. The NSC reps expressed their fear about China hacking their computers and stealing any advances towards possible cures. HHS stayed silent, unengaged.

Ricky unsuccessfully advocated for an international private public search for a vaccine as the best approach. Since this was going to be a global pandemic, containment and broader efforts at finding a vaccine were the highest priorities. No one company or group should have a monopoly on a vaccine. More plainly, Dr. C explained, when people are dying everywhere, finding a solution is the world's problem and needs the world's highest attention. Clark barked something unintelligible about a cure, which Ricky and Dr. C emphasized would be years away, and should not be considered a first line of defense like a vaccine would.

While Derek's shareholders would have preferred a more egocentric approach – let us develop a vaccine and we will all be crazy rich - he was savvy enough to know this administration would never go for a completely public, non-commercial solution. As Senator Sindel really didn't need to point out on the flight down, more energy was probably being expended by Richards' friends on lining up to make money than on developing a solution. Plus, he knew some of the major biotech companies had already sent their $1,000 per hour lobbyists to Congress and the administration to make sure the US government didn't "go all communist" on this problem by taking the private sector out of play. As one highly influential K Street player said at a very expensive dinner with six major Congressional leaders who had Richards' ear, "public health disasters are best solved by private sector profit motives."

So the White House strategy had developed – publicly tell everyone it's fine, and privately push like hell for a vaccine.

The press conference with Richards went predictably horribly, at least from Ricky's and Dr. C's perspectives. Richards stood in stalking position right behind them on the raised stage of the briefing room. When either tried to address the nature of the disease and what may be coming shortly, Richards pushed forward to take over the microphones, and falsely assured everyone that this China flu was totally under control and would soon disappear. When a health reporter from a highly respected US newspaper asked Dr. Cooper how long he thought it might take to develop a cure for the virus, Richards almost grabbed him and pushed him aside. "We have a cure already. I have directed the FDA to fast-track approval of a very effective malaria drug, hydroxychloroquine. It's already here. Been used for years and years. We have this controlled so everyone go out, have dinner, enjoy your lives. The economy has never been stronger. Thank you everybody." With that, Richards ended the press conference. Everyone in that room with a medical degree or any immunovirological experience knew there was no scientific basis to believe the coronavirus could in any way be treated by chloroquine or hydroxychloroquine. But as Richards barked at them from the hallway behind the press room, "People don't need science. They need reassurance."

Within days, Clark convinced Richards to announce a vaccine program called "Operation Warp Speed," a Star Wars or Star Trek type allusion that Clark made up to make it sound like the administration would deliver a solution at record speed. The fact that the government itself was not actually working on a vaccine was secondary. This Operation, dubbed OWS, would distract from the enormous amounts of money the government was giving to huge biotech companies to do the research they would gladly have done anyway. Plus, as a consummate PR guy, Richards agreed with Clark that it's better to tell people a cure was on the way fast than telling them to do the hard stuff it would take to keep the virus from spreading at alarming rates. And they knew Congress would appropriate almost any amount of money they asked for. While the parties pretty much hated each other, no one would go on record voting against money for a COVID vaccine. Richards' friends and supporters, as well as his son-in-law, were salivating about the potential to make huge bucks on this project, and knew it would move way too fast for bureaucrats to catch up to what they were doing. Bloomberg News would later report that in the week after OWS was announced, more LLC's were created than in any month in American business history, and the shell companies had shells that had shells. Like those Russian matryoshka dolls, each LLC was embedded inside another to hide who the true owners were.

Chapter 34: Mid-May 2020: DeeLu's theorem

By mid-May, the virus raged in the US and across the globe. Richards had managed to turn simple public health steps – wear a mask, stay out of crowds, wash your hands – into a culture war. Politicians who disagreed with him and closed schools and shuttered businesses were anti-American, were communists, were stealing your freedom. NewsFirst ran story after story, stoked by loud and uninformed guests, on how masks didn't work, how they could cause asthma, how the only way to defeat the "China flu" was to get extra vitamin D, which you get from just being outside in the sun. Several so-called experts, including radiologists parading as immunologists, pushed unproven cures and fake science. A handful of people died or got severely sick from drinking their fish tank cleaning chemical, chloroquine phosphate, believing it to be the miracle cure for coronavirus Richards and several websites portrayed it to be.

A few so-called education experts came on NewsFirst with unvetted statistics, as more and more schools moved to virtual learning, that Americas kids were losing ground to our competitors, not learning, even regressing. One even suggested that "virtual learning can cause mental retardation" to the shock of even the prime time host. News-

First quickly posted a retraction on its website. As guests, Joe O'Day hosted marriage counselors and divorce lawyers who hyped a coming huge wave of rising divorce rates if unhappy couples were forced to suffer inside with each other as they either worked from home or were laid off.

Several states run by Richards' allies touted their low case numbers and lack of masks and open bars, laughing at the earliest hit states as mismanaged and run by freedom robbers. At least three governors and 10 mayors held press conferences and tweeted out saying "we're not New York."

As the misinformation spread from the White House to millions and millions of residences, the virus raged and spread across the country. Dr. C unsuccessfully attempted to launch a CDC ad campaign to boost mask use and bar closings until positivity rates dropped under five percent. His suggestions were fiercely rejected by the White House. Instead, the president took to social media to tout a variety of unproven cures and stoke his followers to not let communists steal your freedoms. One tweet falsely claimed "Cases, numbers and deaths are going down all over the Country!"

On May 15, 2020, the Defense Department issued a press release announcing that the administration was pushing a historic, once in a lifetime effort to deliver safe and effective vaccines through Operation Warp Speed:

OWS is an unprecedented leap toward a historic breakthrough that will save countless lives. It is leveraging the best experts from the federal government and private industry to develop effective vaccines and therapeutics quickly without compromising safety.

The public was being overwhelmed by contradictory messages coming from the press and the White House. Richards leaning outlets insisted the "China virus" was under control, that its effects were being overhyped by the liberal, Richards-hating media. NewsFirst hosted several physicians who alleged that private hospitals and doctors in blue states were artificially boosting COVID diagnoses to inflate reimbursement by insurers. An all-out publicity war was raging as quickly as the virus was spreading. In the meantime, away from the glare of false facts flying, several companies, including CNOVation, continued their work on trying to find a vaccine. A number of clinical trials accelerated. Each company that made any advances kept its work more closely guarded than the nuclear codes, because this was now a competitive race of cures for cash, not a cooperative effort to save lives. OWS signed up several companies and gave money to a few for research with no commitment to sell to the US government. Money flowed everywhere, flying around almost as fast as COVID-19 itself.

Multiple news outlets began reporting information about the vaccines under development and in clinical trials in the US. Information was seeping out from the British Medicines and Healthcare Products Regulatory Authority too. The MHRA, a kind of cousin to the American NIH, under the stewardship of Professor Dorchester, was investigating a serum that could be delivered by messenger RNA, or mRNA. This approach, known as protein wrapping, stood as unique, even unprecedented for wide scale use, because this vaccine would not include any of the actual virus.

Ricky and many health experts well knew that in standard vaccine epidemiology, you would inject the patient with small amount of the virus, but given how much was still unknown about this COVID, he understood this reluctance. Ricky had been looking into an mRNA methodology for a few weeks before the news of this prospect had become public. If an mRNA strand could be properly coded to trigger the immune system to produce protective antibodies, protein wrapping would also enable the vaccine to disperse into the blood stream at a highly efficient absorption rate. Ricky was also optimistic such a vaccine could be more portable and therefore able to reach poorer countries in a stable state. Of course, as with any major advance, downsides did exist. Introducing a foreign chemical compound too quickly could cause serious side effects, and if spread too slowly could quickly lose efficacy and leave the patient exposed to infection after a short period of time.

While Ricky's team kept looking at potential delivery systems, Ricky affixed his analysis on the odd effect COVID-19 was having in many patients – the loss of taste and smell. He thought back to his days working with Dr. C at NIH on various strains of the avian flu after his groundbreaking work in 2005, and later consulting from time to time on mitigation of Bovine Spongiform Encephalopathy, more commonly known as mad cow disease. This particular virus uniquely causing loss of smell and taste in upwards of 75% of patients confounded him. How was this virus attacking these developmental senses? Smell and taste have basic genetic imprints, sure, but they can be altered, trained and fooled. How was this CoV-2 doing that, and why?

At dinner that night with his team, Ricky was ready to propose a new approach. "What if…" whenever Ricky began what-iffing, everyone quieted and leaned in to listen – he was the EF Hutton of virologists, a cultural reference no one present was old enough to get – "what if we focused more on the coding of other senses to see if they can be impaired by a mutated strain of the CoV-2? Historically we know these viruses will mutate, and if we solve for CoV-2 are we left exposed to naturally occurring mutations, or to new stains, a future CoV-3 and CoV-4 and so on?" All of his eight team members nodded almost in rhythm, but only Jeanne and Shimon really could follow. Ricky continued.

"The cultures we have seem to be slightly variant of each other, with plenty of similarities, at about 98.3% of identity. If we only solve for the respiratory complications, yes we will have averted this awful disease and saved millions of lives. This virus will die off as it runs out of potential hosts to infect and use as spreaders. But we know the path of these types of viruses is to mutate and evolve and return. So, what if we attack the genetic code in DNA that makes us susceptible to sensory loss from such a disease and recode the DNA? Could that let us fight off this and any similar strains that might later develop?"

"DeeLu's theorem." Jeanne was first to speak. "C'mon Ricky, Everything gets a name, a label, a shorthand. Let's name it in honor of your mother's ancestral family name, Ricky." Ricky was very touched by this sentiment, and choked back tears since she had nearly died last year from what may well have been an early variant of this disease. "So we're agreed. Let's tag it DeeLu's theorem; study the sensory imprint in the double helix and see if through genetic manipulation we can kill the virus."

"Well, not exactly." Shimon chimed in. "In theory at least, we'd be creating a vaccine that has traditional virologic benefits – nothing can actually keep the virus out. We'd be preventing the respiratory arrest and complications that come with infection, while creating a form of backdoor that kills the virus at the genetically coded sensory level."

"Agreed" said Jeanne.

"Agreed" repeated Shimon. No one else spoke, as the six others with advanced medical degrees wore "what the hell are they talking about; I'm going to keep my mouth shut" expressions. Ricky broke the silence.

"Okay, Finish your dinners. Tomorrow morning, let's get to work. Be back at 7am. I have some coding to do."

| 35 |

Chapter 35: We are the world – or are we?

By 6 o'clock the next morning Ricky was in the SCIF, along with Derek, Shimon, Jeanne, Herman and Anis. Last night, Ricky had reached out to the WHO and multiple European public health agencies. Professor Dorchester was the first to respond. The Wuhan Institute of Virology (WIV) declined the meeting.

Before President Bursan, the idea that a US private corporation, the NIH, the CDC, the WHO and the WIV would work together and share information was unheard of. But by 2014, there were numerous such joint collaborations. However, Richards had so poisoned relations between the US and China, the US and Europe, and the US with the WHO that Ricky had to call on his personal relationships to find the brave few who would agree to meet.

To make matters worse, President Richards continued to escalate his war of words with the WHO by blaming it for failing to protect the US from this "China flu." He started to cut US aid to the WHO and his derisive choice of words further alienated China. He went so far as retweeting the theory that COVID-19 was hatched in a lab in Wuhan for potential use in biological warfare, but somehow escaped or may even have been purposefully released to see what effects it would have.

Had Richards known that Dr. C had already received emails from some researchers noting that "Some of the features (potentially) look engineered," and could be "inconsistent with expectations from evolutionary theory," he would have released them. Ricky basically begged his peers not to be sidetracked by such issues – yes, the source of the virus was important, but finding a workable vaccine had to remain the focus. Plus, Ricky had already ruled this out as a man-made biotoxin, and General Lind had secured DoD sign-off for commercial exploitation by CNOVation.

Ricky truly appreciated that Derek was allowing him to confer with his colleagues in searching for a fast, safe and effective vaccine. None of them were legally obligated not to share Ricky's thoughts, but were honor-bound to do so. Ricky trusted that they would keep his concepts and research private. CNOVation had secured commercial exploitation rights for this vaccine and the Senator was convinced the US would be a ready buyer. Derek and his board knew the risk of losing any proprietary data was very low by consulting with this group, and they might be able to advance the development process. By now there were at least three private-public partnerships seeking a vaccine that Ricky knew of, but none of those efforts had made it into the press. Derek knew that several biotech companies had already partnered with each other on both research and production. The concept of vaccinating an entire planet was mind-boggling, and the monetary value of this endeavor almost beyond calculation. The board knew that CNOVation would need a joint venture partner when the time was right – production on such an incredible scale was beyond any existing company's capabilities, especially a relatively small company like theirs.

Corporate espionage remained a way of life. The most secure facilities remained vulnerable. Hernan had given several briefings to all CNOVation employees about the increasing cyber-attacks against their company, and the important steps they all had to follow without fail to avoid a cyber intrusion. If Ricky had his way, all of the research everyone was doing around the world would be in the cloud in a shared silo, given the implications of finding a vaccine. But he knew from his father and his own keen awareness that the profit motive would not allow that.

Shimon and Jeanne commented on the unmatched brain power assembled for this call: two Nobel laureates, one in bioethics and one in medicine for advanced immunology, two Wolf Prize winners for advances in gene editing, and three Shaw Prize winners in life science and medicine. These scientists were conducting their own parallel analyses, but none had the time for day-to-day testing. This group was more akin to a think tank. It was an opportunity to try out ideas, harness expertise and 300 years of combined medical research.

After the standard salutations, Ricky posited his theory, illustrated with an animation of just a few culture slides: could a vaccine be developed that would attack the gene coding to disassemble the virus at the sensory level, rather than just immunize the body from the attack of the symptoms? The combined brain power of this collective paused. No one wanted to be the first to admit it, but none had seriously considered it, at least not yet. "I have not started work on this as yet, so I have no preliminary findings or even a virologic approach to suggest. This is purely theory at the moment." Professor Dorchester, perhaps the most experienced in gene splitting methodologies, answered first.

"Wow! Good Lord, Ricky, that is an awesome concept. Are you talking about genetic manipulation through a vaccine? An injection that would affect widespread genetic recoding?"

"Widespread, no, not widespread. Highly targeted. We know with a high degree of certainty that CoV-2 routinely causes side effects of loss of taste and smell, with varying impact, duration and extent of recovery. We know those senses are genetically coded at a primary level, but then disparately develop, such as in differing degrees of acuity and sensitivity. Maybe, this is just maybe, the RNA of the virus can be mutated by planting a protein that alters the sensory code in a way that destroys the virus if and when it attacks the patient."

Professor Dorchester responded. "I, ... I mean... wow. I'd have to see some data. Lots of data. But in theory? Taking the work we did on micro gene editing and advancing it by about, I don't know, 20 years to a massive scale? And in just a few months? I mean, of course, why not ask if we can. But, Ricky, esteemed colleagues, who are the bioethicists among us? What would the effect be of mutating sensory genetic coding? How would it affect our primary senses? And once we know, we have to ask should we do this?" Ricky was silent but looked at his mentor, then Hernan, whose head nod denoted it was time to take down the slides from the screen. "Of course Ricky has thought this through, and he desires our feedback. So, let's give it to him, to his team. They appear to be on to something."

No one else spoke for nearly a full minute. They really had nothing to add. Ricky did not expect such awkward silence. He had not considered that what he was proposing was anything more than answering a series of logical questions, or that this concept was really so far ahead of current thinking. He broke the silence. "I thank you all for your input and guidance. My company asks I remind everyone that this is not yet for public disclosure. We realize that there remain many, many questions to answer. Perhaps we can chat again in a few weeks and I can update you on what we have determined about whether this can even move from the theoretical. Be well and stay safe my friends." With that, Hernan terminated the video conference.

| 36 |

Chapter 36: June 2020: We have to move on this

June 1 arrived with Ricky at his desk at 5am, poring over slides and data. He noted with particular interest how much the genetic sequence of the current CoV-2 had in common with the virus that had infected his mother. He ran several diagnostic tests to try to decipher if what she had could have been an early form of this virus now raging around the world. Ricky's concerns over the similarities between the current COV-2 and what hit his mother were not just a son's continued worries. If the two were truly linked, the progression of mutations would be a challenge they had not seen before, and should be taken into account in developing any vaccine.

COVID-19 cases now topped 6 million worldwide. The WHO issued a report detailing suspected cases of a multisystem inflammatory syndrome (MIS) in children and adolescents thought to be related to COVID-19. Containment efforts were not going well, failing in Ricky's opinion. Americans and Europeans were rejecting wearing masks and social distancing at an alarming rate, contributing to the growing rate of spread. So-called experts appeared on television and social media, arguing that masks were ineffective or caused breathing difficulties, and that mandates were communist. Ricky empathized with Dr. C, who appeared day after day on television and online imploring, almost begging, people to wear masks, socially distance, and wash their hands. For giving such simple and safe advice, Dr. C received death threats and required a security detail for himself and his family. Ricky and Dr. C and many others knew the pandemic would only re-escalate during the fall and winter. Cold weather was a killer - literally

Richards punted on the appearance of concern. He tweeted how he was right and all the "Experts" were wrong, that the virus was magically disappearing during the summer. The CVTF stopped meeting. The White House kept pushing false miracle cures, blaming China, even mocking people who wore masks. A "doctor" associated with CVTF even made several appearances on NewsFirst questioning if masks even worked, leading millions of Richards followers to parrot the same on their social media platforms. Once again, the White House was at war with science, and millions of Americans were casualties. Not only that, Richards continued his battles with US allies by postponing the G7 summit dedicated to forging a global COVID response, over a fight about bringing Russia back into the group despite international sanctions.

Shimon stopped in on his way to the company pool for his morning swim. "So. New?" He put on an extra thick Jewish accent, trying to cheer Ricky up, who seemed in a trance. "So, Ricky. New?" That time was much louder, and Ricky craned his neck up over his laptop.

"Sorry. Deep in thought."

"Aren't you always?" That was really not a question. "I'll be finished by 6. I'll come back then and we'll go over where we are."

"Yes. Please. Let's." With that Ricky was back looking at his laptop and the 3D imaging rotating on his larger second screen.

At 6am, Jeanne sat at Ricky's work table, sipping her second cup of coffee as Ricky steeped his second cup of tea. Shimon bounded in, refreshed from his swim as usual. Jeanne looked up. "Sit our friend. DeeLu's theorem has made a major advance."

"No way."

"Way." They both laughed. Ricky still did not get the pop culture reference.

He took out his pen laser pointer, his most recent birthday gift from his mother. He had three DNA helixes rotating in his modeling. The first focused differential coloration on the genes responsible for the sense of smell, the second taste, and the third color. Ricky explained. "I've been looking back at some of the work from geneticists at the New Zealand institute for Plant and Food Research in Auckland. About seven years ago they were testing 187 people's sensitivity to 10 chemicals found in everyday food, including the molecules that give distinctive smells to cheese, fruit and flowers. They found, as expected, that how the subjects sensed smell varied greatly. So they sequenced the subjects' genomes and looked for differences that could predict people's ability to detect each chemical through smell. Their report was published in *Current Biology*." Jeanne chimed in.

"Sure, I know a few of those guys. One of the lead authors, Jeremy McRae, was affiliated with the Illumina Artificial Intelligence Lab in San Diego. I met him at a few conferences. Really bright, super nice guy." Ricky nodded, then continued.

"He also did some advanced follow up AI work with some of the same researchers and published a report last year. They were looking into the cellular machinery for splicing pre-mRNAs and how to better predict the proper splice junctions within the pre-mRNA sequence as a diagnostic tool for genetic disorders. Their baseline concern was that while the current art of exome sequencing had led to major advances in clinical diagnosis for rare genetic disorders, the basic efficiency of the exome sequencing was maybe 25% to 30%, leaving the majority of patients undiagnosed." Shimon set his coffee cup down, his eyes widening.

"Sure, yes. We were looking at his work for a paper I was collaborating on in Israel on theoretical viral hemopathology but I had to bow out with our work here. McRae's team made very solid advances in high-throughput screening of potential splice-altering variants in looking at random mutations of genetic diseases..." his voice trailed off, as he looked up at, now stared at Ricky. "Holy shit. He was advancing the science on examining the splice-altering mutations that might occur in a pre-mRNA sequence. They were able to evaluate 10,000 nucleotides of the contextual sequence to predict the splice function of each position in the pre-mRNA transcript." Jeanne jumped in.

"Wait. Wait. Ricky, are you saying you think we can sequence the virus, sequence the olfactory genes, find the correct splice points, and use an mRNA based chemical to kill the virus by embedding a protein based vaccine in the sensory code?"

"No … well certainly not yet. Remember, we are potentially dealing with the olfactory cortex and its reliant portions of the nervous system for smell and potentially the sense of taste. This impacts functionality of the central nervous system. But we can certainly test this. We have the nanobot technology here to do some live testing now. Remember when we started? Derek's goal of nanobots uploading a terabyte of data in 247 zeptoseconds? We're almost there. I think we can do some pretty reliable live culture testing and get some fairly solid results using nanobots with a 750 zeptosecond response time. The team tells me they can extract up to 512 meg of data in that time. So, perhaps we can harness the splicing advances we already know about with live culture testing and factor that in with AI analytic tools we have available." Shimon nodded.

"Sure the major science pieces are there – but there are still some big pieces missing from this jigsaw puzzle – like a vaccine."

"Of course. Of course. But I think the theoretical pieces are there. Perhaps we should update Derek? I am comfortable laying out this theory for him if you both are." Shimon tipped his coffee cup to show Jeanne and Ricky it was almost empty.

"Let me get a refill while he's on his way. First, I need another cup. Second, it's a good simple science experiment. I'll bring three. Even as smart as Derek is, we need to lay this out in less technical terms."

By the time Shimon was back with the coffees, this time with lids, Derek had arrived. "Did Ricky bring you up to speed?" Derek looked at Shimon, his eyes semi-glazed. "Okay, I can see he did. Here, take this cup of coffee. But keep the lid on."

"Thanks, Shimon, but I've had plenty of coffee already."

"No, it's a simple experiment." He handed Derek and Jeanne their cups, and took a few sips of his. "Experiment is for you, not me. I need the caffeine. You will need to really concentrate for this. Ok, Derek, take the lid off and smell the coffee, first through your nose, with your mouth closed." He did. "Now, close your eyes, and take a sip." He did. "Great. Now, pinch your nose closed and smell the coffee only through your mouth, and then take a sip with your eyes closed again." He did. "Did the coffee smell differently each time?"

"Yes."

"Taste different than it smelled both times?" Derek looked quizzical.

"Yeah, actually it did."

"Yup, so blame my friend, Dr. Anne Marie Helmenstine. She holds a Ph.D. in Biomedical Sciences, and a B.A. in Physics and Mathematics. She also loves coffee. She wrote an article last year for *Thought.com* on why coffee doesn't taste as good as it smells. Part of the reason is saliva destroys almost half of the aroma molecules before your nervous system lets you enjoy the taste. Bummer right?"

"I ... suppose, yeah."

"Ok so, we know this corona virus has short term and maybe even long term effects on your senses of taste and smell. Maybe it functions something like the saliva that impacts the taste. Maybe it functions like nerve receptors that communicate the smell. We are going to try to isolate the genetic coding to see if the virus is attacking the nervous system in a way we can prevent, by embedding a protein that alters the smell and taste genes and kills the virus upon entry into the body." Derek drank some more of the coffee.

"Sure, okay, that's what you guys talked about on the VC call a couple weeks ago. DeeLu's theorem right? I mean it sounds great." Jeanne interrupted, seeing Shimon was being too coy with Derek, something he really enjoyed doing.

"We think .. credit to Ricky of course, Ricky thinks he's figured out how to do the testing. And if we can do the testing ..."

"Ask the questions, get the answers." Derek finished his coffee. "How long?" Ricky weighed in.

"In our knowledge base, we have a fairly good series of platforms of research that has been done for other purposes. We can build on those. We have highly developed analytics here to quickly extrapolate from what is known thus far. Your nanobot technology is well suited for what we want to do. But, we are contemplating a substantial leap forward from as advanced as you already are. So ..." Shimon stood up.

"He's saying play time is over. It's time to get back to work. How long? Like most incredible break throughs, we'll know when we know. And not to get ahead of my dear colleague, but I personally would love to get a dozen or so more cultures to work with."

"I'll ask General Lind. And when I do, he'll want an update and a time line."

"Sure boss. If it were up to me? I'd have the General and Major Rainey come here in a week." Derek could see that gleam in Shimon's eye whenever her name came up.

"I'll make the call. He'll say we have to move on this."

Chapter 37: Like schmaltz for chicken soup

General Lind and Major Rainey arrived in Boston at noon. The pair chose to drive the nearly seven hours rather than taking Amtrak. They preferred to stay at a sterile guest house built by CNOVation during April of this year, instead of at a hotel or at Derek's house in North Brookline. While the White House continued to downplay the raging global pandemic, most federal agencies had cancelled or postponed almost all in-person meetings. Use of public transportation and lodging were also discouraged.

By 12:30pm they were meeting in Derek's office, the most secure location outside the lab and the SCIF. Everyone wore N95 masks. General Lind was anxious for answers, cranky from the long drive. "So, where are we? It looks like there are a few private companies getting close to a vaccine, and I'm getting a ton of heat for why you guys are not in Warp Speed." The General took a deep breath. "I know you guys are doing everything you can, and that you maintained commercial rights, but some of Richards' political guys are threatening to call me to testify to Congress as to why DoD has funded a biotech company to do research but we don't have you in Warp Speed. I really, really don't want to have to go to the Hill and testify about the work you're really doing."

Derek had not seen him quite this frustrated in their dealings, but Senator Sindel had and understood exactly what he was and was not saying.

"General, you know we are keenly aware of the need not to go down that road. Look, I was probably one of the bigger assholes to you in Congress, and I know some of the ... newer members up there," Sindel did not want to say clowns, even in this private setting, "who would have no idea what damage they would be doing to score cheap political points."

"Thanks, Teddy. So tell me where we are. The pressure is going to grow more intense now that the CDC and HHS have gone public with there being vaccines in advanced testing stages." Everyone knew that these agencies had intentionally convened public meetings of the CDC's Advisory Committee on Immunization Practices (ACIP) to review the data on COVID-19 and potential vaccines. Richards let it be known to Clark and his senior advisors how pissed he was that of the two leading contenders one was not in Warp Speed. He stood ready to fire everybody, including the heads of the FDA and CDC, if he were embarrassed by a company not under DoD contract having the first approved vaccine. Dr. C, the CDC head, and acting HHS Secretary had been allowed to speak publicly on how the ACIP process would be completely free of political pressure to obtain emergency use authorization, but, still, Richards let his inner circle know he wanted the government-funded company to get the first approved vaccine, and to damn well do so before the election.

Ricky started, and drew Lind and Rainey's attention to several 3D animations on Derek's 46" UHD screen. The first image captured the protein layering, spiked steel wool ball seen around the world:

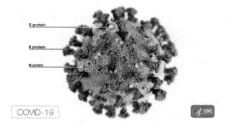

E protein

S protein

M protein

COVID-19

CDC

Ricky then showed layers of images that dissected the protein from various angles, and explained how these resolutions were made possible by the nanobot technology CNOVation had developed. He also narrated as microparticles gyrated on the screen, referring to them as exomes.

"So, basically, a human genome consists of 3 billion nucleotides or tiny bits of DNA. But only a very small percentage, less than 2%, of these tiny microparticles translate into proteins, which are the engine that provides the functionality in the body. An exome contains the genetic coding portions. The way the SARS CoV-2 works, as the first slide reflects, is through what is called a spike glycoprotein, which creates, really encases, the virus that causes the coronavirus disease. While we have been able to sequence the entire human genome down to the functional part of the genome, the portions that encode proteins are really what we need to look at very, very closely. These will aid us the most in studying such things as genetic elements, or genetic codes, that may cause or contribute to genetically induced diseases. Does that make sense so far?" The General and Major were smart enough, and had been steeped in this long enough, to have a decent understanding of what Ricky was laying out. Ricky moved on to a few more 3D illustrations.

"So, here is what we know about the vaccines that ACIP is looking at right now. As you likely have read, they are not the traditional type of serum, where you inject a small dose of the virus in the body along with chemical enablers to induce the body's own immune system to kill the virus before it causes significant complications. These vaccines, partly because of the speed of development and partly because of fear of injecting CoV-2 into humans, are a lipid nanoparticle-formulated, nucleoside-modified mRNA vaccine." Shimon poked Ricky in the shoulder.

"In English, Ricky."

"Right. So, mRNA … messenger RNA is genetic material that contains instructions for making proteins. The vaccines being studied consist of synthetic mRNA that once in the body will penetrate human cells, and the genetic coding instructs the actual cells to produce the spike protein found on the surface of the CoV-2. But then the body will recognize the spike protein as an invader, and produces the antibodies necessary to destroy the invader. That way, if the patient later contracts the actual virus, the antibodies are already present and can destroy the CoV-2 protein before it damages the body. The synthetic mRNA is encased in lipid – basically fats – that will break down and release the protein." Shimon jumped in.

"General. Major. Do you like chicken soup?" They riveted their heads to him, not sure how serious this question is. "Please, indulge me." General Lind answered.

"Sometimes, sure." Abigail nodded her head.

"Chicken soup. Good for the soul, no? My bubbe – back in Israel - she made the most delicious chicken soup. The old world way, with lots of schmaltz. Maybe you heard of?" They both seemed lost, but Ricky, Jeanne and Derek knew Shimon was about to make an important point, and figured where he was likely headed. "Schmaltz is rendered chicken fat. It will cling itself, adhere, to the chicken in the soup. Chicken we all know is a protein. Schmaltz is fat. So the fat wraps itself around the protein, and oy, delicious." He kissed three fingers of his right hand in what he thought was the international symbol for delicious. "So, that's how these mRNA vaccines work. Create the spike protein that causes the COVID virus, wrap it in lipids, like schmaltz around chicken, and then inject it in the body. Antibodies are created by the body's immune system, so that if the actual COVID protein is detected, then boom, it's like a river of chicken soup is unleashed to kill the virus." All in the room nodded. General Lind then looked back at Ricky.

"Okay, now I'm hungry on top of being tired and cranky. Ricky, can your team make this ... chicken soup?"

"Sir, that is not the direction we are going. Not exactly. You don't need us to make this vaccine. There are several very good studies under way and I am fairly confident they will reach the point by the end of this year, maybe early next year, where they will be ready to seek emergency use authorization. I know many of the scientists working on these projects, and I assure you they are the best in the world." Derek chimed in.

"Ricky is also one of the best in the world. He has ... well he has a somewhat different idea." Ricky continued.

"We are looking ... I will try not to be too technical. I am not as eloquent as my good friend Shimon. Although I do enjoy a hot bowl of chicken soup." Ricky squeezed out a toothy grin. "We are looking at a treatment that is directed at the sensory systems. We know that CoV-2 attacks the sensory systems in addition to the respiratory. Most COVID patients experience loss of taste and smell. This is well documented. We are trying to answer why. We are conducting submicroscopic genomic splicing to determine if the DNA coding can allow us to ... well basically, trick the sensory system into rejecting the virus by eliminating the genetic codes that the COVID protein attaches to and replicates from." Jeanne felt compelled to speak.

"This is some really ground breaking stuff we are looking into. I know there are a couple of PhD students who are doing somewhat similar research in theoretical immunology at my old school, Berkley. But, I won't understate it. This is a pretty significant advance in genetic sequencing if we can pull this off." The General stepped forward towards Jeanne.

"If is a pretty big word. Especially how fast this virus is spreading all over the world."

Ricky added, "And mutating." All eyes darted to Ricky. Jeanne jumped in.

"We have no confirmed cases of mutations."

"Correct." Ricky went on. "Not yet. But I keep going back to the virus that struck my mother, the one no one has diagnosed yet. The

Wuhan health ministry would not confirm if there were other strains like it. I have run multiple models to determine if it was an early variant of this CoV-2. My results have been inconclusive to a scientific certainty." Abigail looked at Ricky.

"But?"

"But, I have run models that would account for the variation, but none predict them. I have also run models that predict mutations of this CoV-2. Given everything I've seen in this and other SARS type infections, and even avian flu strains, we can be pretty sure it will mutate. Remember, while it does not have a brain per se, it is a living organism, and survival is its basic instinct. It does not want to kill the host, but it does want to replicate. The work we did to eliminate this as a man-made agent makes it all the more likely it will evolve, and in my humble opinion has already mutated. So, the vaccines being developed will very likely arrest the strains we know about, as well as mutations we can reasonably model for. But there has to be caution about how effective the vaccines can be given the circumstances under which they are being developed..."

"At warp speed."

"Yes, General, at warp speed. We have to account for mutations that we cannot properly test for, since we are not able to run full scale clinical trials." General Lind shook his head.

"Well, that's depressing. Give me some good news."

"Oh, no, please do not take me the wrong way. The vaccines that will be coming on line will have very high efficacy for the known strains and almost by necessity for multiple mutations that will follow similar genetic patterns. The testing and research must be done properly and thoroughly vetted before any vaccine is allowed to be widely used. Remember – we will not be using actual CoV-2, but synthetic spike proteins. That means they can be – well encoded, programmed if you will, in several variant forms that would likely account for the mutations. You will also likely see efficacies that vary based on the impact of the virus if it does strike a vaccinated patient. Most of the time, we are happy with a vaccine that is 60 to 65% effective. This new mRNA will likely test out much higher, since it is artificially created and does not depend on bits of the actual virus. That efficacy will have a very high yield, meaning it could be 95% effective to prevent death, while 80% effective to prevent respiratory arrest, and 70% effective to prevent any symptoms from presenting. Vaccines do not in themselves prevent the spread of the virus, just the effects. So we live with this CoV-2 as a risk until the virus itself dies out."

"Ok I'm lost now. So why are you not working on another vaccine?" Ricky took off his glasses and rubbed his eyes before putting them back on.

"It is a matter of scale, and technology. Delivery systems. We have worked on multiple public health emergencies before. Those times, we sought to initially isolate the disease so as to limit the population that would need treatment. The first thing we did on Ebola - controlling the epidemic at its source, that is really step one in any public health emergency. Here, we have a worldwide pandemic that means we have to vaccinate several billion people to truly destroy this CoV-2. I think, please remember this is highly theoretical at this point, but I think if we can do what we are studying now, we will have a much simpler means of delivery than injecting a synthetic mRNA wrapped in lipid. We would not have a protein wrapped in Shimon's bubbe's chicken fat. Ease of delivery translates to a far more expansive reach, particularly in parts of the world where you cannot send enough doctors or nurses with enough properly stored vaccine to inject enough doses to have a meaningful impact once the virus lands there." General Lind was clearly intrigued.

"And your delivery system? How do you get the vaccine in people's arms?"

"We do not." Ricky took a deep breath. "Water. Water would be our delivery system. If at all possible, rain water. My father once told me there are only four things that are everywhere in the world. Hope. Fear. Sun. And rain. In varying degrees, to be sure, but in populated parts of the world, you will find all four." Everyone remained silent. Derek, Jeanne and Shimon had heard DeeLu's theorem rolled out before, discussed it many times, and each recalled how it first hit them. A water based vaccine. Ricky has gone mad. It finally happened. So many geniuses crushed by their own brain power and need to heal the world. But, Derek, Jeanne and Shimon had all come around. They believed it was feasible; not likely, not probable; but just feasible enough to spend the next however long it took to try to make it a reality.

"Jesus H. Christ! A water based vaccine? Jesus. I need to lay down. All my years in the military. I need to lay down. I need to think this through. Can we meet again in two hours?" Derek patted the General on his left shoulder, the stress evident in all the wrinkles on his face and forehead.

"Of course, General. This is a lot to absorb. Amanda will take you to your rest areas. We'll send coffee and anything else you need." He stared directly into Derek's eyes.

"I don't know about the rest of you, but I could use some water. Plain water, bottled water, whatever you have. Just no experimental vaccine water." Unsure if this was an attempt at humor, no one laughed. "We'll meet back here at 4pm?"

"Yes, sir" answered Derek.

"Send him some chicken soup, too," Shimon added. "It may not help, General, but it couldn't hurt."

| 38 |

Chapter 38: Color blinded

On June 15, the General and Major returned to CNOVation for their now weekly in-person meetings. Their seven hour drive was uneventful, especially considering how little traffic there was on I-95. When they arrived, the Principals were set up and ready to go, this time with notebooks containing slides and encrypted flash drives for their guests to take back to the Pentagon. After the standard greetings, Derek began.

"So, we have made some significant advances since the last meeting. Ricky will explain, but there is something significant we need you to consider?"

"Just one thing?" The General half laughed, half snorted. Those in the room could not miss the growing frustration on his face, even under his mask, the lack of sleep in his eyes, the troubling concern in his voice. "Tell me this, before your presentation. How do I convince the folks in Washington that the current flattened curves of case numbers does not mean we are through this pandemic? I've got Richards seriously talking about instructing the Secretary of Defense to shut down all bio programs not related to COVID. How he even managed to wrap his microscopic attention span around the work we are doing is beyond me. But remember I told you he had installed loyalists in the Pentagon? They've been getting closer and closer to figuring out the actual work you are doing, and Richards want to divert money to his friend's company that's promoting hydroxychloroquine." The Principals were aware of Richards' bent for pushing miracle cures, shiny objects for many of his supporters -- scared people desperate for an easy fix to latch on to. "And, Lord help us, he's directed the NASA Administrator to see if they can get the space station to shoot UV beams at the US, since some idiot convinced him UV light can kill the virus. Jesus H. Christ, guys, we don't have much more time to solve this." All remained silent, knowing his anger and fear were not directed at any of them. Jeanne went first.

"General, if it would help at all, we have included predictions of US and world spread in your notebooks and flash drives. Obviously, you can share with the White House. There are several models, with variations for social response. We suspect NIH and CDC are doing similar modeling, but we understand if you have ... less confidence in what they are releasing. The fact that the curve is relatively flat now during the summer is mostly due to people being outdoors so much more, which is a positive. But we do not detect a significant increase of social responsibility – mask wearing, social distancing being the primary ones. We think ..." Jeanne looked at Ricky and Derek, who each nodded, "we think the CDC numbers may be too low. Their predictions for the curve. We see two probable scenarios where the case numbers just in the US could go up 10 fold, from the approximately 20,000 per day to over 200,000 per day by the end of 2020. The death toll," the General looked at Jeanne, more despair than frustration on his face, "the US death toll could easily exceed 400,000. 400,000 General, by year's end. Up from where we are now at about 115,000." Ricky joined in.

"We are fairly certain also, that there is at least one new strain in Africa that is starting to circulate, and perhaps new strains in South America, likely Brazil." Ricky paused, fearing overload in his guests." Abigail asked

"Is that all."

"Well, no, apologies. We consider there to be a significant likelihood of variants in Europe, in Germany or France. This is not unexpected. You will have a very difficult time getting confirmation through ordinary channels, given the US withdrawal from WHO funding and ... well you know the rest." The General sipped his coffee.

"And the good news?" Ricky continued by clicking on the screen. The first few pages were charts and graphs, the statistics they had led with. But his presentation also included devastating numbers as well, up to 100 million cases worldwide and two million deaths by the end of 2020. The numbers were staggering, each slide was footnoted and annotated to show the sourcing and projection methods. The next slides were 3D graphics of the genomes they had discussed in the prior meeting. Ricky stopped at animated slide 16, and paused it.

"General, Major, what you are about to see is still theoretical. We have done a lot of predictive coding, run multiple AI scenarios, but this is all still theory. Please understand, okay?" They each nodded. "As the prior slides indicate, we have isolated the protein particles that CoV-2 affects that cause loss of taste and smell. We have imagined a spike protein that simulates this impact and an antibody response that neutralizes it. Our analytics tell us this is possible, not so different from the mRNA that protects the respiratory system." Ricky paused, not for dramatic effect, but because each time he has said this out loud to Jeanne, Shimon and Derek, he could hear himself doubting his own words. General Lind walked around, and place his hand on Ricky's right shoulder, to put them both at ease.

"Go on, Ricky. Please. I've got a president who wants to shoot space lasers of ultraviolet light at US citizens. If yours is more far-fetched than that..."

"It is, General, a bit ... well, exotic." Ricky took a deep breath and clicked play. "Slide 16. Here you see the mRNA enter the cell at a spliced locus where we have isolated the sensory gene coding. We have identified a universal genome through advanced exome sequencing that we believe we can alter with a chemical compound that will modify the genetic sequence in a manner that will then trigger the body's immune system to release antigens that should be fairly effective against the CoV-2." He handed the clicker to Jeanne.

"Slide 17. More specifically, the chemical we would introduce would generate red blood cell protein antigens. Now, we know that antigens can either be proteins or sugars, depending on the blood type of the patient. The various blood group systems contain antigens that are controlled by a single gene, and blood types are genetically distinct. While most people think of blood groups as A, B and O, there are actually 22 blood group systems. We believe at this point, that we can introduce an artificially created, blood protein antigen that can be genetically coded to cause the sensory system to trigger the body's immune system." Jeanne handed the clicker to Shimon. The General and Major looked around, almost beseeching Shimon to use some kind of homey analogy about chicken soup or something. He obliged.

"So, you know my background is in theoretical viral hemopathology. I specifically study viral diseases and disorders that affect blood cells. I won't use big words like flow cytometric immunophenotyping and immunohistochemical immunophenotyping. Although," he cracked a big smile, "that's some pretty cool shit. What I will tell you is this. We ran lots of studies and tests, using some wicked cool and advanced toys Derek has here. I agree with Jeanne and Ricky. We believe using a sensory system altering protein can disarm the virus so it won't hurt many people. That's the simplest way to look at it." The General nodded, let out a deep breath.

"Ok, so, I asked you last time, why is this different from the vaccines being developed? You told me you hoped to deliver this by water, this... is it even a vaccine?" Ricky answered.

"For our purposes, yes. We have debated that, but for the sake of our discussion, yes. Consider it a vaccine. And, yes General, our focus is on a water based delivery system. We hope to have more details soon, and even some, further testing results, but we are optimistic right now." The General bear hugged Ricky, violating COVID protocols, but what the hell, then Shimon, then Jeanne then Derek. His enthusiasm nearly brought him to tears as his anxiety began to melt away. The Principals and Derek were clearly not ready to high five, so General Lind sat down, nearly slumping in his chair.

"Okay, now the bad news right?"

"General, we will tell you what we know." Ricky clicked through a couple more slides, showing the introduction of the protein and then its effect on several genomes. He noted some labeling and colorations occurring as the protein worked its way through what he knew were several microscopically tiny particles. "Again, these are largely computer generated models based on all the ... what Shimon called using all the very cool toys. We are noticing that the introduction in the body of the particular red blood cell protein antigens that our compound creates may impair another sensory system."

"Which one?" asked the General.

"Color. Jeanne, would you take this one please?"

"Sure, Ricky. Happy to. So, here is basic color receptivity 101. When you look at an object, say a cherry, small wavelengths of light bounce off the cherry and hit the light-sensitive retina at the back of your eye. We all have photoreceptors, cones, tiny cells in the retina that respond to light. Most of us have some 6 million or more photoreceptors, and almost all of them are concentrated on a tiny, 3/10ths of millimeter size spot on the retina called the fovea centralis. When the reflected particles stimulate the photoreceptors the resulting signal is zapped along the optic nerve to the visual cortex of the brain, which processes the information and returns with a color." Major Rainey spoke up.

"I had to do some research on this, since color blindness runs in my family. I was concerned about it affecting my ability to fly given the instrument displays in the more advanced planes depend on the yellow-blue-green-red differentiation."

"Correct, Major." Jeanne continued. "There are also many diseases that can cause or contribute to color differentiation deficits including sickle cell anemia, diabetes and Alzheimer's. So, we have long known that there is a significant heredity function to color blindness, meaning again genetics, and an impact of a brain function condition like Alzheimer's." She clicked to the next slide.

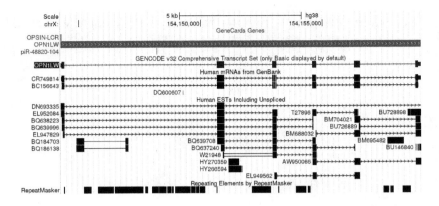

"Is that part of our proprietary data?"

"This. Oh no, General. This is from Google, based on some work done by my friends at the UC Santa Cruz Genomics Project and the NIH. We have isolated mutations in the OPN1LW, OPN1MW, and OPN1SW genes – OPN1 is the basic genetic locus, and LW is long wave, MW is medium wave, and SW is short wave, referring to the length of the refracted light particles. These genomes influence forms of color vision, and breaks or imperfections in the sequencing can cause certain deficiencies." She handed the clicker back to Ricky, who advanced through a few more slides, which he narrated.

"So our observation is that the protein we would introduce has a high likelihood of negatively impacting the ability of the photoreceptors in the fovea centralis to process the light waves." The General stood up, and paced.

"Causing blindness?"

"No, General, it would introduce a color recognition deficiency, not blindness." Shimon perked up.

"Color blinded." General Lind swiveled to look at him, then Derek, then Ricky.

"Color blinded? This vaccine could make people color blind?"

"Quite possibly. Likely. Yes." Ricky stood with the other members of his team, watching as General Lind and Major Rainey processed this information. He knew enough about how scientists spoke to translate Ricky's cautious admonitions to if we do this, millions and millions of

lives will be saved, and millions and millions of people will be color
blinded.

| 39 |

Chapter 39: June 22, 2020 in the Norwegian rose garden

Early on June 20, Clark landed in Oslo to meet the Leaders and restore calm. Richards' reelection campaign was reeling, even with no serious competition for his party's nomination and the convention now two months away. The spread of the virus and the devastation to the economy had moderates looking elsewhere. Meanwhile, Richards' base remained enamored with their guy. The Leaders feared a Richards loss would be a major setback for them. Fritzy also grew concerned. He had not completed building the European components of his empire. Sure, the Richards administration had loosened media aggregation rules, but there was more work to be done.

Clark had decided on a hastily arranged meeting to set things right. The locale was outside the EU, and Norway was non-controversial. His staff advertised his trip as a meeting to negotiate a bilateral trade agreement with a non-EU country, part of Richards' overall "go it alone" approach to global trade. The King of Norway was unable to meet with Clark and the US trade czar, given "prior commitments," but wished them well. Clark didn't care since the trade meeting was purely for cover. He and his team ended up meeting with representatives of five of the eight political parties in Norway.

The meeting that really mattered would be held on June 22 at Frogner Park, a popular tourist attraction. They would gather a few hours before Clark went wheels up to Washington. Few would notice. Clark traveled with light media coverage, and his confab with Leaders did not appear on the schedule. Rather, he had his press secretary list "tour Norway rose garden." Clark's wife accompanied him so his side trip had the veneer of an afternoon spent sightseeing. No one would be on the lookout for three European nationalists with an eye and nose for a rose collection, the pride of Frogner Park. Plus, amid a sea of face masks, detection would be even more difficult.

Clark's security detail scanned the crowd and did not separate him from his three rightwing compatriots, as they strolled among the colorful and sweet smelling vegetation. Ulf Knutsson, Nordic in looks and bearing, had quietly made his way from Central Europe. Knutsson was accompanied by two tall and blonde Europeans. All three held high office in their home countries, and were high ranking officials within the Leaders. In Norway, they all fit in quite easily. All had agreed there was too much risk for Deng Xu-Pei to make the trip.

As Clark leaned forward to inhale, Knutsson began a short conversation. "We are very worried your man is losing his grip on power, and we have a long way to go to racial purity. We need assurances." Clark nodded.

"Understood. I am hearing word that we may have an unbelievable development on fighting this virus that can help us." Knutsson was clearly confused.

"Have you figured out a way to cure white people and not others? We know minorities are more susceptible to this virus." Even to Clark, that sounded harsh; he believed in domination, not annihilation.

"Jesus, no, not that. My preliminary information from my people … well you don't need details. We may be able to develop a vaccine that will cause color blindness, allowing anyone who receives it to only see shades of white." The three ultranationalists were clearly astonished. Could this be possible? A vaccine that would immediately make the entire world look white?

"How do you sell that to the bleeding hearts who oppose racial purity?" Clark looked directly at Knutsson and adjusted his face mask so the three could see his lips for just a moment.

"Watch me." He re-covered his face. "As I said, this is preliminary, so don't get too excited. But be prepared. We will need you and the others to be ready to take to the streets to force your countries, the rest of Europe and Asia to use this vaccine if we can get it developed and ready for delivery. Saving tens of millions, maybe hundreds of millions of lives, saving so much suffering, rebuilding our economies – isn't that worth it just for trading away not seeing colors? Enjoy the flowers, Ulf. Could be your last chance." With that, Clark grabbed his wife's arm, pointed to some yellow roses, and began slowly strolling through the rose garden, towards the exit.

| 40 |

Chapter 40: Like water for coffee

Ricky, Derek, Shimon and Jeanne carpooled to their command performance at the Pentagon. Derek had arranged for a "tricked out" bus,
what Shimon called a travelling hotel once they got inside. Rumor was
that Garth Brooks had been using it for his USA tour, which COVID
had sidelined. Derek knew somebody who knew somebody, so this 55
foot behemoth sat in the CNOVation parking lot at 7am on June 25,
ready for a comfortable ride down to a very uncomfortable meeting.
The owner had no problem with Derek installing portable HEPA filters
to aid in air circulation and lower the risk of infection. Senator Teddy
Sindel arrived at 7:15am as agreed, as did Marc Hale, Hernan Diego and
Nancy Lauren. *"Friends in Low Places"* was softly playing over the sound
system as the sunglass adorned, black suit, white shirt, black mask and
black tie wearing driver asked Derek if everyone was on board and
ready to go. His name plate said Vince.

"Let's rock and roll Vince!" Derek responded.

"Shall I change the CDs out sir?" Derek chuckled.

"Nah. We all love us some Garth" and winked. "But once we hit 95
you should lower the volume."

"Of course sir. And if the temperature needs to be adjusted just let me know. You can hit any of the intercoms buttons. No need to walk up. In fact, we prefer it." With that Derek joined his team sprawled out more than six feet apart on various leather captain's chairs and love seats. Derek's assistant Amanda ensured there would be fresh coffee and tea, water bottles, bagels, scones, fruit bowls and bottles of hand sanitizer, all laid out on counters behind the conference table. She also placed a box of CNOVation's logo-emblazoned masks near the food, which had the same specs as the N95's that people had been scurrying to get. Even though CNOVation was COVID testing its employees twice a week, he was taking no chances with this crew.

For several weeks, Derek had noticed how masks had become a branding exercise. Shimon's bore the Star of David, royal blue on white, Sindel's posted the Red Sox logo, in red on dark blue. Marc Hale boasted the Hale Firm, LLP insignia in gold on a black background. Derek instructed his marketing and development teams to look into whether they could go into commercial production of company logo masks, after making two dozen samples by hand.

"Hey, everybody, grab some coffee, fruit, whatever you'd like. We'll huddle up at the table in 15 minutes." Derek sat down, checked and returned several texts, and enjoyed *"The River"* as he sipped coffee. He texted Amanda good job on the bus, and asked her to order the Garth Brooks' Ultimate Hits CD set, which he saw sitting by the five-disc player. For a high-tech guy, Derek was somewhat old school in his music formats; he even had a stereo at home that played record albums.

The team sat masked at the table by the time the bus entered the I-95 on ramp. On cue Vince lowered the speaker volume by half. Derek started.

"Ok to summarize where we are. 4pm we meet General Lind and Major Rainey in the General's office. That's a debrief. Then it's 5pm in a secure conference room within the Defense Contract Audit Agency wing. This is supposed to be a low key meeting and inside DoD is listed as a defense contractor audit. But it is very high level. Richards' chief of staff, JB Clark, set it up for after most of the employees would have left. We know somehow word leaked out that we are working on an advanced type of vaccine and the General thinks the administration has been clued in on our research. He's been warning us for a while that this could happen." Senator Sindel responded.

"It was only a matter of time. Richards had installed loyalists in every major government agency. My intel is that it's more than just a general understanding that Clark is aware of. He's been briefed on the fact that we are looking at a water based vaccine, and the possible side effect." Shimon shook his head.

"So, he's going to try to shut us down?" Sindel answered.

"Oh, heavens no. With COVID cases over 20,000 a day and deaths approaching a thousand daily, my sources think he's going to try to get Richards to invoke the Defense Production Act and force us to mass produce for government use." Marc Hale interjected.

"Essentially, what that means from a legal standpoint is that the federal government can set the price at which we can sell the vaccine and force us to sell to the government as a priority contractor. So, while we keep commercial exploitation we have a forced-sell requirement and the government sets the price." Ricky jumped in.

"Hold on, wait. We have not completed work on the delivery system, let alone examined potential side effects. As for clinical trials, we have a way to go. And then there is the ethical issue of causing people to go color blind." The Senator responded.

"Cards on the table, Ricky. This type of discovery is almost impossible to keep from a world scared to death about this virus. Plus Richards is not interested in a nuanced debate. He wants a vaccine on the market weeks before the election so he can take credit for it. His poll numbers have been crashing and Clark has him convinced he needs this to have any chance of winning. And he's right. And for icing on the cherry on top – he gets to steal this amazing discovery from a lefty liberal company in lefty liberal Massachusetts. Sorry, guys, that's the politics of the situation." Shimon nodded his head.

"Israeli leadership would do the same. Most countries in the world would too, Ricky."

"So who gets to decide the ethical question?" Ricky seemed on edge about losing control over the ethical dilemma of his lifetime. Nancy looked at the Senator, then Derek, then answered.

"By the time we get back to Brookline, it very likely won't be us."

"And what about production? We are nowhere near equipped to mass produce at ... well, at worldwide levels." Derek fielded that one.

"Ricky, we will partner with two or more biotech companies we can trust. They share our ethics. I've got meetings set up for next week, with SCIF calls for as soon as we get back from DC. If this is going to happen, and it seems likely, we need to be ready. Even if we lose control over whether this will happen, we at least can retain control over how. Perfecting the vaccine, roll out, distribution." Shimon jumped in.

"Distribution? It's like water for coffee. You put the grinds in the water, poof, you brew coffee. The sheer genius among the many geniuses of this here is how easy it is to distribute. I mean, the whole thing is brilliant, obviously, but a water delivery system? No needles, no injections, no field hospitals in poor countries administering shots?"

"So, really, this is impossible to stop?" Derek placed his arm on Ricky's shoulder.

"Ricky, you and your team are about to save millions and millions of lives here and who knows how many all over the world. Why would we want to stop that?" The furling of Ricky's glabella between his eyebrows evidenced the struggle he was experiencing, his lips concealed below his mask. After nearly a minute of silence, he exhaled a few times.

"Ok, so our focus needs to be on medical purity and equitable distribution. We can't let the United States take all the product first, we have to make sure poorer countries can also get help. Assuming we can satisfy ourselves that the vaccine is safe and effective."

"On safety you're absolutely right, Ricky." Senator Sindel sought to reassure him. "Not even Richards would try to push this vaccine ... well, not even the people around Richards would try to push this vaccine out without independent CDC and NIH sign off. This is a radical development and it just won't happen without independent study and review. But on making this available worldwide? Richards won't give a damn, but our biotech partners will help with that. We'll debrief you on that on the way back – less info is more right now." Ricky nodded, and looked down for a few seconds before continuing.

"I'd like to see if we can get Professor Dorchester to consult with us. We have a tremendous team, but he would be a great addition." Derek nodded.

"Of course, Ricky. Listen, you three are the best of the best, but if there is anyone else you want or need for the team, just let me know." Derek paused. "And I realize this is not at top of mind right now, but if we do go forward as the lead contractor on this, even under Defense Production, none of you will ever have to work for a paycheck again. Our ethics advisory board said we should not amend your employment contracts and we have not. So, you have no economic incentive here whether this works or not. But, I don't have that moral dilemma and I owe it to you to tell you that. But a contract like this will make everyone on this bus a ton of money – except Marc, but I already pay him too much." Derek chuckled. Marc must have grinned since his Hale Firm logo extended out. "And we fully intend to reward the three of you and your entire team. That means whatever is going to be your next life-saving project, you can do pro bono if you wish." Shimon reflexively grabbed his coffee cup, knowing taking a sip would be a good cover for the ear to ear grin he was now sporting, then remembering he was masked. Jeanne's eyes broadened. Ricky simply sat and pondered, thinking through the ethical issues.

"I will re-review my slide presentation. I understand where we stand. Thank you for explaining it all to me." Derek broke the meeting up.

"We'll regather when we get to Baltimore to go over any last minute issues and the order of presentations. Until then, get some rest, enjoy the ride." With that, Garth began singing "*If Tomorrow Never Comes*".

| 41 |

Chapter 41: Hate the Yankees

The Garth bus arrived at the secure parking entrance to the Pentagon in Alexandria, Virginia at 3:07pm. Second Lieutenant Wallace, dressed in her Army fatigues, exited the security guard booth, and looked up at this monstrosity pulling in. Fortunately, her team had been alerted that a large vehicle would be arriving for a scheduled meeting, but she was thinking more of a school bus than a glam RV. Derek stepped off to show here his DoD contractor credentials. "I'll need all passengers to exit the vehicle and stand over there" she said pointing to a series of spots marked "Wait Here," each set 8 feet apart.

"Of course," Derek answered. With that, he stuck his head back in and shouted, "Ok everyone out." As they proceeded, Lieutenant Wallace waved to her inspection team, two of whom began to scan under the bus for explosives with long wands that looked like what beachcombers use to find coins, and one entered the vehicle with a bomb sniffing German shepherd. While that went on, a sergeant began patting down the visitors, knowing that each would go through a more sophisticated screening device once at the outer door to the Pentagon complex. This pat down was more for the surveillance cameras to detect any body language or discernible facial expressions that might call for a more thorough later screening. The sergeant recognized Senator Sindel from prior visits when he had been working the inside magnetometer. After patting him down, he saluted, and when the Senator saluted back, he pretty loudly stated, "Red Sox suck, sir." Sindel had to laugh.

"Nats fan?"

"Sir, yes sir!"

"Can we agree to hate the Yankees?"

"Most definitely sir!" They both laughed. Once he finished the pat downs, Lieutenant Wallace walked over near Derek.

"You're good to go, sir. Please follow the jeep to your designated parking spot. Enjoy your visit to the Pentagon." With that, they reboarded and followed the jeep waiting on the other side of the now raised security arm at the second security booth. The walk from the parking spot to the outer door was just four minutes. They walked across the highly sensitive yet invisible bomb and gun detection material built into the flooring. The sergeants working the metal detectors with thermal scanners droned out the same speech they gave dozens if not hundreds of times a day.

"All large items go on the belts. All items must be removed from your pockets and placed into the buckets. That includes cell phones, watches, wallets, keys and coins. Nothing can remain in your pockets. If you are wearing a belt please take it off and place it in a bucket. Shoes must also be taken off and placed in a bucket." The sergeant made his speech eight times as the CNOVation team cleared through the dual security lines, and were handed faceless "Visitor" badges. They walked up to Airman First Class Xi, sporting an Air Force mask adorned with the insignia of his rank, wings sprouting out from a blue circle inside and outside a five winged star. He had been dispatched to escort them to General Lind's office. Derek checked the time as he restrapped his watch; 3:46pm. A few minutes ahead of schedule.

All followed Airman Xi to the elevator bank, where Airman First Class Rodriguez waited, similarly masked. "Three with me please, three with Airman Rodriguez. Social distancing is required in the elevators. We will be right back for the rest of you." With that, the Principals followed Airman Rodriguez, while Derek, Nancy and the Senator accompanied Airman Xi. When they exited on the 7th floor, Airman First Class Jones was waiting.

"Please wait here please for the rest of your party." The elevators descended, and within a minute were back with the rest of the CNO-Vation visiting party. Airman Xi led the delegation, with Airmen Rodriguez and Jones at the rear. At 3:55pm they entered the outer entrance of General Lind's office. Major Rainey was waiting. Each Airman saluted her, and held in place until she returned a salute. With that, they pivoted with military precision, and exited.

No one shook hands with the Major, a common COVID precaution, nor did they salute. A simple exchange of "good to see you" and "welcome" as she led them into General Lind's private conference room. He, too, welcomed them without handshakes or salutes, and invited them to be seated. The table that could seat 28 was encircled with 14 spaced chairs, enough for this and most meetings. Major Rainey sat several feet to the General's right. "I trust your ride down was uneventful." Derek answered.

"It was fine. Very comfortable. Thank you."

"Let me get right to the point, then. Clark moved our meeting up to 4:30. As you all probably know, the administration is now generally aware of your research on the water based vaccine. We don't have time to talk about why or how they know, but they do. The purpose of this meeting, as I see it, is to make sure they understand how sensitive this project is and how preliminary your studies are. I don't want to turn on CNN or NewsFirst tonight and see Richards announcing a miracle vaccine that you can drink from your sinks at home. Clark and his team are somewhat responsible but once they tell the President, well ... honestly, who knows at that point. And, for the record, I say that with the utmost respect for our commander in chief." The General's white mask encrusted with four silver stars neatly covered his smirk. Sindel answered.

"We completely understand, General. Thank you. Our team would never suggest going forward or going public at this point. And, sir, if I might speak for Ricky, he would like to know if someone is going to address the ethical issues associated with such a vaccine. What warnings of the side effect of causing color blindness will be given? Will the vaccine be distributed equitably so that the poor and the rich have equal access? Will poor countries outside the US have access as well?" Ricky nodded in appreciation.

"Of course, and I plan to raise all of those issues. Ricky, feel free to stress those concerns. But, I have to be honest with you. I cannot promise you that ethical issues will win the day with those currently in power. I owe you that." Ricky answered.

"I appreciate that, sir. I know this is a very grave and sober dilemma. I just wish for it to be treated as such by this administration."

| 42 |

Chapter 42: Space Force?

The CNOVation team, the General and the Major all headed into e conference room B-11 in the subbasement of the Defense Contract Audit Agency wing, a drab and forgettable place. The space usually hosted meetings with outside defense contractors. It was both large and secure. Tons of steel and concrete provided shelter away from peering eyes and curious ears. In pre-COVID days this room could seat 50. Defense contractors on major projects usually travelled in large packs – technical, financial, legal - bringing a lobbyist or two was not unheard of – for a meeting with three or four audit specialists. So a room that could seat 50 was repositioned to socially distance for up to 24 attendees. Clark brought two of Richards' allies, each of whom had gone from major campaign donors holding millions of dollars in defense contractors stocks, to high level political appointees in the civilian leadership in DoD. One of these allies also happened to be Richards' son-in-law's brother. Clark had also brought a woman who introduced herself as Dr. Esther Nie, a senior atmospherics research scientist with NASA, and Major Ted Kunkel, the Chief Mobilization Assistant to the Chief of Space Operations for the US Space Force. The USSF had been a pet project of Richards, who pushed to establish it as the newest branch of the Armed Forces in late 2019.

Clark brought no one from CDC or NIH. Ricky did not have a good feeling. No medical scientists were present. Major Rainey had a flat out bad reaction, since Major Kunkel also happened to be her ex-husband. The rest of the CNOVation team maintained the skepticism they had since this meeting was set up.

Derek introduced his team. They sat around a series of tables arranged in a rectangle, each seat spaced six feet apart. The air conditioning ran at a low hum. Microphones were not allowed in the room. Instead, speakers were forced to stand up and project so they could be heard. Monitors were strategically placed so everyone had a decent view of any power point or other presentation. The room came equipped with two air-gapped lap tops, meaning they had not been nor would they ever be connected to the internet. Ricky plugged in his jump drive to begin his presentation. Ten minutes in he reached the parts the administration side wanted to know most about.

"So, what we have been experimenting with, and our research is by no means complete, is an mRNA vaccine that once in the body should interact with the sensory system to replicate the CoV-2 virus and trigger the body's natural immune system. Thus, it is similar in that regard to the mRNA vaccines we understand to be in development and trial stages at several biotech companies now. But, again, the mode of delivery would be completely different – in fact, you could fairly call it radical. It is intended to have a very simple delivery system – water. And as with mRNA, there are likely to be similar side effects common to many flu type vaccines, allergic reactions and the like, but no injection site soreness as there is no injection. But, as I have said, its genetic profile would be quite different as it is not intended to interface with the respiratory system as other vaccines would. But because it is designed to interact with the sensory system it could well cause other complications, and our best data to this point is a very high likelihood that it would trigger color blindness. That is one of the primary issues we are focused on, given the obvious bioethical issues that poses." Major Kunkel stood up, his mask decorated with the same single, golden oak leaf as his ex-wife's.

"Hang on. Are you sure you can deliver this vaccine in water and that it will cause people to become color blind?"

"Major, we are not at the point of scientific certainty, but if we conclude the path we are on, yes, both are likely outcomes."

"And would someone have to drink the vaccine, like from a water bottle? Or would you take it from a bottle, like cough syrup? And what's the dosage?"

"Major, we are not at that point where we can directly answer that with scientific certainty." Kunkel sat back down. Dr. Nie stood up.

"But at this point, Dr. Tsang, you cannot rule out drinkable vaccine?"

"No, we cannot rule that in or out." Dr. Nie sat down. Clark jumped up, surveying the room as he did.

"So I take it you also cannot rule out delivery, say, from tap water or rain water?" Ricky had been very careful to not include a rain delivery system in any of his written reports, as he had been instructed. But he would not lie. Derek and Sindel looked at each other, and simultaneously figured out why NASA and USSF were here. Clark had jumped ahead, way ahead, to vaccinating the whole country by rain, a fast if not imprecise delivery system. Had they actually run studies or models on doing that? Derek stood up.

"Mr. Clark, if I may ask. We of course noted no one from the ... medical or immunological community here. No NIH, no CDC. May I inquire, what role might NASA or USSF have here?" Clark appeared more than eager to answer, even with his mouth and nose covered.

"Of course. We had understood from some of your team's reports to General Lind that what Dr. Tsang had just laid out could put us in a position to have a water- based vaccine. Given our desire to vaccinate 300 million plus people as quickly as possible, I asked NASA and USSF to be here to consider delivery systems. I mean, what could be faster, cheaper and easier that using rain water to get everyone protected? Plus, we avoid all the nasty issues of how to prioritize delivery. Do we treat cops and teachers first? Food workers? People over 65? We can avoid all of that by just telling people to just go outside tomorrow when it rains." Shimon stood up.

"Respectfully, sir, we are still very, very far away from anything like that. Not only are we still analyzing efficacy and safety, we do not yet know the proportions we would recommend to administer."

"Ok, sure, so we tell everyone take a tablespoon or a dixie cup outside tomorrow and don't drink more than whatever amount you say is enough. Look, I get it. There's still a ways to go before your guys and our guys would sign off on letting anyone take this stuff. But we have Warp Speed up and running, and I'm not ... and more importantly the President isn't gonna wait one day longer than necessary. I don't have to tell you how bad this virus is and the numbers are staggering. So we are tasking Major Kinkel and Dr. Nie to your team at CNOVation and they are going to study how to get this miracle drug out to all Americans just as fast as humanly possible. You figure out how to make the stuff; they'll figure out how to make it rain. I have to go, but you get my drift." Marc Hale rose.

"I'm not sure it's quite that easy. This work by my client is not part of their government contract. It's carved out as commercial exploitation. So we can do some kind of information sharing memorandum but we can't just have your people park themselves at my client's offices." Clark was halfway to the door to leave, and he whirled and shouted.

"It's either that or we Defense Production your client. Look, you'll have a contract RFP on your desk in 48 hours. Figure out how much you want to sell this stuff to Uncle Sam for and put it in the proposal. If we like your price we'll do it. If not, well I've got opinion letters from White House counsel and the Attorney General that says we can basically make you do this and set our own price. So, let's all play nice, yeah?" He paused, not really waiting for a response. "Great. Get to know each other, and update me every 12 hours." With that, Clark was out the door, headed back to the White House. He knew he couldn't say anything to Richards yet, but when the time was right, they would hold the mother of all press conferences. The 4th of July would be great for an incredible announcement like this. That gave the white coats another 10 days to get it all figured out before he would have Richards stand in front of the world offering COVID vaccine, baseball, hot dogs and apple pie.

| 43 |

Chapter 43: The other Boston

By 6pm Derek stood in front of the mega-bus, the rest of the team plus two trailing behind him. He told Vince there would be two more for the ride back. "No problem, sir. We could fit eight more if we needed. I hope the meeting went well." Derek may have been the only one in the group who thought it had been a very good meeting.. Well, maybe the Senator and Marc Hale thought so also. They were losing some scientific independence, sure, but getting to basically set the price for a captive buyer for a lifesaving, world saving miracle? Yes, Derek nodded, as if to say the meeting went quite well.

Major Kunkel and Major Rainey walked out of the Pentagon complex together, and seemed to be making limited small talk. She would not be boarding, but he would, along with Dr. Nie. Marc's office would have an MOU on General Lind's desk before they arrived in Brookline at roughly 2am, which could be signed by 9am. Clark's instructions to Richards' lackeys was very clear – get the deal done, get CNOVation under contract ASAP, and he'd get their companies cut in later as part of the supply chain. Conflicts of interest continued to be a low or no priority in this administration.

Major Rainey stopped a few feet before the bus, having a last chat with the Senator, as Shimon peered at her ex. "What a schmuck" ran through his head, for about the fifth time. Major Kunkel lingered awkwardly, so the Senator waved at them and boarded. "Wow," said Kunkel, "is this the Boston bus?"

"No," said his ex-wife. "Well, sort of. Headed to Brookline."

"No, the other Boston. Remember?" She looked confused.

"Don't you remember? Boston came and played down at the Annapolis Dock? Graduation week? Free concert for our graduating class?" Abigail Rainey had a look of near horror. Yes, now she remembered, sort of. While *More than a Feeling* blared, she slugged down her 3rd ... 4th Sam Adams? Graduation exercises were in two days, her parents driving down the next day. She remembered walking past a huge touring bus, about the same size as this, and them sneaking on to invade the band's supply of beers with a few other firsties, or graduating, midshipmen. She also remembered waking up in a local chain hotel with him snoring, her head pounding, and an engagement ring on her finger. They were married two months after graduation. He grew to be jealous of her advancing faster than he did, her graduating first in their class from the Naval Academy at the age of 20, and her being dispatched to fly in Desert Storm. He languished at Andrews Air Force Base, later to be known as Joint Base Andrews, flying with senior government officials on trips abroad. While that experience helped move him up the ranks politically at DoD, he always wanted the battle theater exhilaration she had lived. Their divorce was inevitable, particularly to Abigail's friends who didn't understand the marriage at all. Six years after graduation to the day, she filed for divorce.

"Oh, wow, yes. Boston concert at the Dock. Long time ago, Ted. A galaxy far, far away." He nodded.

"Yeah, true. Anyway, look, I know your mission here and you know mine. Let's not cross sabers, okay? We're all on the same side on this. I know you have a contractor to protect, but Clark is way, way far up our butts about this, so let's make this happen." He seemed almost apologetic for six years of being an ass to her, and sincere in his desire to work together.

"Not self but country, Ted. Not self but country. Have a safe trip. I'll see you when you get back." He saluted her, and she reciprocated.

Once aboard, Kunkel selected a comfortable looking captain's seat near Shimon. He could tell Shimon didn't care for him, and did not want animosity to get in the way of this project. "She's an exceptional person, Shimon. I screwed up a long time ago. If you two have something going on, go for it." Shimon nodded his head.

"Long ride ahead, Major, and long day already. Derek wants us to meet at 8:30 at the conference table. He's got a dinner order meeting us up ahead, so let's get some rest." With that Shimon inserted his ear buds, pressed play for his favorite up and coming klezmer jazz musician, tilted his head back, and closed his eyes.

The soft but sudden stop of the bus in Wilmington, Delaware wakened Shimon and most of the passengers. The sound and smell of the food being brought on the bus woke up the rest. Amanda had arranged for a curb side pickup, sort of, of a combination of seafood and Italian food. Within 10 minutes everything was set up on the kitchen counters, and after Derek gave the two servers $100 each. He announced, "grab some food, and we'll gather at the table in 15." All willingly complied. Vince announced he would be leaving, and a new driver would shortly join them. Amanda had also ensured this crew would have a fresh driver for the balance of the trip home from Wilmington.

Precisely at 8:30pm, Ricky took the same seat he'd had on the way down. The others gathered once they finished their linguine with clam sauce, baked ziti, conch salad, and a few premade poke bowls. Senator Sindel opened the dialog, rather than one of the scientists or Derek. He understood intergovernmental turf fights the best, after all of his years in Washington. "Major, so how does this work, as you see it?"

"Sure, well, as you may know, USSF has operational capabilities on both coasts. We are gearing up to provide operational support to and safety control for DoD and NASA space launches, as well as for the private sector. I'm sure you are all aware of the extensive commercial applications in orbital and suborbital craft now, and the momentum developing behind private space flight. Part of our mission has been partnering with NASA and private sector operations for low vulnerability and autonomous operations, including securing weather and navigational data." Sindel nodded.

"Sure, yes, I am aware. I was on a budget subcommittee that was involved in appropriations for Space Force."

"Yes, sir, mostly opposed as I recall."

"Only to what I thought was unnecessary expenditures to prop up the private sector. But that's history. Where are we going with this?"

"Well, on the unclassified side, one of our public private operations along with our good friends at NASA, such as Dr. Nie, involves atmospherics and dynamic cloud seeding. Dr. Nie, would you elaborate on what has been declassified? And, of course, once I get the go ahead there will be more we can tell you that is currently classified." Dr. Nie began.

"Yes, of course. We have been consulting with several academics who have been studying cloud seeding. This technology is not new, but the main problem has been lack of accuracy. When farmers want to generate rain, they are not usually concerned with accuracy of flow volume. They just want rain for their crops, and they use on the ground irrigation system to capture and flow the rain water. So a team at the University of Colorado Boulder has been doing some very good work on precisely measuring how much extra precipitation is produced through dynamic seeding. We have been looking at this as well. Once USSF became operational it made sense to move some of these atmospheric studies to their jurisdiction." Jeanne jumped in.

"NASA does big rocket ships. USSF has air force capacities, so a lot of ways to deliver seeding materials to make rain."

"Precisely," answered Major Kunkel. "Look, a couple of years ago some guy got on YouTube with a video claiming to show NASA had developed a huge cloud seeding machine. NASA sent its Earth Science Advisory Committee members out to disavow any such thing. Well, no one from the Air Force said anything about it." He paused a few seconds, letting that sink in. "So, as you have all surmised by now, if your vaccine is water based and can be delivered by rain, we think we can figure out how and when and where to seed rain clouds, so we can literally drop vaccine all over the country." Ricky spoke. Shimon made the hand gesture he'd seen on several casino and sports betting app commercials.

"Make it rain!" Ricky then spoke.

"I see the theoretical aspects, in simple terms. But we have many, many considerations – acidity, dosage, precise delivery mechanisms." Shimon jumped back in.

"We cannot, as you might say, just turn on a fire hose and douse the whole world in vaccine water."

"No, of course not." Major Kunkel spoke with a bit of a hostile edge. "That is why we are on this trip to your offices. Dynamic seeding is a pretty delicate science. As I said, some of this is classified, but trust me, no one is suggesting we do a rain dance and hope everyone doesn't OD on vaccine." While this analogy was crude, Kunkel made his point. Derek thought he needed to smooth out a conversation growing rough.

"Look, it's been a really long day. We are all on the same team now. We understand we are, in your parlance, creating payload and you are figuring out how to deliver it. We get it. We'll get you set up when we get to Brookline and start fresh in the morning."

"Sure, but let me just add one more thing." Kunkel added. "We are well aware of the advances you have made in nanobot technology. Our working theory – and, Dr. Tsang ..."

"Ricky, please."

"Very well. Ricky. Our working theory is to see if the nanobots can become the delivery mechanism. Properly spaced, specifically loaded with the vaccine, disbursed in a precise dynamic seeding operation. That is the working theory." Derek and Ricky nodded their heads, and looked at each other. Neither said out loud, that could work; but both felt it. By 9pm, Garth's 2016 "Gunslinger" CD dropped into play mode, the volume low enough to not disturb anyone. The rest of the ride to Brookline was quiet and uneventful.

| 44 |

Chapter 44: End of June 2020:
Race to the beginning

They worked through the weekend, nothing new for the researchers or Major Kunkel. On Monday June 29, the eight of them gathered in the SCIF to update Clark - Ricky, Shimon, Jeanne, Major Kunkel, Dr. Nie, Derek, Hernan Diego and Nancy Lauren. CNOVation presented its proposal to DoD to price the vaccine by the dose, the only way Derek and the legal team could envision things working at this point. At $15 / dose and a minimum of 300 million doses, the price tag was $4.5 billion. The figure was mind-numbing for CNOVation, but actually cheaper per dose than the rumored price of the two other leading vaccines. Derek and his team struggled with but had ultimately agreed to Clark's two non-negotiable demands: First, the US be given a priority buyer status, meaning at least three-quarters of the first 300 million doses be delivered to DoD, which would be the lead distributor under OWS. Second, the production chain include Richard's son-in-law's brother's company – clearly that was graft as Senator Sindel called it, but all relationships were fully disclosed as federal ethics rules and laws required. As the vaccine would be a single dose, Clark wanted Richards to be able to boast that he had secured enough to vaccinate every American over the age of 16. They all understood that testing on children would need to be conducted ASAP, in Phase II if at all possible.

Sindel knew these were no-bid contacts. Given the pandemic, there was no time for snail paced government procedures. He also realized, as did Derek, that once they disclosed the existence of this serum, they would have as many contracts with other countries as they could want at a hefty price tag. Derek, his sister Melissa, the Senator, and the other equity owners in CNOVation had done some rough math, which they could do as a private company without making any public disclosure. They roughly estimated the potential profit of the US contract alone at $1.8 billion after paying their joint venture partners for supply and production. They could also make four or five times that much from worldwide agreements, even factoring in Ricky's request that poorer countries be able to get the doses at lower prices, and the poorest areas get it free. Derek began to think realistically of the prospect of him and his sister becoming billionaires.

Everyone on this secure call knew that the two leading biotech joint ventures, major companies that had partnered up, were still in their Phase I clinical trials, with the Warp Speed contractor running out ahead. Still, Richards had repeatedly made known that he wanted a Warp Speed player to be first across the finish line with an approved vaccine, and now wanted at least half the country vaccinated before Election Day. In fact, if he had it his way, his voters would be vaccinated first. But all indicators were that neither of the two "conventional" shots in arms suppliers would finish Phase I and II clinical trials before Labor Day, and the odds of finishing Phase III before Halloween were bleak. Richards knew and cared little for the science, but he understood the calendar. With large amounts of early and mail in voting antici-pated this year due to the pandemic, he needed a miracle cure delivered by Labor Day.

CNOVation's procurement team worked with supply chain manu-facturers around the world, including the son-in-law's newly formed LLC. They needed to; the essential ingredients for mRNA could not ex-actly be ordered from Amazon. In fact, as Ricky had expressed to Derek for several days now, they were about to run out of suitable monkeys for pre-human trials. Derek would be on SCIF calls later today with the two European biotech players. The two had thus far been left out of the vaccine sweepstakes, but each of which he believed could scale up to produce enough vaccine to meet US needs in a matter of 60 days. His choices were limited. Every major US company had already partnered up with a domestic or foreign company. Neither of Derek's two choices was in a clinical trial but both were consulting with the British Ministry of Health, which would make Ricky's request to bring Professor Dorchester even more beneficial. Going to Asia for partners was not viable. China had been excluded from any US contract, and Japan could barely meet its own demands. Derek and the Senator would be leaving tomorrow to meet with the potential supply partners, assuming Marc and Nancy were satisfied with the NDAs. Fortunately, Derek had been able to keep the White House completely out of these discussions.

Hernan triggered the SCIF call. Clark spoke first.

"The President wants to be on the next briefing and he wants assurances that this project is a go by the 4th of July." Ricky responded, probably out of turn but that would be ok with Derek.

"By a go, Mr. Clark, what precisely does that mean?"

"Well, best case, that you are ready to recommend to the CDC and FDA to approve the vaccine. But we all know we won't be there, so Richards would settle for your recommendation to the FDA and HHS to approve your beginning clinical trials. The institutional review boards that will look at your product would very likely be comprised of the same people who have already approved the major studies underway." Ricky paused, deliberate as always.

"I understand, sir. I cannot at this point give you that assurance. I am also awaiting an advisory opinion from a panel of bioethicists that we can ask people to meaningfully consent to a clinical trial knowing the high likelihood of losing significant color perception. We cannot race to the end with this, with all due respect."

"Race to the end? Son, you're in a race to the beginning. You of all people know all that has to be done once you start the paperwork to ask for clinical trial approval. We're almost at the end of June. Our COVID cases keep rising, and it's early summer. We've all seen the CDC modelling. If this keeps going on the current trajectory, we're looking at ten million COVID cases here by Halloween, and 100,000 deaths minimum."

"We are painfully aware. And I believe the projections you have released publicly are, well, conservative."

"Of course they are. We don't want to scare the shit out of the whole country and cause a panic."

"Of course, sir. But still, the ethics of causing color blindness..."

"How is that any different than giving them the laundry list of other possible side effects, just like in the other clinical trials already underway, and having them sign a waiver? The IRBs review the adequacy of the informed consent document before they green light the clinical trial. Just make sure you write it up correctly. You've got very talented lawyers. Figure it out." Shimon stepped into clearer camera view, seeing that Clark was not really as interested in asking questions as he was in dictating the answers.

"The difference – the vast bulk of the other known and possible side effects, those are all temporary. Chills, fever, loss of taste or smell, hives, fatigue etc. – we are 95% plus sure if they occur those will be temporary - maybe a few days, maybe worst case, in a very low percentage, a couple weeks. This color blinding, it may be permanent. All of our indicators right now is it is likely to disable the ... well in plain terms, it makes everything you see white and gray." Clark was not only undeterred by that possibility, he was enthralled. No more black, no more brown, only shades of white and gray.

"We're fronting all the research money you need and paying you guys 4.5 billion dollars to make the vaccine happen. So, make it happen. I've got to go in 2 minutes. Major Kunkel, how are things looking on the delivery side? Can you make this stuff rain?"

"Sir, we are very pleased by the research we are seeing here on deploying the nanobot technology."

"Great. Dr Nie?"

"Sir, if USSF can get this payload loaded in a stable state, we believe NASA can deliver it for the dynamic seeding. We are still testing but we are cautiously optimistic it can be done."

"Also great. See, Derek, is it really that hard to get some good news? Work on your guys, will you? Ok, I'll bring Richards up to speed and he'll expect a further update Friday. Remember, the 4th of July is Saturday. He's really hoping to make an announcement then. People are sick and tired. They have COVID fatigue and they need a shot in the arm. This would be it. 9am Friday." With that, Clark's side disconnected, so Hernan did the same. He catalogued the call, and set the reminder for Friday's call on the calendar so everyone would know it was blocked.

Derek had about 10 minutes until his next secure call to speak with his Principals. He excused Kunkel and Dr. Wei to head back to the lab, keeping everyone else in the SCIF. "Look, deal's the same. You do the science. Nancy and Marc do the lawyering. The Senator and I do the politicking. Clark's a pit bull. That's his job. He does his, we do ours. Ok?" His team all nodded. "Great. I've got to do this call and then will be gone for a few days." He texted Amanda to make sure their return flight landed by midnight Thursday. She had to arrange the meetings in a country that had yet not imposed quarantine restrictions on US travelers, meaning the entire EU was out. So, Derek and the Senator would be spending three days in Norway, an accessible country with a low number of COVID cases and no quarantine. Neither Derek nor Amanda was aware at the time that Clark had himself just been there on what had been called a trade mission.

Before Derek began his next meeting, Clark was on the phone with Fritzy. "Yeah, we don't know for sure yet. I'm not gonna let him do a prime time with O'Day and promise this as the next new thing. The last couple of things he promised blew up on him. Drinking bleach. Space UV lasers. Jesus Christ." Fritzy laughed.

"Yeah, he stepped in some shit with those. I still can't believe there's 20 million or so people who believe any stupid thing he says. But you know his idiot son-in-law or the brother is gonna leak it. Get drunk at some Georgetown cocktail party. Try to be the big man in town. How much do you think those morons stand to make if this really works?"

"Don't know. A butt load. More than I've made in my lifetime."

"C'mon, JB don't BS me. I know you've got pieces of pieces all up and down the supply chain and on the distribution side. And if this works, on top of all that money, you'll have world domination." Clark smiled a broad, toothy ear to ear grin.

"Controlled leak then. Your guys get the exclusive, he's already booked. We'll set it up. Shit, this really better work, or he's a one and done." Clark ended the call, and headed to his next meeting.

| 45 |

Chapter 45: July 2, 2020: No more monkeys jumping on the bed

Derek, the Senator, Nancy Lauren and Marc Hale nestled comfortably into their first class pods for the long flight back to Boston. The meetings could not have gone better. Marc's law partners texted him how ecstatic they were to have traded their hourly legal fees for a fractional interest in CNOVation's vaccine contracts. This move would net his firm $45 million on the government contract alone. On top of that, Derek agreed to pay all travel expenses. Derek remained true to his philosophy of loyalty and rewarding his team. He had not yet told anyone besides the board that Ricky would receive a $50 million bonus, with Shimon, Jeanne and the Senator getting $25 million each. When you have $1.8 billion nearly guaranteed coming in, it's easier to be beneficent, although many business people would not share so well.

Marc started revising the memorandum of understanding with the manufacturing partners, which his office would securely transmit before the flight landed. For security purposes, the agreements would simply be with Marie Curie, NV, the code name for France-based ONA de Sciences, and Einstein, for Netherlands based RGNZ.

The flight would have them land at 10pm Eastern time on July 2, as they would recapture six hours on the 13 hour flight home. At 3pm Eastern, Derek and the Senator received nearly simultaneous emails that at first seemed unrelated. Derek's was from corporate security, notifying him that there had been a local power surge, which triggered their electrical grid sensors. Given the number of kilowatts it took to run their lab, SCIF and security systems, in addition to the normal demands, they had installed a sophisticated power usage monitor. They would know in advance if they needed to fail over to back-up generators in the event of a brown out or black out. Summers in Boston can get "wicked humid" so electricity spikes were pretty common. Derek's team had sent a first alert, with a promise to send updates.

Sindel's email caused him concern. A couple of retired Secret Service agents had been asked by active duty buddies to "grab a few" after they "bunk down in Beantown." Sindel immediately assumed what they did – that someone very high level, maybe even Richards, was coming to Boston. Sindel placed his mask on, an airline requirement if he left his personal pod space, to talk to Derek. Once he saw him, Derek slid his on also. "What's up Teddy?"

"You hear anything from Clark about a surprise inspection?" Derek shook his head, perplexed at the question. "No emails from corporate security about a request for a Secret Service advance team coming through?"

"No, nothing like that." Derek added. "We did get a temporary power surge alert, but our guys are monitoring."

"Check again." Derek looked down at his phone as a text came in from Amanda to check his secure emails. He logged in to the VPN and then into his secure emails. Sure enough, his corporate security team had just hung up with the Secret Service who would be arriving tomorrow at 7am to do a sweep. That was all the info they had been given. Derek updated the Senator.

"That asshole." Sindel said, then rubbed his chin.

"Clark?"

"No. Richards. Let me check a few things, but my guess is he's coming to Boston to announce your vaccine."

Derek looked upset, but not surprised. "So, why the power surge? Is that related?"

Sindel answered, clearly annoyed. "Could be. If I'm right, it's for a major press event. So, it could be media vans plugging in to test for a remote press conference." Sindel emailed Clark, who didn't respond right away, so he went back to his pod.

An hour later they had their answers. Clark confirmed that Richards had decided to showcase CNOVation by holding a press conference on July 4 at 11am in front of their offices, after Richards does an inspection inside. Sindel emailed back. "JB, is that wise? I mean you heard the scientists. They may not be ready to launch then."

Clark's response email was curt – "Get them ready. This is happening." Sindel remasked, and went back to Derek.

"It's a power play by Clark but honestly he is right. This is too huge a deal not to leak, especially if the moron son-in-law blabs about the millions he's about to make." Derek pondered for a few seconds.

"Well, at least this way we get some control of the narrative."

"With Richards? He doesn't know a hypodermic from a hypothalamus. But, yeah, the lid can't stay on this much longer. I'll tell Marc, you tell Nancy."

"Will do. I'll let the rest of the team know at our morning briefer. Since security confirmed Secret Service sweep for 7am, I'll move the team briefing to 6:30am. I'm not chancing this to texts and I'd rather tell them in person."

Sindel nodded and went over to Marc's area while Derek went over to Nancy. The conversations were low key and low volume after carefully checking around to make sure no one could overhear. Marc whispered "I'll expedite the draft MOU to our manufacturing partners and send it before we land. My office has already confirmed no EU regulations currently prohibit them supplying us for a US product – but my guess is we'll start to see those type of restrictions as retaliation for the administration's requirements that the US receives 75% of the first doses."

"No doubt. I'll talk to my EU markets friends as soon as I can to give them a heads up and try to calm them down." The Senator went back to his pod. Derek had finished bringing Nancy up to speed, then had Amanda change the scheduled Principals meeting to 6:30am. The gave each other a thumbs up. Ricky texted a few second later.

"All went well?"

"Yes. Full debrief in the am. Any news you can share on text?"

"No more monkeys jumping on the bed." They both knew this was silly, but agreed to only communicate in simple code by sounding like a nursery rhyme, even though both had no kids. This was Ricky's way of saying the supply of test monkey had run out. Derek had started working on a source, so he went back to that.

| 46 |

Chapter 46: Count on it

The morning debrief with the Principals went about as Derek expected. All were very excited about the ability to deliver the vaccine in huge quantities, and equally disappointed that the President was coming to force their hand on the timing. Ricky objected to being told he would be standing near Richards when he made the announcement. That queasy feeling was somewhat made better when Sindel said Dr. C would likely be there also. "Try to smile. Otherwise it will look like you're making a hostage video. And we need the public to have immediate confidence in this, which is hard to sell if the primary scientists look nauseous."

Hernan hooked in a New York based PR firm for a few minutes via a scrambled web chat, not as secure as the SCIF but better than not being involved at all. Two account executives from the Boston office would meet later in the day with Derek and his team. By that time, press releases would be ready to go; they expected this gargantuan news would likely leak. While CNOVation had excelled at keeping its work off the grid, once a 4th of July Boston trip showed up on Richards' daily calendar and the limited press gaggle he allowed to travel with him was invited to fly on Air Force One, all sources would be hit really hard to give up something.

The Secret Service advance team visit was fairly uneventful. They saw no need to wear antibacterial suits, or locker their guns. Richards had assured them he had no interest in entering the lab. The whole sweep took 50 minutes, only half of which Derek had stayed for.

By the time the agents left the building and emailed the "All clear" to the special agent in charge, Clark was on his burner phone planting the story with Fritzy. Jim O'Day would be front and center at the presser at the front door of the CNOVation building, and would get an exclusive afternoon interview with Richards; this could not wait until nighttime. The first and only question would go to Analise Simmins, the light skinned black NewsFirst reporter. O'Day and Analise were dispatched to Boston and told to arrive at the lab by 4pm Friday for an exclusive pre-air interview that no one at CNOVation yet knew about. They thought the element of surprise would make for a more authentic visceral response.

NewsFirst was taking no chances of being scooped, not on a story this huge. O'Day knew generally what he'd be asking about on his prime-time exclusive, but would lean on the expert science contributor from Harvard. NewsFirst had been asked by Harvard several times to stop promoting Dr. Loey as a Harvard researcher, since he did not earn a degree from there. In fact, Dr. Loey had only spent five weeks in an executive MBA program, which he didn't complete. His doctorate was in history, not medicine. Fritzy's legal team told Harvard to stuff it, since Loey had technically trained at Harvard – they never said he graduated or had a medical degree from there. Besides, Loey worked cheap and would convincingly and loudly express the right opinions – once told what they should be.

Clark was finishing up some work at 3pm when his non-government issued burner cell lit up with a secure chat. Deng Xu-Pei's second in command, known only to Clark as Mike, texted as expected. Even through an encrypted text Clark would be extra cautious. "Needs?" Clark responded.

"Large scale. Maybe 2000 for actual, but get 6000 total for now."

"When?"

"Very soon. Few weeks."

"Done. Meet?"

"If can. Moving the cookies is delicate. Will need 40,000 more served later."

"You deliver the cookies. We will serve. Size of party is No problem." That ended the conversation. Through a series of cryptic messages, Clark had gotten word to Deng that a large scale human trial of a vaccine would be required, the type that in the US would be bogged down by laws and regulations and bureaucratic red tape – a phrase Deng objected to since red tape was still a synonym for bad things in America but red was the color for happiness in many Asian countries. Deng led a country sanctioned by prior US administrations for human rights abuses, which sanctions had crippled the economy for 15 years. These sanctions had been eased but not completely eliminated under Richards. Deng expected a quid pro quo for providing the first clinical trial: Washington would scrap all remaining sanctions.

Clark had gamed it all out, and devised his plan to get the first 20,000 doses to Deng's autocratic regime. His basic outline was simple. Richards would announce this miracle, and how millions of lives would be saved. Operation Warp Speed would be declared a ground breaking, unprecedented success. The liberal press would complain about not politicizing a COVID vaccine by rushing the science, and how awful it was to be color blinded. They would also ask why would anyone agree to that? The Richards does-no-wrong side of the media, led by NewsFirst, would praise his incredible leadership in getting a vaccine in months, not years, and criticize the liberal press for making this miracle a political issue. By Richards launching this political football, and the ensuing hysteria that would follow, the FDA, CDC and NIH would have to issue a joint press release announcing that no vaccine would be approved for use in the US without going through the full phases of study for efficacy and safety. Countries around the world would instantly take varying practical, medical and ethical positions. On one side, why rush into causing people to go color blind when several safe and less impactive vaccines would be arriving soon; on the other, this disease was still spreading and by fall would again be ravaging the world at alarming rates, so who can afford to wait?

Clark calculated that US public opinion would trend to we could not afford to wait, and put enormous pressure on the approval process. The administration had simple talking points prepared to be distributed: "Why not save millions and millions of lives and countless suffering, especially in poorer countries and regions that may never get a properly stored vaccine delivered by a clean needle? We're all sick and tired of COVID fatigue. We're ready for getting back to our lives, even if this is the price."

With the 24 hour news cycle and all social media platforms on the verge of melt down from nothing but this game changing vaccine being debated and argued and discussed, Deng would step forward and make an incredible offer: his country had arranged for a large scale, "voluntary" 40,000 person human trial. Half would take the vaccine, the other half would receive a placebo. The US and other major powers could even send their scientists to audit the study to make sure it was all on the up and up. The scientists would debate and agree on a smaller Phase I – maybe 4,000 to 6,000 total, and if that showed promise, then a second phase. For this first study, seeding the rain clouds would not be required. The scale would be small enough for a more traditional yet still unusual delivery system – a drink of water. While the clinical trials were underway, USSF and NASA would test the cloud seeding for use in the third phase of the trial.

The studies would be quick and of course a major success, prompting Richards to take executive action to remove the remaining economic sanctions, and forcing the FDA's hand to give emergency use authorization. In a move NewsFirst and others of a similar bent would tout as sheer genius, Richards had already gotten a promise of 300 million doses for the US, saving the country from this terrible Chinese plague. How could liberals, how could anyone oppose saving lives and stopping suffering? And this could all lead to getting doses out in the US by Labor Day, more than enough time to rocket Richards to a second term, and deliver the Leaders the colorless world they so desperately wanted – well, that most of them wanted. Clark had received reports back that not all of the Leaders were satisfied with a solution that allowed minorities to move freely around them. To some in that group, it was not acceptable that the "lesser races" would retain their freedoms and it would just be harder to tell who was white and who was not. Clark knew that a compromise solution was always inevitable, and he truly believed this was the best possible outcome without massive wars and bloodshed.

At 3:45pm, Clark called Derek to advise him that O'Day would be arriving to do some advance work, and to be fully cooperative. "Let him in the damn lab if he puts on the clean suit." These were no longer requests; these were commands. And since the DoD had signed and retuned the overall contract for the $4.5 billion in purchases, to be drawn down by purchase orders, Derek knew he had virtually no legal or practical ability to decline. He did refuse any recording of any type within the building, as the agreement allowed.

When O'Day arrived with Dr. Loey, Analise Simmins, and his producer, after clearing security, Amanda escorted them to Derek's office. Derek and the PR team were waiting, along with Nancy and Marc Hale. NewsFirst would not sign an NDA – no actual news organization would. But they knew they would get no audio or video recordings, so received the limited information CNOVation would provide. Derek had to give O'Day ten minutes of access to Ricky – that's the deal he made with Clark. O'Day could have free access to Kunkel and Dr. Nie, but they were under strong NDA's so could not really say much. Simmins knew she was there to give the black person's perspective on the story after tomorrow's press conference, she just didn't know perspective on what – until now.

Ricky joined the meeting as scheduled. The PR team did the set up – a couple of minutes on Ricky's background, and the ground breaking vaccine research his team had been undertaking. Everything was bathed in glowing yet vague generalities. O'Day looked at Ricky.

"So, tell us Dr. Tsang, what is the promise of this vaccine?" Of course the answers had been scripted. Ricky gave a generic highly technical response, laced with words like promising yet still in early stages, not yet tested on human subjects, potential for significant side effects. "I'm sorry, but I don't know why I'm here or why the President of the United States is coming here tomorrow. You make this sound like something that may never work and if it does it will be awful for whoever takes it. Yet our government has agreed to pay you four and a half billion, billion, dollars. Why? You're obviously holding back – I get that – but right now my story is government makes horrible decision to invest in unknown Boston company." Everyone in the room knew O'Day was a blow hard, an agitator, not a real journalist. Ricky had been prepped for that. Plus Ricky had almost no ego, so a prompt like "what the hell makes you so special" would not work with him in any setting, much less one where he had clear misgivings. His answer was pretty much what he had been encouraged to give.

"Sir, I do not wish to go outside my area of expertise. I do not get involved in the company's business or the government contracts. I am in public health and I have been asked to work on a CoV-2 vaccine. I am doing that with a highly skilled team. I am thankful for this opportunity to be of service. Ours is one of many studies underway, but I can say quite different from what is publicly known of the others. What we are working on has great promise, but as with any new advance certain drawbacks." His tone, his pattern of speech, his volume never changed. He would not let himself become the story – mad scientist working on secret cure. He stood and looked at Derek. "May I go back to work now?"

"Yes, of course." Derek stood, and walked Ricky out. His thumbs up was given in front of Ricky and thus blocked from everyone in his office. He returned and remained standing. He stretched out his closed fist to O'Day. "It's been a pleasure meeting you. As my team explained to you, there is very little we can discuss right now. I hope you have enjoyed your visit to CNOVation. Amanda has a press packet for each of you to take with you. It even includes one of our logo branded masks. The air filtration in it is comparable to the N95s, and we are in discussions with the government about producing masks for the military.

You can report that out. We look forward to seeing you here tomorrow. Perhaps after the President speaks we can talk again." O'Day stood, buttoned his suit jacket, and firmly bumped Derek's hand. Under his NewsFirst mask, he grumbled, "count on it."

After Amanda escorted them out – O'Day left his goodie pouch on the conference table –Nancy said what everyone had surmised. "He already knows what we're doing."

Derek answered. "Probably so. He's always had an inside track with this administration. But if he knows it from their side so be it. We can't control that, but no need to confirm it. Plus Loey is an idiot, and bringing him here is an insult. It's like sending your 8 year old son out to bat against Roger Clemens at Fenway. He's so out of his league, he probably didn't understand a word Ricky said."

The PR execs started to head out. "We have our full team ready to roll on a moment's notice. We'll blanket the major media outlets the second Richards starts talking and can have anyone you want on the Sunday morning talk shows." Marc Hale stopped the executive.

"I always thought Saturday the 4th of July is a dead news day. Everybody is out at picnics or barbeques. Why did Richards pick it?"

"Conventional wisdom? It makes no PR sense. But we are clearly not in conventional times. A huge number of people are stuck at home, gatherings will be way down. Virtual fireworks and web parties? This story will grab every headline. No one is working, no school. The people who will be out partying but shouldn't be are already predominantly his supporters. The socially responsible and complaint folks who will be home watching streaming services or baseball games in empty stadiums will get the shock waves of this news. He only needs to win 10% of them to cruise to reelection. That's it, that's what all the polling is saying. So, 4th of July? Independence from this awful virus? We see why he's doing this."

| 47 |

Gored on the 4th of July

The media starting assembling at 10am in front of CNOVation.
The press conference had been called for 11am, likely meaning noon
with Richards. Satellite trucks lined the streets for three blocks. On a
business day, several nearby companies would have complained, but
their offices were closed today. It was Independence Day after all. The
Red Sox game would be the Sunday Night ESPN game, so many bored
Bostonians who had been stuck at home gathered in the streets nearby
for this media spectacle. They stood behind the yellow security tape
with a large group of Richards' supporters, who had disembarked their
"Richards 2020" campaign bus at 8:30am.

The onsite reporters did their stand-alone set up pieces, while anchors and pundits gathered to talk about this obscure but highly regarded Brain Belt lab. They speculated about the announcement,
noting the addition of Dr. Tsang Yi DeeLu and his team's history
of work in infectious diseases. Several "highly placed" administration
sources "who were not allowed to publicly comment" were being
quoted as saying DoD had signed a massive contract with this company,
larger that the size of all contracts in Warp Speed – which was true,
since DoD did not count the Defense Production Act orders for ven-
tilators and PPE as contracts for reporting purposes. Only O'Day and
Analise knew this was all about a new and different type of vaccine,

but even they didn't know the magnitude of what was about to be discussed.

Ricky and Dr. C enjoyed the chance to catch up inside and away from the media circus outside, while the government team was installing the final touches on the bullet proof glass and teleprompters. Dr. C was actually awestruck when Ricky told him the details of this discovery; and for a man with over 40 years of public health experience and serious, serious infectious disease chops, it had been a long time since anything literally made his jaw drop. "Ricky, my lord, this is ... I just ... I mean wow! You'll get me in to the lab and analytics later?"

"As soon as this side show is over, yes of course." Derek walked in to Ricky's office.

" Dr. Cooper, so great to have you on our team, even if on loan. I've admired your work my whole life. Thank you so very much." Dr. C was gracious as well.

"You've got one hell of a company here. I've been aware of your advancements for several years. And you made a terrific decision bringing Ricky on board. He is world class."

"He speaks glowingly of you as well. Any chance you'd consider coming to the private sector? There's always a spot here for someone as talented and respected as you." Dr. C had received and rebuffed many similar overtures over his career.

"If I was going to go anywhere, it would be to work with this young man. But, no, thank you, that is very kind."

"Well, I'll let you two continue to chat. I've got to go to wardrobe then hair and make-up for my 15 minutes of fame out there. I mean, I'm happy in my jeans and tee, but PR says I should look a little more corporate when the leader of the free world strolls in. Honestly, I don't even know my jacket size anymore, but ... well, small problems, right? See you in a bit." With that, Derek left as Shimon and Jeanne strolled in. The four scientists talked about the science behind this discovery. Amanda popped in at 11:30, an hour later than Richards was supposed to arrive.

"He's here." Two Secret Service agents walked in, doing their third pat down of the morning.

"This way, please." Derek arrived, almost unrecognizable in a blue suit, white shirt and muted red striped tie. The eight of them walked towards the security desk, now occupied by Secret Service, Boston PD, and Massachusetts state police. Clark waited there with Major Kunkel and Dr. Nie. He hollered for all to stay back, except Ricky; Richards would be photographed and videoed walking in alone, greeted at the open door only by the guy he called "the lead researcher." The broader photo op shots would be taken as they exited and lined up behind him on the riser. Clark looked at his government phone; a text from Richards as he prepared to exit the Beast.

"Dr. Nie and Major Kunkel, please join me." They stepped forward, and Ricky back. The two lead Secret Service agents opened the front door wide, and Kunkel and Nie went half way out, each shaking hands with President Richards. He swiveled, placed an arm around each, and let the cameras click and videos run for about 20 seconds. His grin was wide as could be. He then removed his arms, waved both hands, turned his body, and walked in, trailed by his agents, Clark, Kunkel and Dr. Nie.

Once safely out of camera view and microphone ears, he looked at his watch. "Fifteen minutes, then back out. Where's the executive head?" Derek led him to the nearest restroom, since his company didn't separate restrooms based on rank or gender. He waited outside after the agent went in to make sure it was "all clear." Richards then went in. One agent waited inside, one agent guarding the door. Derek heard the flush, but was not sure he heard the water faucet turned on and off. Gross!

Everyone had gathered in the secure conference room by the time Richards was done with his business. Clark handed him the envelope with the five index cards, each with just a few words. He eyed Ricky, remembering they had met, then eyed Jeanne, sure they had not. "Alright, two minutes or less, tell me how this vaccine works. And what's the catch." Two minutes or less, to describe what had taken a combined

200 years of education, training and experience just to imagine and try to create. Having no fear of an American politician, Shimon answered.

"Well, we made a vaccine that lets chicken soup drop from the sky and saves everyone from COVID. It's really that simple. We take a protein, like chicken, wrap it in fat, like chicken fat, and serve it up in water. That's the easy part. The hard parts are it makes everyone color blind and we're still working on the dosage to make sure we don't accidentally kill people. Oh, and it hasn't been tested on any humans yet."

"Uh huh. You know they really love me in Israel. I've got a higher approval rating there than your own Prime Minister." Clark jumped in.

"Major, will you pick it up from there?"

"Yes, of course. Mr. President, sir first let me say it's such an honor to meet you." Richards looked at his watch, then looked up. "So, yes, this vaccine can be delivered through rain water. We at Space Force can seed the clouds and make it rain vaccine from the heavens, basically. NASA assures us they can make it rain in the right amounts to have the optimal effect." Richards looked at Dr. Nie, since she was wearing a NASA lab coat, not happy there were now two Asian looking people on this project.

"That true?"

"We are pretty sure, sir. We'd like to run some field tests and some soil evaporation tests as soon as possible, but all of our..."

"Okay. Good fine. Why not just drink this chicken whatever stuff. If it's like water can you drink it out of a bottle?" Everyone looked at Ricky, who shrugged and stepped forward.

"Sir, in theory, yes. This is not being designed as an injectable. What we have devised is a delivery system that even the poorest countries in the world can be served by, hopefully through a simple rainfall. This way..."

"Yeah, son look I don't care about some poor shit hole third world country. We're paying you billions of bucks to save American lives. So why not just put this in bottles and let people drink it?"

"We were told speed of delivery is a key. If this tests out and passes the bioethical concerns, NASA tells us the rain cloud seeding part can be done as quickly as we can get the vaccine manufactured. It is a trade-off. Since we focused on speed we have not fully tested for the effect of plastics on degradation of the vaccine. Our emphasis now is on rain acidity and how that could impact dosing. And we left for NASA to study any possible ground water secondary effects, although we expect the vaccine will not have a long enough effective life to cause any seepage issues."

"Okay, great. I've got what I need. Let's roll." Clark lined everyone up, like a party planner positioning the processional at a wedding. Richards first with one Secret Service agent at his side, then Clark, then Major Kunkel and Dr. Nie, then Ricky and Dr. C, all of whom would gather behind the President in that order. The rest of the CNOVation people could exit however they wanted as they would be outside the main TV images. The second agent opened the doors, and the party rolled out. The first to greet Richards were the governor and the Senator whom Richards had helped get elected. He had not invited the other party's Senator, local Congresswomen or Mayor of Boston. Why should he – they didn't vote for him and often clashed with him.

Richards stepped to the center of the bullet proof glass and the array of microphones. The great seal of the President adorned the lectern. He took out the envelope. Card 1: "Today is an incredible day for our great country." Card 2: "With the great assistance of our Space Force and our NASA scientists," and now the first riff "which I was totally responsible for, the Space Force. No other President ever had the brains to come up with the idea for a space force, and today it pays huge dividends." Card 3: "And due to Operation Warp Speed," next riff, "again, totally my idea, my leadership to do that to get Americans killed by the China flu made safe, to keep America safe and strong." Card 4: "We have developed a safe and effective," the card said, "are developing," but Richards went with "have developed". Card 5: "That you can drink; no shots, no needles, you'll be able to drink it." End of cards, next spontaneous statements. "Folks, this is truly a miracle. With my Space Force and NASA and my leadership, we will have all of America vaccinated by

Labor Day!" With that, his handpicked, invited supporters erupted in thunderous applause, and chants of "four more years! four more years!"

"I only have time for one question." All hands shot up, multiple questions all being shouted, none of which could be deciphered. "Yes, Analise." All eyes and cameras turned to her, and she knew hers would be the only question taken.

"Mr. President, will this new vaccine be safe and effective and how many lives do you think you will be saving." You – not the scientists and researchers – you.

"Absolutely safe and totally effective. We'll save millions and millions of lives and get our economy roaring back, just like it was doing before we got blindsided by this China flu. We had the greatest economy in the history of the world going, and we'll get it back, and make it even greater. I'll let our scientists take the rest of your questions. But remember folks, no administration in the history of the world ever developed one single vaccine this fast – we'll have at least three, including this newest one, in less than a year. Never been done before. But under my leadership, we have totally done this at warp speed. Watch my interview on NewsFirst today for more details." No mention of side effects; no mention of the need for human trials; no mention of the difficult road yet ahead before delivery could occur.

The governor and the one invited senator crowded in for toothy grinned pictures, then Kunkel and Dr. Wei. With that, Richards barreled off the stage. No acknowledgment of CNOVation at all before he was whisked into the Beast, to the adoring cheers of "four more years! four more years!" O'Day, who had ridden in the Beast a few times before, and Analise, who never even dreamed of doing so, piled in behind him. They were headed to the local NewsFirst affiliate for the live exclusive interview that the station had started promoting 24 hours ago with "Major news announcement and exclusive interview with President Richards tomorrow" on the crawl, as well as on all of their streaming platforms.

Derek looked down at his phone as journalists shouted multiple now indecipherable questions. He had a text from Sindel, who was watching from home. "Gored on the 4th of July." Derek managed a chuckle. The spotlight, which Derek never sought, eluded him at a moment when he thought he'd allow himself to bask in it. Ricky and Dr. C were livid, but no one could tell from their calm exteriors. They both had run this scenario in their minds. A perfect, easy, safe and effective vaccine would be highlighted by the president, it's all good, nothing to worry about. He oversimplified the vaccine much the way he mishandled the pandemic when it first hit public consciousness – it's like the flu, will magically disappear. Now they had to bring the truth, the bad news to the world - not only had this miracle not been tested on human subjects yet, it could and likely would cause color blindness. Richards didn't care. The people who wouldn't want to be color blind were most likely not his supporters anyway. They could wait to get the other vaccines.

Fritzy already had a panel of experts, including Dr. Loey, ready to go for the O'Day interview. They would all say the odds of being permanently made color blind were very, very low, and even if it happened, it was better than being killed by the China flu. None would mention wearing masks until everyone had been vaccinated. By the time people figured out if the side effect was permanent, Richards would have taken the oath of office for the second time. The Leaders would have achieved an unimaginable goal of billions of people never seeing black or brown or Asian skin tones again. The big lie, that this was a no risk, totally perfect, easy to get vaccine, had already made its way around the world, before the scientists had a chance to tell the hard truths.

| 48 |

Chapter 48: Now what?

Katie Numoff, Senate Minority Leader and Samantha Elysson, Speaker of the House, had decided to have a web chat while watching the press conference, knowing something major was going to break. As Ricky and Dr. Cooper described the actual state of research and the potentially devastating side effect, Katie chatted "these July 4th meetings are getting to be a habit for us."

"I know. With Richards we always need to be ready to announce what we think Congress should do."

Katie asked, "Do we have anything we should do here?" Samantha waited before responding, putting only a

in the chat box. She then added.

"I don't see any legislative effort on this, and we sure don't want to get out ahead of the science on it. I can schedule a hearing to consider whether a vaccine that causes color blindness is or should be legal, but

I'm not sure that's the right move. Richards has so badly screwed up this pandemic. If we start railing against the vaccine before it even gets to FDA, we look like we're playing politics and jeopardizing lives. This country is already polarized enough about whether to take any vaccine approved while Richards is in the White House. I think we'll have to wait, but..."

"I know. He pulls this off, we may be stuck with him for four more years." Katie ended her chat message with a frowny face emoji:

They disconnected after wishing each other a Happy 4th and a safe trip home.

Thirty-three minutes after Richards, Clark and company had left the premises, Ricky and Dr. Cooper ended the press conference. Ten minutes later, the team had reassembled in Derek's office along with Nancy Lauren, excusing Major Kunkel and Dr. Nie for a few minutes due to "attorney client privilege," even though Dr. C attended. Sindel and Marc Hale were on the phone. Shimon spoke first.

"Well, this is a shit show. What do we do now?" Ricky had retained his calm exterior and resolved his internal anger.

"We go back to work. I do not see what else we should do. Derek?"

"I totally agree. Dr. Cooper?" He answered with his thick Brooklyn accent still intact.

"Look, we do the science not the politics. We told the public what we know, and we'll do the same every step of the way, even if you get to the point of applying for emergency use."

"If?" Shimon had jumped in, the look of exasperation still blanketing his face and physical demeanor. "C'mon, we all know where this is headed. This will be non-stop bullshit until we get to your approval process." Jeanne chimed in.

"Look, we told them and told the world. The hardest part now, not that this hasn't been a huge challenge already, is to find a large enough human test group." From the speaker phone, Sindel asked.

"How big a group do we need?" Dr. C answered.

"Look, I can't be on both sides of this, but here's what I think and you have plenty of other public health experts to consult. The open source data on the two most promising vaccines looks like about 30,000 to 40,000 in each of their clinical trials, start to finish." The Principals all nodded. Ricky spoke.

"We are going to need a lot more materials."

Derek quipped, "We're gonna need a bigger boat." Only Dr. C, the Senator and Jeanne got the *Jaws* reference. "We obviously can't run a trial that large in our facilities. Our European partners can help, assuming they still want in on this. I'm already getting emails about how livid they are over how Richards sold this." At that moment, Amanda came in.

"Derek, you may want to turn on your TV." She clicked the large screen on, tuned to Derek's preferred cable news network. It and several others had cut away from the pretty boring Saturday afternoon programming to carry Richards' live interview with Jim O'Day, a highly unusual practice, but these were quite unusual times. Richards had actually taken a call during the interview – yes, on air, a phone call from a world leader.

O'Day announced it. "Ladies and gentlemen, on this incredible, ground breaking day, we can now tell you that President Richards had just received a call from Prime Minister Deng Xu-Pei. We think he's a fan of the show." Awkward self-congratulatory laughter – another sign of the bloated ego that had made O'Day and Richards such natural friends. Every current and former senior member of the State Department watching cringed, as did the majority of the US national security apparatus. World leaders live on TV talking about who knows what? No advance work, no going through channels, not even a classified call worthy SAT phone. Richards treated such protocols with the disregard of a teenager who details his first underage drinking binge on social media despite multiple parental warnings about privacy. Richards didn't even leave the set to take the call.

"That's great, so awesome, Deng. Hey, I'm on live TV – you mind if I put you on speaker and you can tell the world what you just told me." He pressed the speaker icon, and there it came, for the world to hear:

"Mr. President, our countries have had many differences and we still do. But with your incredible leadership we have made great strides to have a better relationship. Our nuclear talks have been very productive. Our goal remains to be a major trading partner with you. And our country, too, has suffered from this terrible virus and our best scientists are hard at work on a cure also. After your incredible announcement today, I assembled our scientific leaders, and they tell me without doubt that we can arrange for a very large, voluntary human trial of 40,000 of our patriotic citizens. In fact, thousands of calls have already come in to our ministry of health offering to volunteer." Richards hoisted the phone up, like he was showing off a grandchild, like how Rafiki extended his arms to hoist Simba up high on Pride Roc for all the kingdom to see. Everyone in Derek's office felt the nausea at the same time, even before Richards began to speak again.

"You see that, folks? See what real leadership looks like. Deng, that's spectacular. Totally great. We'll get our people to get that done. Can't wait til our next meeting."

"It is an honor and privilege, Mr. President, for our humble country to be a part of this truly historic event. A tribute to your unmatched leadership skills." With that, Deng hung up. Richards resumed gloating and congratulating himself. Clark, back stage, started receiving encrypted text messages of congratulations and thanks from his racist, populist, far right believers all around the world. A few did point out "too many Asians," but Clark was of no mind to quibble. He even received "way to go!" from two former Grand Wizards of the KKK. His government phone was blowing up at the same time, with congratulatory texts and email messages from party leaders wanting to stand with

Richards, and industry leaders wanting in on the deal. Fritzy strolled over. Neither spoke. Neither had to. The sheer joy and elation expressed more than neatly arranged sounds could.

Mainstream world leaders were reaching out to each other, setting up secure video conferences to address whether to allow their companies to participate in studies of the vaccine, and whether they would let it be distributed in their countries. An incredible dilemma, as new cases and deaths were up in some countries and down in others. Mutations and new strains were starting to appear. No other solution was on the horizon, perhaps for the rest of the year, or longer.

With not much else to say, Derek simply looked at his team, and mostly whispered, "I guess we get back to work." Sindel added the obvious.

"The pressure to get this done was incredible an hour ago. It will be unimaginable now." In a few minutes, Derek, his sister Melissa, Sindel, Nancy and Marc Hale would be on a grueling secure call with executives and lawyers from ONA and RGNZ, as well as their PR firms. They had planned for this venture knowing that once word of this possible vaccine got out, there would be a whirlwind of activity. They all believed they would have more data to support the safety and efficacy of the vaccine. All knew that talk shows, news shows, social media, group chats, kitchen tables, pool parties, mostly empty and way too full bars and restaurants would be talking about nothing else. Every American would talk, argue, advocate for or express horror over this stunning 4th of July announcement. They felt like the fate of over 7 billion people rested in the labs of these three companies, on the shoulders of a handful of women and men – that is exactly how these researchers and executives now felt, and precisely how Clark, Richards and the Leaders wanted it.

When Ricky finally got to his apartment at 1:30 the next morning, he called his mother. He had missed too many of their regular calls. Both she and his father had texted and emailed him periodically, but he had been unable to respond quickly, if at all. She worried for him, knowing how much stress he was under. "You do not look very well, son. Are you getting any rest?"

"Not enough, mother. But this is a very big job we face." She smiled.

"It always is for you. We know how important your work is." She paused, smiled that motherly smile she always had for him. "With this big news, do you see getting a break? Can you come home for some rest?"

"I suspect, mother, that I may be on my way to Asia soon." Mae seemed pleased by this notion.

"Can you come home after your trip? You will be so close." Ricky smiled, knowing she would soon be planning a menu of his favorite meals.

"I will. I promise." She beamed.

"Good. Your father and I will be so very happy to see you. He is at work, but I will tell him when he comes home tonight. Send him your flight information when you have it. We will pick you up. Stay longer this time." Ricky smiled.

"As long as I can, dearest mother." They just looked at each other for a few more seconds.

"Sleep well tonight, my son. Save the world tomorrow."

| 49 |

Chapter 49: Late July 2020: One shot, two shot, red shot, blue shot

The intensity did not let up. Ricky's team worked virtually round the clock and side by side with experts from ONA and RGNZ. Under orders from DoD, CNOVation had to quickly produce 20,000 samples of the DeeLu vaccine, as everyone except Ricky had agreed to call it. DoD had counter-signed the first purchase order, and had wired the first $300,000 to CNOVation. Clark refused to advance more than the agreed $15 / dose for the first 20,000 doses, just to make sure they remained hungry for a successful test. Once that occurred, Clark had ensured Derek and Sindel that money would flow like, well, rain if the first tests were successful.

The public relations battles waged on outside the labs. COVID cases and deaths continued to rise while the WHO and US public health officials announced the discovery of at least two new variants. No other vaccine showed enough promise and had progressed through enough testing to be available even for emergency use before January 2021. COVID fatigue impacted personal behavior. Bars were packed, fewer masks were being worn, and fewer precautions taken. People were yelling at home and fighting in public about the vaccine, about masks, about bars, restaurants, gyms, businesses and schools being opened.

The WHO and the British Ministry of Health were now predicting that without a wide spread vaccination effort beginning soon, by the end of 2020, COVID infections would likely hit 80 to 105 million cases causing 1.2 to 2 million deaths. CDC and NIH had similar internal numbers, with a third of all cases and deaths potentially being in the US. Clark made sure these drastic projections were leaked, to help drive the demand for a vaccine, any vaccine. All of NewsFirst prime time programming the week of July 6 featured talking heads spreading gloom and doom around the bleak prospect of 30 million Americans infected and at least 500,000 dead by year end, an economy in ruins, rampant joblessness and homelessness without immediate action. They even had a couple of fringe mental health experts decrying a coming wave of suicides. An administration that had been downplaying COVID in March through June was in full "break the glass" emergency mode in July.

At 8:25am on July 15, Hernan Diego prepared to initiate the largest SCIF call he had yet attempted; Derek, Ricky, Jeanne, Shimon, Senator Sindel, Anis Eljim, Nancy Lauren, Major Kunkel and Dr. Nie from CNOVation. In addition, Professor Dorchester and two colleagues from London, General Lind and Major Rainey from DoD. Also, Clark with Attorney General Farraday and White House counsel Max Gold, together with several underlings, from the White House would be there, too. Clark unceremoniously began.

"Are we there yet?" He generally was not a patient man, and today was far from an exception. As agreed, Derek answered.

"My team here has finished its analysis and we are ready to start production in three days at RGNZ's labs in The Netherlands." The Attorney General inquired.

"Why there?" Derek didn't recognize him, but knew he would be on the call.

"Purification, supply chain issues, technical science side reasons. It's all in the executive summary we transmitted a few hours ago." Farraday remained undeterred.

"I read that, of course. It explains the processes, what will happen. I asked why the decision was made to initiate production outside the US." Derek remained California cool.

"Again, sir, we all agreed it would be the most efficient way to create the 20,000 doses as required by the purchase order. Transport to the first testing country is also frankly easier from there." Clark jumped in. This was not a pissing contest he had time for now. Farraday wanted domestic control of the product. He didn't trust Deng to keep to his promises of open testing and onsite inspections. The AG wanted this vaccine stored at a US military base while in clinical trial mode.

"When do your guys leave for The Netherlands?"

"My team leaves in 24 hours. They stay with the RGNZ folks through production. Then Ricky heads to Asia to monitor the first test, along with Professor Dorchester. There will be others going as well, as I'm sure you know." Yes, Clark was fully aware of the testing protocols. He'd written half of them himself. Clark only cared about the details to the extent they assured the outcome he so desperately wanted.

"Make sure everything is ready to go and you're on the ground in seven days to begin the clinical trials. That's it. One week. July 22. No later." With that Clark left the call, but let his AG and White House counsel talk through some other details.

The size of the on-site inspection team would make a visit from the International Atomic Energy Agency delegation under the global Nuclear Non-Proliferation Treaty look like bridesmaids picking out the venue for a bachelorette party. If not for COVID restrictions on international travel, there would be thousands of inspectors, moderators, conciliators and journalists. As it was, the newly named and created town of Deng-Khot would accommodate 4,000 "volunteers", along with the 237 monitors from 26 countries who would stay for the duration of the trials, expected to run six weeks. Based on the Mongolian word for city, Deng quickly built Deng-Khot in his own honor, moving with the speed of an autocracy. Workers built enough temporary housing to keep the visitors safe and well fed in what any of his subjects would consider lavish surroundings. Each guest would have their own room with a kitchen and bathroom, a COVID requirement of the agreed protocols. The trial subjects would share two to a unit, since part of the trial also considered transmissibility while the vaccine took effect. The patient monitoring areas were outfitted with high speed, fiber optic video surveillance equipment, rivaled in Deng's kingdom only by what he had in his primary palace that he used to keep an eye on his countrymen. To Deng, everyone could be a dissident or try to spoil his shining moments of glory.

To make this a truly double blind setting, another major feat Deng pulled off was creating large barns that allowed for simulation of rain, all of which had to be done indoors. Clark had retooled the initial drafts of the testing agreement to allow Deng-Khot to simultaneously run Phase I where subjects drank from cups into which their water was poured, with a Phase II test to simulate a cloud seeding effect to test for raining the vaccine down on a second tranche of volunteers. Because NASA was still not prepared to publicly acknowledge that it could create rain cloud effects, the parties agreed to build a hydroponic plant watering system. Pure rain water would be captured and carted in. One barn would deliver pure rain water and the other rain water mixed with the vaccine. Each subject in Phase II would be given a 2 oz dixie cup, brought in to the silo during a short simulated rain event, and told to fill their cups half way then drink it.

All of the testing would be live streamed, except the filling of the Phase I water cups and the actual seeding of the Phase II hydroponic barns. The whole world would literally be watching the trials on a live stream. Who could question such an open process? Of course, none of the rampant starvation or human rights abuses would be on display while the world shone a 100,000 mega-watt spot light on Deng-Khot. Deng even let himself imagine a Nobel Prize nomination, or hosting the Olympics.

As observers and monitors began to arrive, no one on the ground was surprised to learn later that day that Joe O'Day was to be the only American "journalist" allowed on site. Under the so-called Deng-Khot Accord, each participating country, meaning those that supplied goods or materials, including the actual vaccine or the equipment needed to deliver, test or monitor, was allowed three scientists and one journalist. Le Monde of France, Der Spiegel of Germany, Yomiuri Shimbun of Japan, De Telegraaf of The Netherlands and the Times of India each sent their top medical correspondent. No Chinese state reporters were allowed in, given the continued clashes Deng had with the Chinese government over some disputed territory well off the coast of mainland China. The WHO, the British Ministry of Health and CDC / NIH were allowed to send three each. Of course, the companies creating the vaccine could send their own teams, as could Space Force and NASA.

The initial 20,000 of the colorless and odorless DeeLu vaccine arrived on time under tight security on one of Deng's military planes. Ricky and his counterparts, one French and one Japanese, were also aboard, accompanied by three armed guards. Even whose plane would be flown had been the subject of intense negotiations. Clark forged an agreement under which Deng's plane would carry the precious cargo, accompanied by two American F-35 fighter jets. The observers arrived with the actual cups that would be used along with the vaccine. For consistency's sake, the protocols for Phases I and II provided that the placebo and vaccine cups would be color coded. Only Ricky and the two other control observers would know what went in which cup. The code was simple. The placebo in a red cup with one shot of two ounces of water, the vaccine in a blue cup with two shots, one ounce of water one ounce of vaccine. One shot, two shot, red shot, blue shot rhymed the French scientist, thinking of his four and six year-old boys at home. A similar color coding would be used for the hydroponic silos.

The agreed protocols followed the same procedures as were used for any major new drug or vaccine, with three notable exceptions: the speed at which all of this ran; the homogeneity of the volunteers – while they aged in range from 17 to 75, they were not racially or ethnically diverse; and perhaps most importantly, 100 members of each of the four groups would actually be exposed to CoV-2 seven days after receiving the dosage, all of whom would remain isolated for 14 days for post-exposure observation. None of the participants knew the group they were in.

The protocols were designed to ensure compliance with US, EU and Japanese public health requirements, each of which were more stringent than any other country that might buy this vaccine. However, each country would be left to determine how to best solicit their own volunteers. Clark had pushed hard for this, arguing it was a matter of national sovereignty. Derek very proudly told Ricky before taking him to Logan airport that CNOVation had already been granted patent protections by the US, the EU and Japan, under an international agreement that allowed for the formulation and process to be sealed under lock and key with both the WHO and the World Trade Organization. Derek had promised Ricky that this most valuable trade secret would be released to open sources as soon as CNOVation and its partners had sold 2 billion doses, and all three companies agreed to deliver the vaccine free to the most impoverished countries of the world, even paying for crop dusting airplanes to drop the vaccines in the most remote of areas if those countries' governments would allow.

The trials went as smoothly as anyone could have hoped.

On August 11, 2020, Ricky's 36th birthday, with the world watching the press conference live, after the results were checked, cross checked and triple confirmed, the three observers reported out the following results:

From the unexposed placebo study group: none contracted COVID or had any side effects; from the exposed placebo study group, seven contracted CoV-2, one of whom had a severe case, attributed to her comorbidity of being overweight, itself a rarity in this country. The other six complained only of fatigue, headaches and minor muscle pain. This 7% positivity rate was slightly higher than the reported infection rate in the country, but actually lower that the averages being reported in developed nations around the world, including the United States.

COLOR BLINDED - 259

No one who received the vaccine and was exposed to COVID became infected. Of those who received the vaccine, whether or not exposed to COVID, less than 10% reported any immediate side effects, which were limited to fatigue, headaches, muscle pain, chills or fever. Those who experienced those symptoms reported side effects lasting under 48 hours. However, as Ricky expected and feared, all reported varying degrees of inability to differentiate most colors along the color spectrum other than white and gray starting within 48 hours. This color differentiation deficiency increased at slightly different rates. By the end of the observation period, this color blindness was nearly total.

Before any reporters were allowed to ask questions, Deng turned his microphone on and proudly announced: "We are prepared to allow this miracle to be widely given to all 80 million people in my country. And we welcome anyone in the world who wants to come be part of the final phase of this trial. We can accommodate 50,000 more volunteers for a final trial, but I am satisfied as is my parliament that this miracle should not be withheld from anyone." Deng knew that Ulf Knutsson and similarly minded members of The Leaders stood ready to send tens of thousands of volunteers to Deng-Khot for the final phase of the trial, as would at least two unscrupulous leaders of African countries who were promised millions of dollars to offer up some of their citizens. Clark had made clear his goal of all testing being completed by Labor Day, and the vaccine being ready for wide scale distribution soon after. The last piece would be the dynamic cloud seeding. Clark was joyful the testing would be a success under the controlled environment of Deng-Khot.

Jim O'Day posed the first question to the panel, most of which was a speech by him about how incredible a leader Richards was and how gracious Deng was, how incredibly well this test went, and how safe the vaccine is. Before O'Day had finished his question, Derek was receiving an email of a second purchase order from DoD, this time for another 40,000 immediate doses and 20,000,000 doses for delivery by September 3 at a price of $900,000. He barely had time to print the orders when another rolled in for 30million more doses by September 10,

for another $45million. Within an hour, after the panel answered a se-
ries of scientific question, a fourth purchase order came in for 100 million more doses by September 30, for a purchase price of $1.5 billion.
Derek's eyes swelled looking at an order of this magnitude. He texted
his sister, "passed the Bn in orders."

She texted back:

CNOVation, ONA and RGNZ had already discussed scaling up production with a 24 hour production cycle, but had not yet projected
scaling to this volume. Derek received a series of emails from biotech
companies, large and small, offering to join forces to speed up production. That would have to be discussed ASAP with his current partners.

Sindel texted Derek "congrats great day." Then "check twitter.
Richards active." Derek opened his twitter feed and did a search, since
he didn't follow Richards. As expected, Richards had jumped the gun
and announced "USA buys 150 million doses. COVID solved.
#4moreyears" The inevitable and really unrelenting PR and media blitz
continued. The biopharma companies involved in their shots-in-arms
trials released statements complimenting and congratulating the "rapid
progress being made on this alternate form of vaccine" without naming
the companies behind it, and vowing "our work to help stem this global
scourge continues on time."

Within an hour after the press conference had ended, Ricky formally signed off on the study's results. Everyone from the science and
business worlds who had gathered for this event and had planned to
leave would meet in the specially built dining hall for farewells. Some
agreed to stay on for the final phase study that would start soon. New
observers were already en route. Cleaning crews were again sanitizing

all of their rooms, and security forces continued ensuring that nothing left this city or country that Deng did not permit.

Deng entered the dining hall flanked by a reporter and camera crew from his state controlled media, a smile so broad his mask could not contain it. He headed directly to Ricky, his right arm outstretched. Diplomatic protocol and manners required Ricky accept his handshake, COVID protocols notwithstanding. Several in the hall were aware of stories of people Deng had executed for refusing his handshake.

"Dr. Tsang. Me, my people, and the world thank you. This is a most auspicious day."

"Thank you, sir. I am pleased that the tests went so well."

"A humble man, just as I was told." Deng held Ricky's hand in his for longer than normal even in pre-COVID days. "There is still much work to be done here. Would you reconsider and stay?" Ricky retrieved his hand, still respectful.

"Prime Minister, you are very kind. Your hospitality has been outstanding, and you have built an incredible facility. But it is time for me to move on, and there are so many talented scientists here to finish this work." Deng pulled Ricky in closer by the shoulder.

"I understand you have concerns with your vaccine's side effects. I share them, believe me I do. But we will always be able to recognize each other as Asian – our features will always set us apart. Our skin tone has never defined us. The whites, the blacks, they choose to stand on phony ground and fight because of their color differences. For those who loathe you and me for our heritage and our appearance, your vaccine will keep them safe but not cure the hate in their hearts. We must rise above those petty differences, and achieve our rightful place in the world. Do you not agree?" Ricky paused.

"Prime Minister, if I could create a vaccine that eliminated hate, that would be the crowning work of my lifetime." Deng let go of his shoulder, and stepped back.

"Then travel in peace, my friend. Go in peace." With that, Deng nodded, and two security officers approached, asked permission to take

Ricky's bags. They then escorted him to join four other scientists waiting on a government helicopter for a lift to the airport.

| 50 |

Chapter 50: We've been set up

Ricky managed a much needed deep sleep on his flight to Beijing, barely staying awake during his meditation. He had answered a few congratulatory texts from Derek, Sindel, Shimon and Jeanne, and the clearly mixed message from Dr. Dorchester. Dorchester acknowledged the truly remarkable discovery, but expressed disappointment that the ethical questions were both unresolved and now most likely politically neutered. His mentor knew Ricky would long tussle with the difficult questions. He suggested perhaps in a year when the disease had been defeated and largely forgotten they could look back and try to determine if this what we should have done.

Upon landing and awakening, Ricky powered his phone back on after the pilot announced it was safe to do so. He had several more text, email and phone messages. The one from the manager of the local bank branch in Boston he used for his direct deposit and paying bills caught him off guard. He returned that one first after deplaning, using the phone number in his contacts, not the one on the message, for security. "Yes, this is Ricky Tsang. I am returning a call from Mr. Edmunds." After a brief hold, he heard a voice he did not recognize, as he had no reason to talk with the branch manager.

"Dr. Tsang, yes thank you for calling me back. I just want to let you know that our branch offers a full range of investment options through our partnership with a major investment house."

"Yes, thank you Mr. Edmunds." He rubbed his eyes, looking at the text from his father confirming he was at the airport and would meet him outside of international arrivals. "But, I don't imagine needing those services."

"I see. Certainly, that is fine, it's just with such a large deposit, I wanted you to know what our branch offers." Ricky did not understand, but thanked him for his call. He then opened his secure mobile banking app, saw the current balance of $20,042,572.20, with the most recent deposit of $20,000,000. He called Derek.

"Ricky, hey you land okay? Flight good?"

"Yes, thank you. Everything is fine." Derek heard the concern in his voice.

"Your mom ok?"

"Oh, yes thank you. My family is fine. Derek, there is an accounting error in my bank account." Derek didn't realize the transfer would go through that fast, but was happy Ricky received it.

"Yes, hey Ricky. Yeah, that's the first half. We'll send the rest once we get the other purchase orders in, probably a few weeks." Ricky was still confused, and then it hit Derek – he had planned to tell Ricky about his bonus when he returned to Boston, and then didn't have a chance while he was at the trials. "My bad. I meant to tell you after the trials were over. We are giving you and your team bonuses for the extraordinary work you have all done. We took out 20% for taxes." Ricky now could not find words. "You should hire an accountant." Derek laughed.

"Derek, that … I do not know how …"

"To thank me? Jeez, man, no way you're thanking me. You know the size of the deal we made, and no way we're doing any kind of deal anywhere near that size without you and your team. Remember, I made you a promise that if this vaccine was as successful as we thought you'd never have to work for money again. You can keep doing the good for the world you've been doing, but not worry about where your next good meal or pay check would come from." Ricky heard one of Derek's other phones buzzing. "Speaking of your team, Shimon and Jeanne are on their way in. I want to tell them before the money hits their accounts. Their bonuses will be smaller, just FYI. You want me to put you on speaker?"

"No, Derek, that's ok. I plan to call tomorrow or the day after and catch up with them. I just ... well, this is quite generous of you and the board."

"Take your parents out for a nice, socially distanced dinner. Send my best." With that, Ricky joined the customs line for Chinese nationals, speeding through the highly efficient system. The customs agent looked at his well-worn, now fully stamped passport, and looked at him three times. In perfect Mandarin, Ricky asked if everything was in order.

"It is, and welcome home Dr. Tsang. I saw you on television. Your work is quite impressive."

"Thank you."

"Enjoy your stay, sir." Once through the passage way for arrivals, Ricky spotted his father. They hugged, an unusual spectacle for grown men in public here, but Wai knew his son had quite the past few weeks and months.

"Your mother is quite excited you are home. We both are. We hope you can stay longer."

"I hope to this time, father. I hope to." Ricky wheeled one bag, and his father carried his backpack. "I may need some investment advice, father. I'll explain in the car." And he did. Wai barely knew where to begin to discuss that amount of money, but he did have a trusted financial advisor he promised to set Ricky up with. Could he be any prouder of his son? Ricky also explained that he would not need to closely follow the next clinical trial of the vaccine. There were many gifted scientists there to do so, and he had little reason to think the outcome would be any different. He had told Derek and the team that he was available should he be needed.

When they arrived at the apartment, Mae embraced her son for a full minute, tears streaming down her face. She knew he would be tired, but would enjoy a traditional dinner of Chinese mud carp, his favorite. They ate, drank, and shared stories. His parents knew he would rather not talk about his work today, or maybe even tomorrow. They were just delighted he had come home.

Ricky slept very well, but at 9:15 am when he awoke to use the bathroom and brush his teeth, he could smell fresh minced pork stuffed buns and tea. He checked his watch and phone again. Breakfast this late, on a Thursday? He entered the kitchen to find his parents at the counter laughing and smiling and sharing a late breakfast, or early lunch? He rubbed his eyes and scratched his head, remembering his father had said he'd be taking a few days off. Mae fixed him a plate and a cup, and they sat and talked. Mae told stories of when he was so precocious at seven years old, his first chemistry set, entering the academy at nine instead of the proscribed age of twelve. Ricky did not truly realize how much he missed warm moments like this.

At noon, as promised, he accompanied his mother to the nearby gourmet market. She picked out the items she wanted. He carried the basket. She seemed to be stocking up given the quantities she selected, but he didn't mind. Even with his mask on, he could sense that people recognized him, but none bothered him.

When they returned to the apartment, he helped his mother put the groceries away. Ricky then went to his room, returned some texts and meditated for a silent 30 minutes. He promised to call his team in response to Shimon's "Holy Shit!" text and Jeanne's "Wow! Wow!" He smiled; they must have gotten their money also. After talking to Shimon and Jeanne, neither of whom could contain their excitement and thankfulness, he decided to take a nap. When was the last time he had that luxury? Although he planned to be down for just an hour, he was awakened at 5:11 p.m. by the sounds of laughter in the kitchen and more than two voices. He freshened up, stretched, and opened his door to see Mae, Wai, and Mr. and Mrs. Yung. He remembered them from parental visiting days during his time at the academy. He did not recognize the striking young woman with them.

"Ricky," sang out his mother, "you remember Li and Shia Yung?"

"Yes, of course." He hugged them each. "Thank you for your concern during my mother's illness." He addressed Shia. "And I am so sorry about the passing of your mother." They both nodded and expressed thanks. Mae spoke again.

"And you remember their daughter Caihong" Caihong? She looked very different from when she was 13.

"A rainbow in the sky. Caihong, how are you?" They started catching up on the many years that had passed since the academy. Then Ricky saw six place settings at the table, the extra leaf having been inserted to make more room. The extra food his mother had bought. This was pre-planned. His mother winked at him – she never winked. He smiled.

They sat down at the table, the women helping to serve the food. With the soup still steaming in front of him, Ricky leaned over to Caihong. "I've been set up." She smiled, and whispered.

"We both have. But I don't mind. Do you?" Ricky shook his head no.

After dinner, while the adults told stories and laughed some more, with the sun still high in the sky, Ricky asked Caihong if she would like to go for a walk.

"That would be nice. Where to?"

"I was thinking Beihai Park? Is that ok?" She smiled, grabbed her purse, and they headed out.

THE END